A Heart Torn Apart

Coyote Creek Book Two

Katie O'Connor

-A Heart Torn Apart-

-Coyote Creek Book Two-

This book is a work of fiction. Names, characters, places, and incidents either are products of the author's imagination or are used fictitiously. Any resemblance to actual events, locales, or persons, living or dead, is entirely coincidental.

Copyright © 2020 by Katie O'Connor

Published: July 2020

Katie O'Connor and Snarky Heart Press (katieohwrites.com)

ISBN: 978-1-989816-07-3 (Digital Edition)

ISBN: 978-1-989816-08-0 (Digital 2)

ISBN: 978-1-989816-06-6 (Print Edition)

ISBN: 978-1-989816-42-4 (Digital Edition 2)

Design and cover art by P.S. Cover Design.

Editing by Terri St. Clair.

Dedication

For Linda Brown.

Friend extraordinaire, confidant, and fabulous nurse.

The universe was smiling on me the day I met you. Nobody makes me think about my actions and their impact the way you do. You inspire me to be a better person, to dig deeper and write better books. You are the sister of my heart.

And yes, I named Coyote Creek's Doctor Brown for you!

And to the lovely staff at the Toole County Library in Shelby, Montana. Thank you for the information and photographs allowing me to make my characters' visits there real.

·♥·♥·♥·♥·♥·

About this Book

Missing teens, broken hearts and an undeniable love.

RCMP Constable Amy Baxter, retreated to Coyote Creek to escape an enormous mistake. She wants to do her job as a police officer until the scandal passes and she can further her career in another large city. Her attractive new neighbor is secretive, doesn't seem to have a job and keeps weird hours. His behavior triggers her law enforcement warning bells and his body sets off sensations best forgotten.

Justice Flint is a man on a mission and Amy is an unwanted distraction, poking her nose into his business. His teenage daughter is missing. With no idea if she's run away or been abducted, he's spent the last two years searching for her. His broken heart won't allow him to give up searching until he finds her.

When Amy catches him breaking the law in search of clues, she has two choices: arrest him or team up to search for his daughter. Either way, she needs to ignore her attraction and protect the walls she's built around her heart.

· ♥ · ♥ · ♥ · ♥ · ♥ ·

Chapter One

The crisp fall breeze whipped strands of hair into Amy Baxter's face. It was days like today she debated cutting her mid-back length blonde hair into a pixie cut. She rifled in the pocket of her jeans for a hair elastic and with deft fingers plaited her tresses and flipped the braid over her shoulder. She scrambled back up the ladder, spread her feet to the edges of the rung, braced her shins against the top platform and stretched up on her tiptoes to reach the eavestrough.

The five-foot ladder tilted and swayed beneath her. Crap. She'd hoped it would give her enough height to hang the seasonal orange lights on her new house. She shifted her stance carefully, the ladder steadied and she tried again. It tilted precariously. She wanted, needed, the lights up. Today. Before the guys from the station helped her move from her tiny rented apartment to the white and green, three-bedroom, bungalow she'd taken possession of last week. It was bad enough she had to ask for help lifting her furniture, she wouldn't ask anyone to bring a ladder just because one wouldn't fit in her compact Honda. She could do this. Alone.

She'd found this stepladder in the backyard shed along with a few other gardening tools and couldn't wait to make her mark on her first real home. Decorating for Halloween seemed the perfect way to start her new life. It was already October 29th. She had to get the lights up before the guys arrived with her furniture. They'd helped her load it in a U-Haul last night. Today, they'd help her lug the large pieces of furniture inside. Between work and moving in, she wouldn't have much time to prep for Halloween and she really wanted to go all out for her first Halloween.

She couldn't wait to see the lights on the house she'd been saving for since she moved out of her last foster home and started working as a bartender at eighteen. At twenty-two, she'd decided on a new career and entered the RCMP academy; changing her life for the better. Life was grand until she met the man she'd thought she'd fallen in love with. Ruthlessly, she pushed her ex out of her head. That relationship had died an ugly death and she'd never go back there.

This small, updated bungalow was her dream home and it was fast becoming a reality. She was off duty for Halloween and couldn't wait for the trick or treaters. She spread her feet, one against either side rail of the ladder, stretched on tiptoes and inched upward. Almost, just a little more.

The ladder wiggled. She reached again. Maybe if she leaned, just a bit.

"What the devil are you doing, woman?"

"Crap!" She jerked and tipped ominously backward, arms wind-milling. The ladder steadied but unable to catch herself, she flew into the air. Her hand whacked something hard on the way down. Strong, solid arms caught her before she hit the ground.

"Oof," she grunted.

"Woah! You're heavier than you look." Justice Flint's smiling green eyes caught her gaze and the remaining air in her lungs burst out in a rush. His smile turned to a frown of disapproval. "You know you shouldn't be standing that high up on a step ladder, right? Never higher than the second step from the top." He made a soft sound of censure. "I'd have thought an RCMP officer would have a better grasp of personal safety. If I hadn't spoken, you'd have climbed to the top, wouldn't you?"

She wiggled in his arms, trying to get down. "Put me down, Flint. I'm fine." Physically, she was undamaged, but it would be a frosty day in Hawaii before she admitted to him she was shaken up. Nearly breathless, every single inhalation flooded her senses with the soft, masculine scent of his aftershave. Tufts of dark brown hair peeked out from under his black felt cowboy hat. He was all male and every inch of him was pure, rock solid Flint. His hair, his eyes, his height and his strong build. The Flint men were similar enough you recognized them on sight, but different enough and once you knew them, you could easily tell them apart. Justice Flint's distinguishing feature was his lone left dimple. A very sexy dimple.

"I could have you arrested for assault," he chuckled, not putting her down. "You punched me in the face."

"I wouldn't have hit you if you hadn't tried to kill me by startling me off the ladder." She struggled against his firm grip. "I assume you're man enough to take a punch?"

"I've taken punches from people a lot tougher than you." He lowered her to the ground facing him. "What exactly are you doing?"

"Decorating for Halloween." His hands remained on her shoulders, warm against her bare arms which were icy from the rising breeze. Until he touched her, the air had been invigorating, now she wished for a jacket. His touch made her cold and much too warm all at once. Goosebumps erupted on her arms. She rubbed her hands up and down her arms before shoving her hands in her pockets.

His brow wrinkled and his arms dropped to his sides. "This house has been vacant for months. Since the Tamaracks retired to Texas in May, to be precise."

"This house is mine. I took possession last week; the realtor hasn't removed the For-Sale sign yet. I'm moving in today. I just wanted to get a head start on the lights." Why was she telling him this? Even if he was going to be her neighbor, her life was none of his business. She answered to keep their relationship pleasant and on good terms.

"Well, if you own it, I don't have to call the police to have you arrested for trespassing," he joked.

"As a member of Coyote Creek's finest, I'm unlikely to be arrested. I believe it is you who is trespassing and tried to scare me to death. I believe that qualifies as attempted murder," she teased back. Why was she joking with him? She didn't flirt, she didn't date. She had no interest in Justice Flint or any other man. She was done with men. It was time to focus on her career and her own happiness.

"Scared you to death? No doubt." His eyes lit with amusement and he laughed. "Can I help you with those lights?"

"No, thanks. I'd rather do it on my own." Deep down, part of her wanted to accept his offer of assistance, but her independent side refused. There was nothing a man could do which a woman couldn't do, *if* she set her mind to it. "I've got it. I'm not an invalid."

His brow wrinkled as he studied her. She could almost read the questions in his eyes before his face shuttered. "Okay, I was heading out anyway. I've got things to do. There's an extension ladder in my shed, if you want it. It's not locked, help yourself."

"Thanks, I might take you up on it. Where are you headed?" Her question surprised her and if the look on his face was any indication, he hadn't expected it either. Sometimes, the cop in her rushed to the forefront and poked her nose in where it might not belong.

"Going riding west of Smoky Lake. I haven't been out there in months. I used to camp with my daughter beyond the lake. Thought I'd get a camping trip in before the snow flies and hunting season starts." He glanced away, not meeting her stare.

"That's where they found the body of the teenage girl last week isn't it?" She knew darn well it was, she'd been part of the investigation and resulting grid search. Why would he choose to go there? The investigation was still underway but she, and the rest of the precinct, believed the death an accident rather than suspecting foul play, but it did seem weird he'd go in that particular direction and it was late in the year for camping.

"Is that where they found her? I didn't realize." He shrugged and his eyes shifted away again. "I'll grab the ladder for you, unless you want me to put those lights up."

Irritation prickled up her spine. "I can do it, but I would appreciate the loan of your ladder. If you show me where it is, I'll get back to work." She wanted to be finished decorating before the guys arrived. Her fellow officers were great and never treated her as incompetent, but her own competitive nature drove her to prove just how capable she was and her Halloween decorations were just another self-imposed competition. A proving ground.

"Follow me," Justice gestured toward his house.

His yard, front and back were immaculate; the lawns mowed to perfection. A couple of mature trees were the only things marring the manicured expanse of lawn which stretched, unbroken, to the flawless white fence. No flower beds, no shrubs. No ornaments. It was perfect, weed free, and uninspired. He needed flowers to break up the green or maybe a patio, a fire pit and a couple of chairs. The shed was adjacent to a garage which opened into the alley.

"Not much on flowers, are you?" She asked as he rummaged around in the shed. She peeked through the door. Shelves lined three walls, their contents organized and precisely placed. The man must have a bit of OCD in him. She didn't blame him. Everything had its place.

"No time for flowers. I've got ranching responsibilities and personal stuff to do. I love the grass, but flowers are too much work. Mom and Dad have an oversized vegetable garden and fruit trees on the ranch. I help with the gardening in exchange for my produce. Nothing beats fresh veggies, unless it's a big T-bone steak." He glanced over his shoulder before backing out of the shed with the ladder slung under one arm. "Here you go. One ladder, suitable for hanging Christmas or Halloween lights and cleaning gutters."

She felt the blood drain from her face and lodge in her stomach as an uneasy ache. Cleaning gutters? Another thing to add to her autumn to do list and snow was expected any day now.

He walked past her, through the gate and into the front yard. She bristled. Did he think she was incapable of carrying a ladder? She was an RCMP officer, fit and strong. Stronger than many men. She opened her mouth to object and snapped it shut. She'd only been in Coyote Creek nine months but in that short time she'd learned the Flint men never let a woman carry anything heavy or awkward. Nor did they leave them to handle car trouble or physical danger. They had old fashioned chivalry which, somehow, didn't seem out of place or demeaning to those they helped.

She'd watched Justice's father, Robert, the family patriarch, tote loads several times. On one occasion he'd bickered lightly with Sue, his wife, telling her he knew she could carry the box, but with him around, she didn't have to. Sue had passed him the box, patted his cheek and called him her hero. All the Flint boys, or rather men, shared the chivalrous gene and it seemed Justice was no exception.

Justice extended the ladder and propped it against the eave of her house and stepped back. "Have at 'er. I'd appreciate it if you could put the ladder against the shed when you're done, if you don't mind. You're not tall enough to hang it back up."

"I'm not exactly short," she protested.

He eyed her up and down. "No, but I'm six feet, which makes you—what five six?"

"Five seven, actually." She wasn't sure why the extra inch seemed so important.

"I rest my case, I can barely reach it, you'd never manage."

She conceded his point. "I'll put it by the shed when I'm finished. Thanks for the loan." She clamored up the ladder. "You going to be gone long?" she called over her shoulder and grabbed the next light.

"A couple days, more or less." Beside her, he stretched the dangling lights out, untangling them as he stepped to her right.

"Anyone going with you? Does your family know your plans?" She clipped a couple of lights to the eavestrough and clambered to the ground. Lifting the ladder with ease she moved it a few feet to the right. He shifted to get out of the way.

"You sure you don't want me to do that?"

"Ugh. No, thanks. I'm good." She climbed up and down a dozen more times stringing the lights as she went. She hopped down after the last light was clipped. "Wow, talk about luck. The two strands exactly fit. Doesn't get much better than that. Thanks for untangling them for me, it saved me some work, and more importantly time." She couldn't stop the smile of gratitude and satisfaction she felt curving her lips upward.

She'd easily be able to wrap lights around the porch supports without the ladder, so she might as well put it back. If she needed it later, she knew where it was.

She'd done it. Alone.

Okay, Justice had helped a bit, but the lights were up. Before the guys arrived with her furniture. Homeowner victory number one!

· ❤ · ❤ · ❤ · ❤ · ❤ ·

Chapter Two

Justice couldn't deny it; Amy Baxter was one stubborn woman. He'd have been more than happy to hang those lights or return the ladder to the shed. But, if she wanted to do it alone, he'd let her.

She'd been in town the better part of a year and had earned a solid reputation with her RCMP coworkers and the rest of Coyote Creek's residents. Few people messed with her and she'd been known to single-handedly break up a bar fight with just a stare. He'd seen her take down a rowdy tourist without breaking a sweat. He had to respect that.

It would be nice to have a neighbor again, but he'd have preferred a couple or a family over a single woman. She wasn't his type anyway. He preferred soft and feminine, not muscles and tough-guy attitude.

He watched her grab the extension ladder and lower it unerringly to the ground before collapsing it and hefting it up. Before he could move to take it from her, she trotted toward his backyard with the ladder settled firmly under one arm and braced with her opposite hand.

Huh. Maybe there *was* something appealing in a physically strong woman. His ex, Ellen, spent hours at the gym but had very few muscles to show for it. She was lithe, lean and flexible and she abhorred anything physical beyond yoga. When they'd gone skiing, Ellen had spent all her time sipping tea or cocktails in front of the fire while he hit the slopes with his brothers or friends.

He shoved the thought aside. Soft, hard—it didn't matter, he wasn't interested in dating, he had a daughter to find. He wouldn't rest until Hannah was home safely and they'd rebuilt their relationship. His earlier good mood evaporated like water under the sun. Defeat swamped him. No! He was not giving up. He would find Hannah if it killed him.

There was no way he would let a woman get in the way of his search. Besides, at thirty-eight, he'd done the whole marriage and family thing, he had no need to go there again. His life focus was finding his runaway daughter and bringing her home safely.

Brakes squeaked and a horn tooted. He turned from his empty gate to the street behind him. A fifteen-foot rental truck from his brother's garage swung widely on the street and slowly backed onto Amy's front lawn, stopping a few feet from the porch. Whoever was driving was skilled. They eased the truck between two heavily foliaged shrubs without touching either one and stopped the perfect distance from the porch.

"Nice park Danny. Hi, Jeff. Good to see you both," Justice greeted the two thirty-something off-duty officers who climbed out of the truck. He'd gone to school with Jeff, Danny had been a few years behind them. Funny how so many people left a small town for the city and a new career and then ended right back where they started.

"You here to help, Flint? Another set of hands wouldn't hurt."

"He's not here to help." Amy stormed up to them, a frown twisting her pretty face. "This is only going to take an hour. I really appreciate you guys helping with the furniture and I'll get the rest and return the truck to the garage. You guys helped me load the heavy stuff last night is more than enough help."

Justice stifled a chuckle. Amy was as bristly as one of his sisters when they were trying to prove they could do something without help. Women! You had to love them. Even when they drove you nuts.

"Don't be silly. I'm here, it won't take more than a few minutes to help out." He really wanted to get going. He needed to get in as much outdoor searching for Hannah as he could before fall gave way to winter and the snow started flying. Still, chivalry wasn't dead, at least not in his family. He couldn't walk away and let Amy move in virtually unassisted. The guys were help enough; but moving sucked and the more hands, the better. He'd make the time. Just to be neighborly. That truck couldn't possibly hold much stuff, it wasn't very big.

Two squad cars pulled up and Amy's superior and lead RCMP officer, Sergeant Lance Pfeiffer, and two more officers climbed out, fully uniformed. Wow. Most of the detachment had shown up. By his count, there were only another three RCMP officers on duty. Definitely a sign of respect for their fellow officer.

"Hey, boss," Amy called. "I didn't think you'd come but I'm glad to see you."

Her eyes squinted a bit, leaving Justice wondering if she was being completely honest. She had an independent streak five miles wide and probably didn't want any more help than she absolutely had to have. Well, they were here now and he'd pitch in with the rest of them and she could just deal with it.

"Really, guys. All I need is help with the sofa and the bedroom furniture. I can get the rest myself. I loaded the smaller stuff alone."

"Why did you do that?" Justice piped up. "Nobody needs to move alone. Not when they have friends."

"Are you implying I don't have friends?" She glared at him, hands on her hips.

He winked and turned to open the truck's sliding back door. "No way, darlin'. I know better. You stick to yourself a lot, but you do have friends."

"Are you stalking me?" She gaped at him, slack jawed.

Someone snickered behind him. Opening this particular can of worms in front of her coworkers might have been a mistake. Too late now. He better back down. A bit.

"We're going to be neighbors. This is a small town. People gossip. I'm just saying I'm here to help and so are your friends." He hopped into the truck and began undoing the tarp straps holding the load steady for transport. "We'll start with the big stuff and take it from there. I'm just being neighborly."

He groaned silently. Seriously, how many times could he pull the 'neighbor' card in one morning? And why was he still here? She had plenty of help.

Amy joined him in the truck, and unfasted the opposite ends of the straps and the unloading began. With so many hands, the work went quickly.

A short time later, Justice and Lance hauled an enormous dresser into the biggest bedroom. They set it in place against the wall opposite the window as Amy had instructed on their way in. Justice leaned his elbow on the tall, oak dresser. The bottom had space for six drawers, the top had doors which opened for storage. Sweaters or a TV unless he missed his guess. The finish was flawless and it glistened in the dim morning sun brightening the room through the open curtains.

"You've got balls," Lance laughed. "Pissing her off and turning your back on her. I suspect she's got a well-controlled temper under her icy exterior. You might want to tread lightly. I remember how you used to be with the chicks in high school. Flirting and wooing them with all your manly charms." He puffed up his chest and swaggered around the room in mockery of Justice's teenage antics. "I'm not sure you're Amy Baxter's type. If she has a type."

Justice laughed. "I was a bit full of myself." He shrugged. "But the ladies do like the Flint charm." He paused. "It doesn't matter anyway; I'm not looking for a woman. The only person I'm looking for is Hannah. Although with Dad being under the weather, I'm not getting as much search time as I'd like. Extra hours at the ranch are keeping me tied to town. Don't get me wrong, I love the work and family is everything, but having split priorities sucks."

"How is your dad doing?"

"Not as well as he'd have us believe. Spends a lot of time hiding in the shed and won't let anyone else in. Mom's getting worried about depression, despite him claiming he's just looking for privacy and relaxation. His color's off, he's pale and seems weak. We're all pitching in to help out with the heavy chores. Thankfully it's nearly winter which means fewer heavy chores. We use the tractor to move bales and the small grader on the driveway. But there'll be a lot of slogging through the snow and calving starts early in January. With less outside work, he'll have more time to rest and recover. The doc better find something soon."

"I hope he starts to improve and I pray you find Hannah. Although I do remind you not to break any laws while you're searching." Lance smiled, taking the sting out of his warning. "I'm keeping an eye on all the police databases, Canadian and international. If anything comes up, I'll be all over it like Mrs. Adelson on fresh gossip."

They laughed together. Mrs. Adelson, Coyote Creek's biggest gossip was harmless but if there was something to know about anyone in town, she seemed to be the first to catch wind of it. She'd have made a great detective. They waited in the doorway for two of the guys to pass into another room carrying a large desk.

It took twenty minutes to tote in all the large, heavy items and against Amy's protests, they started in on the lighter items and the boxes.

"You guys don't need to do this. I am capable. It won't take me long at all." She took a box out of Justice's hands.

He yanked it back. "Take off those sassy, stubborn pants and let your friends help out. It's what we do."

"Sassy pants? Are you kidding me? Flint, get back here," she demanded.

"Yep. Sassy pants. That's what Mom calls my sisters when they talk back. You're sassy and stubborn, just like they are. Relax. I'll be back just as soon as I put this box in the," he paused to read the label, "in the kitchen." He side-stepped around her and into the house. He set the box on a pile and slurped some water from the tap. He could really go for a beer about now.

"Justice Flint, please go home."

Her voice was soft and almost pleading. He wiped his hands on his jeans and turned to look at her. Strands of her hair flew about her face in tangles, and her T-shirt was dusty. Her lips pursed together and her forehead had scrunched up tension lines. She looked exhausted and frustrated. And more than a little mad. Damn, she was cute.

"Tell me why and I'll consider it." He leaned against the counter, arms loose at his sides, his left ankle crossed over his right.

"Because I want them to go and they won't leave if you're still working."

"Why do you want us to go? You haven't even thanked us properly yet." Her desire to have them gone puzzled him. What thoughts were running through her mind?

"And how, pray tell, do I thank you properly?" He heard an eye roll in her voice.

"Beer and pizza. Everyone knows you feed and water your moving assistants."

She sighed. "Crap, I meant to do that; it totally slipped my mind. I was going to buy beer yesterday. Shoot! I can't leave to get beer now, but I can order pizza."

"You could call for pizza and get a taxi to bring beer. They'll do odd delivery jobs on occasion. They deliver flowers when the florist can't get away. Carl's got two cabs now. He'll appreciate the business to help pay off the new car."

"The taxi delivers beer?"

"Yup, small towns are different from cities. We've got a special bylaw for it. Of course, they never deliver to minors. It doesn't make sense by city standards but it works for us. It often keeps the inebriated off the roads. They didn't mention it at the station?"

She shook her head in disbelief. "I'll never adjust to this place, but thanks for the tip." She leaned against the opposite counter and squinted at him.

"No problem. I'll just grab another box." He stepped toward the doorway.

"Flint?" Her voice was soft with an unspoken question and made him pause.

"Will they ever think of me as a co-worker and not a woman?"

The random question threw him off balance. He pivoted to look at her. Her shoulders were tense, her arms crossed defensively over her chest. "They might. If you act like a man. It's in a man's nature to protect those who are weaker than he is. And, like it or lump it, you are weaker than the rest of the detachment. That doesn't mean they don't trust you or that they think you're incompetent. It just means they'll stand up for you when you need it."

Her questioning expression turned angry. "Oh! Get stuffed. What a load of crap. Women can do everything a man can do."

"A lot of times, that's true. But they are physically weaker. It's the testosterone. But they'll relax if you act like a man."

"Act like a man, so burping, farting and rude jokes?" She quirked an eyebrow.

"Wouldn't hurt. Honestly, be yourself. Do what you can. Ask for help when you need it and pitch in whenever you can. Watch them. Do what they do and you'll slide in before they notice you're a living, breathing, sexy woman under all the bristle and bluffing."

He could almost see her hackles rise like a riled dog. She was so easy to bait. He was enjoying this. For a moment, he almost forgot he needed to get on the road to continue his search. "Relax, if they didn't respect you, they'd have let you move in alone."

Lance stuck his head into the kitchen. "Let's finish the load. Snow's coming. Radio just issued a severe weather warning. Twenty to thirty centimeters of snow in the next forty-eight hours. You'll want to get this truck back before it starts. And we'll need to be back on patrol." He disappeared around the corner.

"Let's get the rest inside," she said with a sigh. "No sense fighting a losing battle. You got a coffee maker?"

"Sure do. Why?"

"I have no idea where mine is. The guys on duty won't have a beer but they'd take a coffee. Can you run along and fetch us a pot?" She smirked at him.

"Touché. One last word of advice? Ask them all over, a few at a time, to repay them with beer and movies. Think like a guy, not a chick. They love video games and poker too."

"Poker I can do. I love poker. I'm a kick ass poker player."

Avoiding the congestion at the front door, he slid out the back and through the gate adjoining their yards. He was back with coffee before the beer and pizza arrived.

"About time you got back, Flint," she drawled when he re-entered the kitchen with a baking sheet laden with coffee, mugs, cream and sugar. "Leave it to a man to take half an hour to get coffee. Where's your apron pretty boy?" He could tell by the help-me expression on her face she was trying to fit in with her male coworkers and wanted him to play along.

"Yeah, Justice, shouldn't you be serving us?" Lance joined in.

"Naw, I'll leave the serving to Jeff. He aced cooking in high school." Everyone laughed.

"And you never would have passed if I hadn't shared my stellar muffins with you in the final," Jeff shot back.

"True enough." They shared a high five and passed out coffee.

Chapter Three

Forty-five minutes later, Amy said good-bye to most of her coworkers. Lance and the other on duty officers left for work promising to take Danny home after he returned the rental truck for Amy. Although tempted to complain, she graciously accepted the offer, grabbed another piece of pizza and settled on the floor, back against the wall, to eat it.

"Need any help unpacking?" Jeff asked around a mouthful of pizza.

"Gross man. Don't talk with your mouth full." Amy threw a wadded-up napkin at him. Men could be such pigs. "Thanks, but I can do it. It'll take me a while to figure out where I want everything. I appreciate the offer but you might as well get home before the roads get bad. Your wife will be waiting on you."

"True enough. Jeannie will pitch a fit if I'm not home in time to watch the baby while she picks up Jaden from school. She doesn't mind taking the baby when I'm at work, but if I'm off, she prefers the alone time. Lets her unwind. I guess."

"Don't sound so certain," Amy laughed.

"It's true," Justice quipped from his lounging spot on the sofa. "When you've got family, and kids, time by yourself can be hard to find." His joviality dropped. "Now, I just wish I had Hannah back."

The ache in his voice brought a lump to Amy's throat. "What happened? If you don't mind me asking. Who's Hannah?"

"You don't know? I thought the whole town knew." His sigh sliced right into her heart leaving her feeling sucker-punched. She had that 'brace yourself for bad news' feeling. Just like she'd had when her sister had called and said she wanted to talk about Amy's ex.

"Hannah is my daughter. She ran away from her mother's house nearly two years ago. I keep searching. Every spare minute I have is spent searching in person, or online. I'll find her. Even if it kills me. I want my daughter back, safe and sound." He uncurled his fists and ran his palms down his thighs. Despite his attempt at relaxing, the tension never left his shoulders.

"It's got to be tough," Jeff said. "I keep looking when I'm surfing the web. If I find anything, I'll let you know. But now, I have to run. Thanks for the beer and pizza."

"Thanks for helping me move in." Amy jumped to her feet, shook his hand and walked him to the door.

Outside, swirls of small snowflakes drifted to the ground melting on impact with the road and sidewalks. It was starting to pile up on the lawn, dusting the blades of grass with sparkling white. They'd finished unloading just in time. She shivered in the chill air. If the wind picked up, this weather front could turn ugly, fast. Even after living in Regina for years, she still wasn't used to freak snow storms. She eased the door shut after Jeff jogged down the street toward his home three blocks away.

Grabbing her beer, she flopped onto the couch at the opposite end to Justice. "Want to talk about it?" She asked. He was silent for so long she assumed he wasn't going to say anything.

"Hannah is almost sixteen. I divorced her mother, Ellen, when Hannah was seven. The court gave the majority of custody to Ellen. I get, got, Hannah one weekend a month and we alternated major holidays like Christmas and Easter. It sucked. Big time. But we made do. I talked to Hannah every night and she talked to my folks at least once a week. I never missed a chance to see her if I was in the city. Ellen was good about letting me have time when I was there."

She winced when his teeth ground loudly together.

"Was it amicable?"

"For the most part yes. We had a few differences of opinion on how to raise Hannah. Ellen came from money. Big money. She wanted Hannah to have her every heart's desire. If she asked for it, she got it. New laptop, new cell phone every year. All of it. My family is more down to earth. We work for what we have. Nothing is free. You learn quickly to value what you work for. That's the philosophy I wanted Hannah to grow up with."

Amy nodded but didn't respond. She'd witnessed the Flint philosophy more than once, watching Justice's nieces and nephews do small chores to earn spending money. They worked hard and were careful with their possessions.

"Where does Ellen live now?"

"Just outside of Edmonton. She returned to her family home when her mother passed away. It's a mega-ranch where they raise and breed thoroughbred racehorses. Hannah wanted to be a jockey. I said no. It's too dangerous for a child."

"Sixteen doesn't seem too young for horseback riding."

"No, but she was only fourteen then and too young to be looking for jockey work. Way too young to be hanging around the racing circuit with all the extraneous money and decadence." His voice was low and dangerous, is glare like a dagger. She sensed his anger was with someone other than her.

Justice continued speaking. "I went to a few parties when I was married. The booze, the drugs, it sickened me. I'm sure there was a lot of random sex, but I never saw it. I didn't want my daughter involved in that type of life. Fortunately, such events were rare and Ellen didn't host them."

Losing his daughter must have cut deeply. "This must be so tough for you. How do you even handle it? I'd go insane missing her."

He jumped to his feet and paced the room. His hands raked through his hair and massaged the back of his neck. "Sometimes I can't handle it. It keeps me up at night but I won't quit searching. Not ever," he said vehemently.

"Tell it to me. From the beginning," she suggested. "Maybe my police experience can help out." His angst and indecision were evident as he paced, sat down, and sprang back to his feet.

"Hannah had just turned fourteen, it'll be two years ago mid-December. It was Ellen's turn to have her for Christmas. Hannah complained she wanted to be here that year. Ellen refused. I thought we'd settled it." He sighed. "Hannah preferred to call me at night. She could call when she wasn't out with friends or doing homework. I allowed it because she never missed a call, and I didn't want to interrupt her studying. She was an honor student."

Those few statements left Amy with a thousand questions, but she kept quiet hoping he'd share more. How could he stand being apart from his daughter? When she had kids, she'd keep custody if her marriage ever broke up. She'd dealt with enough children from broken homes to know the issues they could end up with. Most were fine with split custody, others, not so much.

"She missed calling one night. No big deal. It happens. Then she missed a second and I got worried. When she missed the third night, I called her cell phone but she didn't answer." Self Loathing recrimination laced his voice. His fists clenched so hard his knuckles cracked.

"You were worried. I would be too," Amy commiserated.

"Damn right. I was worried. I called Ellen. She told me Hannah was sleeping at a friend's house for a couple days over Christmas break. She wasn't worried. Hannah had left a note. Ellen hadn't even bothered to follow up with the girl's parents."

Chills raced down Amy's spine. What was wrong with a woman who didn't care where their child was? An only child, she'd lost her parents when she was seven. Some of her foster homes had been great, especially the Englots. Like her birth parents, she'd lost them to a car accident. The loss had been devastating. At ten, she was certain the Englots were going to adopt her, she'd overheard them talking. When they died in a car accident, the loss mentally and emotionally crippled her for years, but at least she had the cold comfort of knowing their fate for certain. She'd bounced from foster home to foster home after that. Most okay, some less than ideal.

"Ellen was wrapped up in her third husband and didn't give a shit that our daughter was missing so I drove to Edmonton to talk to her, to find Hannah. Ellen had thrown away the note. I called all of Hannah's friends. Every contact I could find from school, from dance, from band. I searched the area, I talked to the principal of the school and I reported her missing. I talked to kids in the area until the cops told me they'd arrest me if I didn't stop hanging out around high school kids.

"I came home for two nights, Christmas Eve and Christmas Day, and went right back to keep looking. I looked for months before I came home. I spent a fortune on hotel rooms and take-out food. Don't get me wrong," he whirled around and stared at Amy with fire in his eyes. "I'll never stop looking, not ever. I spend every spare minute searching the internet, going to places we've been together. I will find her. If it's the last thing I ever do!" The final words were laced with certainty.

"I can try searching the files at work." She held up a hand. "I know, it's been done and others are still looking. A fresh set of eyes won't hurt." There was no way she could stand by and do nothing. He was hurting, badly. An answering pain echoed in her own heart. "Promise me you won't do anything stupid or break the law while you're looking."

"I won't make promises I can't keep. I'll do whatever I need to. I'll find her." His arms crossed belligerently and he repeated vehemently. "If it's the last thing I do."

Admiration warred with frustration. Instinct told her he'd break the law in his search. He probably already had and likely would again. The cop in her was cautious and curious. Her compassionate side understood his position entirely even if she couldn't possibly imagine the pain of losing a child. Losing loved ones was bad enough. But not knowing where your child was or even if they were okay? Beyond comprehension. No parent should outlive their child or have to wonder about their child's fate.

Try as she might, she couldn't take a mental step back. She was going to become irrevocably wrapped up in his search and as a result, probably in his life as well. She wanted to be sociable, but hoped to keep from forming deep attachments in this town, the town she was determined to leave in only a few years. She'd yet to figure out how to balance staying alone with setting down roots, but that was a problem for another day.

"I'm sorry helping me move in delayed you. You could be searching by now." Guilt wracked her, leaving her feeling stretched to the limit.

"It doesn't matter, I'd barely have gotten out there before the storm hit." He chugged the last third of his beer. "And I'd have to turn around and come home. No harm, no foul."

"You wouldn't have known the weather was changing," she offered lamely.

"Weather alerts on my phone, I'd have been loading up my horse Buttercup, and never would have left. I'm glad I could help."

"The guys and I would have been fine without you, but thanks. Having you here made things go faster. I appreciate it. Even with extra hands, it took longer than I expected." She glanced away not wanting to share the depths of her gratitude. She wanted, needed, to be strong and independent, like her foster-sister, Mindy. Mindy was the Englot's natural daughter, their only child. After the Englot's death, Amy and Mindy had been sent to different foster homes but had kept in touch over the years. They were fast friends and visited each other often. Mindy never seemed to need anyone's help. She'd achieved the independence Amy strived for. Amy stared out the living room's bay window, barely noticing the swirling snow.

"You're welcome." He grabbed his used plate and beer bottle. "How about if we unpack the kitchen?"

"Why don't you head home? I can manage." She followed him into her kitchen and put her bottle in the case alongside the rest of the empties. "I'd buy this again," she changed the subject. "I've never tried micro-brewery beer before."

"Yeah, Mulligan's makes great pale ale. Their Pilsner isn't bad either and you're avoiding the discussion. I'm free for a while and more hands lighten the load." He saluted. "I swear, on my honor, my cowboy honor, not to tell a soul about it. Your secret will be safe with me."

"Hardy har har. You're a laugh a minute. Even I recognize a boy scout salute. Do cowboys even have a salute?" She hated to admit, even to herself, he was amusing and her fondness for his company would never pass her lips, nor would appreciation of his assistance.

He whipped a jackknife out of the front pocket of his jeans and sliced open the top box. "I'll pass things to you and you can put them away. Deal?" He unwrapped a clear glass salad bowl patterned with daisies and held it out to her.

"Fine." She grasped the bowl and stood staring at the dark brown, wooden, cupboards, unsure where she wanted it. "I'll let you hinder me, if you let me repay you with dinner next week."

"Hinder you? I believe you mean help you." He folded the beige packing paper neatly into quarters and set it on the counter before reaching for another item. The next item was a slightly larger bowl with matching daisies. He unpacked, folded and unpacked again.

She waited until he had unearthed the entire set of six serving bowls. She stacked them neatly on the granite countertop and slid them into an upper cupboard.

"Daisies?" he asked with a smirk. "I thought a rough and tumble cop would have skulls and crossbones, or maybe Harley Davidson dishes."

"Harley Davidson?" She laughed. "Do they even make dishes?"

"Who knows. I just wasn't expecting daisies." He unwrapped the first of a series of plates which were standing, on edge, in the box. "Oh, good gravy. More daisies?" He examined the bright yellow plate patterned with orange centered, white daisies and trailing green vines patterned across the surface.

She shrugged. "What's the matter, tough guy? Do daisies unman you? I'd have thought a rancher was tougher." She hadn't thought anything of the sort, but she liked the way he teased her. Like she was a sister or friend rather than a woman. She set the plate in the cupboard to the left of the sink. She could get used to having a male friend. Someone she didn't have to worry about what he thought of her. Or care if she was untidy when she saw him. Someone she could be herself with.

·♥·♥·♥·♥·♥·

Chapter Four

Flint held out another of the ridiculously feminine daisy plates. After a second, he set it on the counter and looked at Amy. She seemed a million miles away, lost in thought and he wondered where she had gone. She looked pleased and puzzled all at once; she was smiling but her eyebrows were pinched together quizzically. Something was going on behind her light blue eyes. If he knew her better, he'd ask about it but their friendship was too fresh to risk it.

He glanced around the kitchen, giving her time to think. The walls were fresh celery green, the windows sparkling. The house had been upgraded with modern appliances and a top of the line faucet by the previous owners. He set two more plates on top of the one he'd just set down before she moved.

She shook her head and smiled at him. "Sorry, I was thinking."

"You must have a lot on your mind with the move. It's a good thing I'm here because at the rate you're moving, you'd never finish unpacking." He smiled to soften the words.

He flipped over the emptied box, cut the tape sealing the bottom, collapsed it and set it aside. "Shoot. I should have saved it for the paper," he said glancing at the growing pile of neatly folded sheets on the table.

"No worries, I expect we'll empty another one."

"You're going to let me help with a second box?" His voice rose with mock surprise and he clutched his chest. "Be still my beating heart. The independent Amy Baxter is allowing a man to help her. I may not survive the shock."

"Don't make me get out my Glock and shoot you," she warned. "Beer?"

"Sure. It's not like I'm driving home in this blizzard."

"You live next door. I'm sure you can walk that far; even in a snowstorm." She walked to the fridge, popped the door open and bent over to reach inside.

His breath caught in his throat. Geez. Nice backside! He shook the thought off and forced his gaze to the ceiling. He had no right to be ogling her backside or any woman's backside for that matter. It was rude. His mother would slap him silly. Okay, Sue had never hit him, but one look and he'd feel way too much guilt and remorse. His stepmother had the evil eye down pat.

"You'd send me out in a blizzard?" He groaned. "After all I've done to help you? I might get snow blindness and get lost."

"It's less than fifty feet from my door to yours. I think you'd manage." She popped the bottles open deftly and passed him one. "Are you going to wimp out on me? Need a crystal glass for that, pretty boy?"

"You think I'm pretty?" He batted his eyes like a black and white movie heroine. A load of folded papers hit him in the face. He sputtered in shock. "What the heck?"

"You're here to work, not to be pretty," she responded and threw another stack of papers at him.

"Hey, I folded that carefully, so it could be reused." He scooped a pile off the floor.

"And I reused it, to throw at you. Are you going to open the next box or stand there fishing for compliments?"

He laughed. "I guess I know where I stand with you. Right out back of the outhouse."

"You'll be in the doghouse if you don't open the next box."

Another salute. "Yes, ma'am." The box was open and the knife returned to his pocket in seconds. "Oh no," he groaned after unwrapping the first item. "Daisy mugs? Don't tell me your entire kitchen is done in daisies. You're going to have to buy more masculine dishes before the guys come over." Truthfully, he couldn't care less what the dishes he ate off looked like, nor would her coworkers, but he enjoyed the teasing camaraderie they'd developed.

"Too afraid of your feminine side to eat off girlie dishes?"

He threw his hands up in mock disgust. "That's it, I'm out of here."

"Oh no, you are not. You offered to help me unpack the kitchen. You're stuck until we finish. Step up the pace, Flint. I'm waiting."

He did a mental count of the boxes. "There are sixteen boxes here. How many dishes does one woman need? You live alone. You need one of everything. Guests can use disposable."

"That would be really environmentally responsible wouldn't it? Tell me you don't use disposable dishes."

"Of course not, I was teasing. We've only got one planet and we need to take care of her. But, really, why so many dishes?" Couldn't she tell he'd been teasing? Surely, she had a sense of humor. It wasn't like he was Mr. Jolly Jokester, but he did admire people with a sense of humor.

"Some of this belonged to my first foster parents. It has sentimental value."

A soft smile lit her face as she gazed at the dish in her hand.

"I didn't know you were a foster child."

"I was. For eleven years and more foster homes than I want to count." Her tone told him to drop it.

Right, like that was going to happen. She must have mixed feelings about her foster families. "And some of the dishes are from your first foster home?"

"And a few things from my birth family. What of it?" She slid the dish into the cupboard and crossed her arms over her chest, her eyes narrowed.

"Just curious how you managed to keep it. But if you'd rather not talk about it, I understand." Her losses brought Hannah back to the forefront of his mind. Dammit, he should be looking for her. Online if nothing else.

"You'll find her," Amy said, placing a comforting hand on his forearm. "Mom and Dad's neighbor kept a box of keepsakes for me when I went into foster care. When my first foster parents passed away, their neighbors stored a few boxes for their daughter Mindy and I. Dishes and a family album are all I have left of them."

Her hand slipped off his arm and she snatched up her beer and took a long pull from the bottle and stared out the window.

"Sometimes," he said, "life sucks." He tipped his bottle toward her when she turned back.

"Sometimes, you move into a new house and find a friend." She clinked their bottles together. "It takes the bad to help you remember the good."

"That's what Mom says." He appreciated the change of topic.

"Your mother is a very wise woman. And no doubt very patient. She has six children, right?"

"Eight. Dad had five boys. Sue, she's my stepmother, had three girls before she married Dad. Eight all together. We're a big, rowdy brood but we look out for each other."

"I stand corrected, she's a saint." She set her beer aside and hip checked him aside. "If you're not going to unpack, I am."

He grasped her shoulders and turned her around. With a soft shove, he pushed her back the way she came. "I don't know where anything goes. I'll unpack, you put it away."

An hour later they were finished. A neat pile of collapsed boxes sat by the door waiting to be returned to the depot for reuse. One was crammed full of neatly folded packing paper. Amy told him she planned to drop it off at a daycare for the kids to craft with.

"What now?" he asked.

"Now, you go home. I'll get the rest."

"I can help." He didn't understand why he needed to be here, helping her. A holdover from his upbringing, or attraction. Maybe avoiding the loneliness of his own home.

"The rest is private. I'll rebuild the bookcases and DVD stand and then fill them later. Now, I'm going to take a break."

"I can put them together for you." He was enjoying the casual companionship they shared. Being with her was...comfortable. She felt like family; if he disregarded his physical attraction to her.

"I'm sure you could but I'm more than capable of running a drill and screwdriver. You've been a great help, and you've done more than enough. Go home, find something to do. I'll talk to you later in the week. I'm off all week, I'll feed you either Wednesday or Thursday."

"Did you forget, Wednesday is Halloween?"

"Are you getting fussy? About a free meal?" She laughed.

It was adorable when she wrinkled her nose, it was so un-cop-like. "Fine. I'll be grateful for dinner on the night of your choosing. Except Halloween. I have to dress up and pass out candy."

"But your house isn't even decorated!"

"It doesn't need to be. The kids know me. I'm the guy who gives out full sized chocolate bars. I make a special trip to Costco every year to stock up."

"You need decorations."

"No, thank you." He hadn't decorated for a holiday since Hannah disappeared. Sure, he'd only missed one Halloween so far. This year would be the second. Somehow it seemed...disloyal to decorate without her.

"Just a few," she pleaded. "Halloween is magical for kids. Put up a few decorations for the kids. For Hannah."

"Low blow," he growled. "I'll leave you to your unpacking." How could she bring his daughter into this? Guilt and pain clutched his guts and for a moment, he thought he might be sick. He bit back the gag. She wasn't right. Was she? Would Hannah be disappointed he didn't decorate? Would she want him to? Dammit. Wasn't his life tough enough without all the added questions? He pivoted on his heel and headed to the front entry.

She trailed after him to the door, apologizing with every step. "I didn't mean to touch a nerve. I just thought..." She sighed. "Never mind. Thanks for the help."

Anger surged through him and he whirled around to confront her. "You just thought what? You'd stab me in the heart? Test me to see if I really missed my daughter." He ignored the single tear rolling down her cheek. He slammed his feet into his boots.

"I just thought—what if she showed up on Halloween? What if she sees you stopped celebrating the holidays? How would she feel? I think she'd want you to keep celebrating without her."

"She's not dead!" He shouted the words as if volume could make them true. *Oh God, what if she was?*

"She's not. I believe you. I know you'll find her."

Amy clasped his suddenly cold hands in her soft, warm ones. Her eyes glistened with emotion. "Justice Flint. You have to believe. Hope is all you have. Let it fuel your heart until you find her."

He closed his eyes and pictured Hannah's face. Usually, her image came to him, laughter and smiles wreathing her chocolate brown eyes. Today, his vision of his daughter looked serious and sad. Was Amy right? Would Hannah want him to decorate?

"How do I let myself get talked into these things?" He asked when he opened his eyes. "I'm not doing it today. The weather sucks. As soon as it clears up, I'll dig the decorations out of the basement and put them up. For her. For you. I apologize for losing my cool. I'm over sensitive when it comes to Hannah." He opened the door and stormed out.

"Flint? I'm sorry." Her voice, heavy with remorse, bounced off his back. "You forgot your coffee carafe."

He was a screw up. He'd messed up being a husband. He could barely be on the ranch without arguing with his father over how they did things. He was even worse as a father and now he'd hurt his new neighbor. Damn. He wanted a drink. He crashed into his house, barely resisting the urge to slam the door behind him.

Pausing, he closed his eyes and let his hands drop to his sides and forced his fists to open. She hadn't meant any harm; she was trying to help him. One deep breath followed another until a small measure of calm crept over him. He hung up the denim jacket he'd barely remembered to grab on his way out and placed his cowboy boots neatly in the closet and his hat on its peg.

He stepped into the living room. Heavy pine furnishings with leather cushions made it a masculine haven. Pillows and afghans crafted by Hannah made it more feminine. His mom had taught her to crochet and sew. The heavy oak mantle over his wood burning fireplace was lined with pictures. Starting on the left was Hannah's kindergarten picture. They progressed in order to the final one of her in grade nine. Every year her dark brown hair had gotten longer. She refused to cut anything except her bangs. There should be grade ten and grade eleven pictures there. On the right was a picture of him, Hannah and Ellen. He'd rather it wasn't there, but Hannah liked the picture from the one trip they'd made to Disneyland, so he let it stay when Ellen moved out. Hannah had Ellen's petite bone structure, barely weighing in at a hundred pounds, if that; and she had her mother's dark brown eyes. Her hair was pure Flint, though her face contained elements of both her father and mother. She had her mother's cheekbones, her father's stubborn chin and two tiny little dimples.

To the left of the fireplace was what Hannah affectionately called the mug-shot wall. Family photos of his entire family. Candid shots of everyone, individually and in groups, were mixed with professional images and scenic views of the ranch. One of his favorites was Hannah holding the bouquet of roses he'd given her after her opening night performance as Dorothy in the Wizard of Oz. He stroked the edge of the frame, wishing she'd come home.

He stared around their home. It had lost most of its warmth and homey-ness. Gone was the mess and clutter of teenage life and discarded clothing. Strangely, he missed it. Deep soul punching pain slammed into his solar plexus. God, he missed Hanna and the messes she left behind.

It wouldn't be so bad if Amy hadn't been right. Hannah would want him to decorate for the holidays. His mother had mentioned it, once, the first year Hannah was gone, and he'd nearly bitten her head off. Sure, he handed out candy and bought Christmas gifts. The bookshelf in his office held gifts he'd purchased for Hannah in vain hope she'd come home. Valentine's Day, Easter, Christmas, her birthday. They sat lined up in a row, wrapped and waiting for her. Would she like the tablet? The novels by her favorite author, the cute teddy bears? Last year he'd even bought her a costume to match his knowing she loved to help hand out treats. But he'd skipped decorating. Putting them up and taking them down would only reinforce her absence. The year she'd disappeared he'd left their Christmas decorations up. His mother and sisters had snuck into the house and taken them down the next February. He'd cried for days and stubbornly gone without talking to them for months. Only after his father and brothers had ganged up on him had he tried to forgive them. It had taken a while, but eventually he'd come to realize they'd been right to remove the sad reminder of his loss.

It would be different this year, he'd decorate and take pictures. For her.

Renewed resolve washed over him like an invigorating tide. He'd pull out all the stops and go full-on Halloween and then he'd find her. This was the year she came home. He could almost feel it. Maybe his efforts would pay off and his prayers would be answered.

Chapter Five

Amy paused to catch her breath, leaning against her snow shovel and refusing to give in to the exhaustion swamping her. She'd walked to the store and back for the wide edged scoop. The snow plows had been out, the sanding trucks would be along soon, but the roads were still icy. Snow continued to drift down; it was almost up to her knees in only a few hours. With her house nearly unpacked, she'd decided to tackle the first enormous layer of snow. The front walkway was finished as was the route to her tiny garage in the back alley. Now, she was determined to stick with it and clear the path between her place and Flint's, the one leading along the west side of her house from her front yard to her back.

More than anything, she wanted to quit, but she'd bought this house and by all that was holy, she'd keep up with the maintenance. Maybe she should have purchased a snow blower. She scooped and threw another two loads of snow. The amount she lifted was getting smaller with each progressive effort. By the time she finished shoveling it would be time to start again. Mother Nature had a way of putting people in their place. Her foster mother, Mom Englot, had said, "Do it right, do it once. One and done." She'd been so wrong when it came to shoveling snow. Amy chuckled and bent back to her task.

The forecast for the next few days was sunny and warm. If she was lucky, most of the snow would melt. Today was Halloween and she wanted the walkways safe and clear for the trick or treaters. Even if it meant shoveling repeatedly and salting any icy places.

She scooped and paused to lean on her shovel. Her arms trembled with the effort. She'd need a long soak in the tub after this or she'd be too stiff to move tomorrow. She looked up at the sky. Heavy, elaborate snowflakes drifted lazily down obscuring her efforts. She sighed and shook her head to clear the snow clinging to her hair and lashes.

Beside her a light flipped on in Flint's house. Justice, she reminded herself. Somehow, in her mind, she'd started referring to him by his last name, the same way she referred to her colleagues. Besides, what kind of name was Justice anyway? There had to be a story behind that. She reminded herself to ask him about it when she had him over for dinner.

She peeked into the window on the side of his house, the one which faced the tiny window in her dining area. Inside, Justice paced back and forth. He wandered out of the room and returned a few seconds later with an enormous box. She tried to tear her gaze away but the investigator in her kept her glued to the scene.

His back was to her as he set the box down on his desk. His shoulders raised up and down, like he'd heaved an enormous sigh, and he lifted the lid off the box. He set it aside and pulled out an oversized plastic jack-o-lantern. Next came a skeleton and an enormous rubber rat, then a black cat with it's back arched menacingly.

The decorations would delight children. They were as whimsical as they were scary. What else would follow? With effort, she turned her attention back to her shoveling and made short work of clearing the rest of the path. A smile of victory crossed her face. Flint was doing it! He was decorating for Halloween. She knew he'd never give up searching for his daughter, but at the same time, he was moving on. One thing she knew was that moving on was important after a loss, no matter how much it hurt. The grief never went away, but it faded enough to let the happy memories shine through. Halloween with the Englots had always been a blast. Haunted houses, trick-or-treating, candy galore but best of all—a scary movie fest. She'd have to remember to call Mindy and see what she was watching this year.

After her bath, she popped outside to turn on the lights strung across her eaves and the two strands circling the porch pillars on either side of her front steps. She turned on the flameless candles in the five carefully carved pumpkins decorating her stairs. Finally, she plugged in the two long strings of LED lights that hung between her porch and the enormous lilac bushes flanking her sidewalk. She smiled in satisfaction as the orange bulbs made her yard glow festively. She could barely wait for Christmas; she'd already purchased the first of her yard decorations.

She glanced down the street, nearly every home had their decorations out. One or two weren't lit yet, and only one house seemed to have skipped decorating completely; it looked cold, dark and out of place among the festive and glowing homes. From the other direction she could hear the faint clink of chains and ghostly howls of the neighborhood haunted house a few houses down from Flint's. She'd taken a quick tour of the house when she'd gone out to get her shovel the other day. It was scary fun. The kids would love it.

Curious, she turned toward Flint's house. A row of lighted plastic skulls lined the walkway. A skeleton leaned against the base of his lone birch tree and lights serpentined through the railings on his front steps. Three grinning jack-o-lanterns clustered on a bale of straw to the left of his doorway. An inflatable ghost with waving arms stood guard at the corner of his house. He'd gone all out. When Flint did something, he did it up right! Her mind jumped to other, more adult, pleasures and she caught herself wondering how much attention he'd put into them. What kind of lover would he be? If the effort he put into small things was any indication, he'd be attentive to her needs.

She stepped out onto the sidewalk to get a closer look just as Flint came out of his house carrying a wooden rocking chair with a scarecrow sitting on it. He set it in the snow on the lawn and stood back to admire his handiwork.

"Hey Flint. Looking good," she called. "Why don't you come over for dinner? I'm making pasta. We've got just enough time to eat before the kids start showing up." The question startled her. She hadn't intended to extend the invitation, but once the words were out, she wasn't going to take them back. Being around him gave her mouth a mind of its own.

He paused halfway to his house and looked at her. He glanced at his watch and pursed his lips. "Sure, why not? I'll be over as soon as I'm done here."

"Give me fifteen minutes to get it ready." She waved and ducked back into her house, heart pounding like she'd run a marathon. What had come over her? She didn't randomly invite people over. She was a planner by nature, sometimes planning things down to the minute. Was this a mistake? Maybe she should recant the invitation.

Sure, then he'd think she was just another irrational female. She'd heard that story more than once, from idiots she'd dated. She'd shared a few short conversations with Justice since she moved to town and she was beginning to think of him as a friend. No harm in friends sharing a meal. She'd let the invite stand. She brushed the snow off her slippers, wiped the bottoms dry and hurried to the kitchen.

While the water boiled for the pasta, she set the table and chopped some leftover chicken. She hurried to the bedroom and slipped into her witch costume. A flowing long black dress, a cape and a pointy black hat. By the time Justice knocked on her door, dinner was ready. She rushed to the front door to let him in.

"Whoa!" He clutched one hand to his chest and jumped back. "You're not planning on having me for supper, are you?"

His chuckle sent a bolt of warmth through her and she laughed. "Not tonight but I'd watch your back if I were you. After tonight, all bets are off."

"I'll keep that in mind. Will a peace offering help? I hope red wine is okay. Seems I'm out of white." He held out the bottle.

"Oh, Apothic. Nice. One of my favorites. Thanks, you didn't have to."

"Mom told me never to go to dinner empty handed. Always bring something with you and I sure wasn't going to run out and get flowers." He chuckled. "Besides they'd send the wrong message."

"And what message would that be?"

"That I think of you as a woman. Or a date. We're buds. Pals. Neighbors. Friends who don't bring each other flowers."

"I'll try to remember," she said wryly even as she banked irrational disappointment that he didn't think of her as a woman. Wasn't that what she wanted? She stepped back. "Come on in. Dinner's ready. I'll just grab some glasses and open the wine."

She tossed some Alfredo sauce on the chicken and pasta and set it on the table next to the salad and fresh rolls.

"I smell Alfredo. Are those spiral noodles?"

"Yes, Fusilli. Does it matter?"

"Everybody knows Alfredo always goes best with fettuccine," he teased. "Bottled sauce? I thought you'd be a gourmet chef."

"I am, when I want to be. This was a spur of the moment invitation. I did bake the buns today." She spooned some salad onto her plate and passed him the bowl.

"I can tell, I smelled them cooking as I came up the walk. I swear, baking bread is the most welcoming aroma in the world. Going to my brother Jason's butcher shop is murder. It's right next door to the bakery. I end up buying fresh bread and a cake every time I visit." He served himself salad and accepted the pasta dish from her. "So, if this was a spur of the moment invitation, it doesn't count as the meal you owe me. You'll have to feed me again to keep your end of the deal."

"Don't get your hopes up, Flint."

"I do have a first name, you know. Most people do."

"Flint works," she said and after a moment's pause for a silent prayer of thanks, she started eating. "What kind of name is Justice? Did your parents hope you'd become a cop?"

"Oh man," Flint declared after his first bite. "This is fabulous. I stand corrected, you can cook." He took an enormous bite from his well buttered roll.

Amy laughed. "Nice evasion. Tell me about your name, there has to be a story behind it." She waited for his answer. His avoidance of the topic suggested there was a story, and that he wasn't thrilled with it.

"Mom went into labor with me on the highway on her way into town from the ranch. An RCMP officer stopped to help out. Corporal Zebadiah Emanuel Flitbottom delivered me. Mom wanted to name me after him, to honor his help. She changed her mind when she learned his name. Dad suggested Justice as a compromise. I guess there was a Justice Flint over a hundred years ago. Some distant relative. According to Mom, the past and the present blended well."

"So, I should call you Zebbie then?" She asked, pouring them each a glass of wine.

"Not if you want to live." His eyes turned narrow and squinty. "Justice will be fine."

"Anything you say Zebbie Justice."

"I'm warning you," he growled, seeming half serious.

"Threatening an officer of the law, Mr. Flint?" She really shouldn't tease him, but it was adorable how he disliked what could have become his name. The story was cute and touching, not something to be bothered by.

He shoveled an enormous portion of noodles into his mouth effectively ending the conversation. When he emptied his mouth, he took a long drink of wine and looked at her seriously. "Listen, I would seriously appreciate it if you forgot I was ever foolish enough to tell you the story."

"I promise it will never leave this room, Zebbie."

A chorus of children's voices called out "Trick or treat."

"Shoot. I hoped we'd get time to finish eating," Justice groused. "I don't even have my costume on."

"Sit, I'll hand out treats."

"They'll stop at my place if they haven't already." He jumped to his feet sending the chair skittering backward.

"Go, get your treats, bring them back here and we'll take turns handing them out until we finish eating. Is it typically busy this early?"

"Naw, just the youngest ones. The middles come out about six thirty and the big kids around eight. Answer the door, I'll run and get my treats and my costume."

The first family were dressed as Minions. "Is that a dart gun?" Amy asked.

"It's a fart gun," a boy about six years old answered, giggling like crazy.

Amy threw her hands in the air nearly spilling her skull shaped bowl of treats. "Don't shoot me with that thing," she cried, sending the family into a fit of laughter.

"I won't Constable Baxter, I promise."

She studied the youngster. "Sorry, I don't remember your name."

"Brett Green. You came to my school to talk about Halloween safety. I'm in Miss Paxton's class."

Miss Paxton, right. The grade one teacher was engaged to Flint's brother Riley. She remembered the boy now. She shook Brett's hand and those of his siblings and parents. "Nice to meet you, Green family."

Justice loped up the sidewalk, a box of chocolate bars held high. "Hiya, Greens." He'd spiked his hair up and donned a cape and fangs and looked vaguely vampire-ish. He ruffled the baby's hair and pecked her mother on the cheek. "Happy Halloween." He tossed a couple bars in each of their treat bags.

"Two?" Brett cried ecstatically. "You only give one!"

"Special treat to the first kids of the year," he explained. "Have fun."

Brett scampered down the sidewalk and called a distracted "Thank you," as he went.

Amy searched up and down the street. "Nobody else is coming right away, let's finish eating while we have the chance." She debated asking about the double treat and decided to let it rest for now. He'd already brought out the decorations, perhaps the double treat was another way to remember his daughter.

He slipped his fangs into his pocket and they finished eating. Amy refilled their wine and they bundled up in warm jackets and mittens, capes slung overtop to stay in costume. They sat, side by side on her front porch handing out treats and talking quietly. After the fourth group of kids skipped up his sidewalk and back down disappointed, he moved his scarecrow to the end of the sidewalk and gave him a sign reading, 'My treats are next door'. He added an arrow pointing toward Amy's house. Everyone took it in good fun and seemed to enjoy getting double treats at her place.

Amy lit her portable gas-fired, deck heater and they sat companionably side by side enjoying the night. The snow slowed to a stop and the clouds drifted away leaving sparkling stars high above. Beautiful and so unlike the city where endless street lights blocked out the heavenly view. He pointed out a few constellations. When the chill started to get to her, she suggested hot chocolate.

"Only if you put a shot of brandy, or something, in it," he replied with a rogue grin that went straight to her heart.

"Beer when I moved in. Wine with supper and now a shot in your cocoa? Do you always drink this much?" She was teasing, but part of her wondered. She'd had one foster father with a taste for alcohol. He wasn't mean when he drank, just careless and unconcerned about his wife or the half dozen kids they were responsible for.

Justice paused before he answered. "Not really. I drink on occasion, rarely to excess, though I admit to a few drunken escapades as a youth. Since Hannah disappeared, I've never been beyond the legal limit to drive. If she calls, I need to be ready to go." He checked his watch. "Two glasses of wine in three hours. I'm pretty sure another small shot won't hurt."

"I'm not going anywhere, so I'm in. Sit tight and don't be cheap with the treats." She skipped inside, happiness bouncing around her chest. Justice Flint was a man she could get used to. He shared the work and let her do her own thing. She barely knew him and suspected he had a stubborn side and didn't like to see women struggle, but at the same time he was chivalrous and sweet. If she didn't watch herself, she'd become accustomed to spending time with him and that wasn't her plan.

She was staying in Coyote Creek for a few years and then relocating. Regina's RCMP detachment, and the mistakes she'd made while there had besmirched her reputation and she intended to stay on the straight and narrow here. Personal mistakes rarely made employment files and hers hadn't. She'd been lucky, even if the entire department had known about her mistake, it wasn't official. If she kept her nose out of trouble while she was here, she'd walk away clean and clear. People had short memories, perhaps her previous coworkers would forget about her sins if they ever worked together again.

The mistake she'd made falling for a fellow office would disappear, nobody in Coyote Creek knew she had mistakenly dated a married man, except her. She'd believed him when he said they'd marry. She'd never forget how he'd lied to her and hidden his reconciliation with his ex-wife. When her sister called to say she'd seen him with another woman, Amy had ended their relationship, requested the next transfer and fled as fast as her car would carry her.

She sighed as she filled the kettle. She'd been so naïve and stupid, believing him when he said they needed to keep their relationship a secret to protect their jobs. Until that point, she'd always wondered how people fell for the lies of sweet-talking men. She knew better now. The only upside of her mistake was that it had given her increased compassion and understanding for women in difficult situations which sometimes led to bad decisions or the inability to make decisions.

Scooping the cocoa mix into mugs, she pondered the man on her porch. Justice Flint was handsome, sexy and kind. He would make someone a great husband. That someone just wasn't going to be her. After tonight, she'd be certain they stayed on a friends and neighbors status. Nothing more, nothing less. Just friends. She wouldn't let herself desire anything more.

She paused with the kettle suspended over the first mug. She was getting carried away. Again. Flint had no interest in her. They'd barely met. He was totally wrapped up in his enormous family and his search for his daughter, as he should be, and here she was thinking about stalling a relationship that showed no signs of starting.

It didn't matter if he was as handsome as sin with those flashing Flint green eyes, brown hair and that single dimple in his left cheek. No sir. Just because his jeans fit to perfection and he could rock an insulated plaid jacket and ridiculous cape like a GQ cover model. Nope, none of it mattered because they were neighbors. Just neighbors.

She mixed the hot chocolate mix with boiling water, added heated milk and a dollop of Baileys. She topped the jumbo, daisy patterned, mugs with a generous portion of spray whipped cream, one of her biggest vices, and carried them out to the porch.

Justice accepted his mug with a smile and a thank you.

She smiled back, knowing the smile didn't quite reach her eyes. Between the kitchen and the porch, she'd decided to step back to keep her distance from Flint and not let their friendship deepen. She didn't need ties to him or to Coyote Creek. A few years from now, she'd be gone like a streak of greased lightning. Onward and upward in her career.

Funny, she didn't feel as eager to leave as she once had. Nostalgia for the holiday, that's what it was. Simple nostalgia. She was not getting attached to Coyote Creek or her bachelor neighbor.

·♥·♥·♥·♥·♥·

Chapter Six

The reek of industrial cleaner and unwashed bodies scraped at Justice's nose. Gross. Nothing should smell this bad. Cow shit didn't smell like this. Okay, he had to admit manure didn't bother him. It was earthy and musky but not entirely unpleasant. It was as much his mission here at the RCMP station as the smell which had his hackles up and his body in distress. All the cleaning in the world would never remove the acrid stench from the small interrogation room. How in the world had the Coyote Creek RCMP office acquired such a horrific smell?

His sister, Candy, had promised him she was done with this foolishness and yet here he was for the third time in less than a year bailing her ass out of jail. She wasn't a bad kid, just uber obsessed with saving the planet from man's plundering. But this time, dear God, this time she'd gone and outdone herself.

He paced the small room impatiently, waiting for Amy to bring in his wayward sister. The clock tic-ticked, marking time, fueling his frustration until he barely held back a growl. After an eternity the door opened and Candy stepped in. Her blonde hair was a tangled rat's nest. Her chin tipped down almost to her chest. She shielded herself by letting her hair hang down to conceal her face. Bits of leaves and pine branches entwined with the usually orderly strands. Mud stained her clothing and she was shoeless. Had she lost them, or had the police taken them?

"What the hell happened to you?" As upset as he was at being called out of bed in the middle of the night, concern for her smothered his ire.

She flung herself against his chest and wrapped her arms around his waist, sobs wracking her slight frame.

"I'll just leave you two alone for a few minutes. The door isn't locked. Come get me when you're done talking. Candice, don't leave the station." Her words rang heavy with warning.

"Thank you, Amy—Constable Baxter. I appreciate you giving us a moment alone. I know it's not protocol," Justice said.

"Five minutes." Amy stepped from the room closing the door firmly behind her.

"Amy? You're on a first name basis," Candy accused him.

"Skip it, kiddo. You can't deflect this. What the hell happened to your face?" He cupped her chin and tilted her head back and forth, staring at the scrapes and bruises darkening her usually flawless skin. Even under her tan she was pale and washed out.

She stepped back from him. She leaned against the wall, feigning nonchalance and innocence. "Nothing. I'm fine. Just pay my bail and get me out of here." She flashed him a hopeful grin. "Please."

He knew that look, the one that talked him into anything. She wasn't going to play him this time. He was tired of stepping in and trying to hide her troubles from his parents. She already owed him bail money from previous arrests. It was time she stepped up and took responsibility for her actions. She'd been arrested at a demonstration, again, but this time was different. This time she'd been caught in possession of drugs. Not much, only a few joints and two tablets of ecstasy.

"Demonstrations I understand. But drugs? You know better. You barely drink and you're doing drugs? You promised me, twice now, you wouldn't get arrested again." She started to protest and he waved her words away. "I get it, you love the planet, but there are better ways to save Mother Earth. And drugs? Dammit, Candy what were you thinking?" His heart thundered in his ears. "You're twenty-four years old. It's time to grow up."

He was scared. Terrified she'd get hurt and he knew there was no way he'd be able to keep this from their parents. In the past, when rumors found their way home, they'd let her other arrests slide and let him off the hook for trying to protect her. But with drugs involved there wasn't a chance in hell their parents would let it go. He wasn't even going to try and hide this one.

"They aren't mine." She stepped forward and held out her hand as if asking for forgiveness. Her fingers trembled. Nerves? Or was she coming down off something?

He closed his eyes and prayed for strength. "Cut the crap. Tell me the truth." She wasn't much of a liar, at least he didn't think she was. But Candy, on drugs? It didn't make sense. Maybe he didn't know his little sister as well as he thought he did.

"This is the last time, ever, that I bail you out. After this, you're on your own." He could tell by the look in her eyes she didn't believe his lie. Even he didn't believe it. He was at a loss as to how to get through to her.

His fists bunched. Forcing his fingers open, he scraped his palms along his thighs before thrusting his hands into the pockets of his fleece lined, denim jacket. It was Ellen all over again. His ex had been a master manipulator, it was one of the many reasons why he'd asked for a divorce. Now, being the brunt of female machinations again, he was sorely tempted to just walk away. No, he wanted to ride away as fast as his favorite horse could carry him. But Candy was family. His sister. Yeah, she was young, but she was old enough to stop doing stupid shit.

"Come on, Justice. This is me. You know me. The drugs weren't mine."

He glared and her face blanched.

"I swear to you." She dropped to her knees in front of him and pressed her hands together prayer-like. "I swear. I swear on Mother Earth, on this planet's health, they aren't mine."

He grabbed her grimy, dirt encrusted hands and pulled her to her feet. "Look, I don't get it. What happened to you? Why are you doing this?"

"I'm not doing anything I haven't done before. I did what you guys asked, I got a job. I'm sticking closer to home and keeping my costs down. I'm not asking Mom and Dad for money. What more do you want from me?" she snapped.

"I want the truth. No more BS. No crap. Tell me about the drugs." Her denial was killing him. He wanted to believe her but something about the way her eyes shifted back and forth, refusing to meet his, told him she lied. If she wasn't lying, she was certainly hiding something. The question was what. It hit him like a bolt of lightning. Pratt. "Tell me you aren't tangled up with Allan Pratt again?"

"I'm not."

She shifted back and forth on her feet, refusing to meet his gaze. Yup, she was lying. "I can't believe you're hooked up with him again. That's it. I'm done. You're on your own. I won't help you if you're going to keep hanging around him." He turned his back on her, opened the door and stepped into the hall. He wouldn't abandon her, but he was hoping to scare her enough to get the truth. Maybe she'd turn her life around before something seriously went wrong.

"Fine. I saw Pratt at the demonstration. We talked." She grabbed Justice's elbow and turned him back toward her. "I can't help it if he shows up where I do. He just seems to find me. We were talking, I was trying to convince him to leave me alone when all hell broke loose. Some idiot brought a shotgun. Bullets bounced off the tree, right over my head. I nearly crapped myself. Next thing I knew, Allan had knocked me to the ground, and he was gone." Her breath shuddered in and out. "He saved my life. How can I turn him in for putting drugs in my pocket when he saved me?"

Chills raked down his spine. He'd heard the expression that your blood ran cold. This was the first time he'd ever actually felt it. He froze in place. As much as he wanted to walk away, to force her to solve this herself, he had to find a way to get through to her.

"Talk to Constable Baxter. She'll help you out with this. I know she will. You can't keep letting that jerk mess with your life. This time, you could have been hurt. You could have been killed." His voice rose in alarm. "I can't put this behind me. Deal with it or I'll deal with him."

·♥·♥·♥·♥·♥·

"You'll deal with who?" Amy asked, stepping back into the room.

"Nobody," Candy blurted. "He's just being all big brother bossy. I swear he thinks he's my dad."

"Indeed." Amy stated blandly, ignoring Candy's eye roll. "Seems to me he's doing you a favor, coming out in the middle of the night to get you out of jail. Only the best brothers stick their noses out for their siblings. Most would let their little sisters call their parents..." she trailed off with a shrug.

"Tell her about the drugs," Justice demanded.

Amy looked back and forth between them. Something was up here. As a police officer, she always had one ear open for gossip and innuendo. She'd never heard anything about Candice Flint and drugs. Not a single word. Justice on the other hand, spent way too much time hanging out around the high school, talking to kids. Why was he pushing his sister so hard? Was he trying to get her to pin the drugs on someone else, to take the suspicion off him?

She didn't want to believe it was possible. But so many things about this man didn't add up. Multiple trips out of town. Dozens of packages coming and going from the post office all the time. No real job, just work on the family ranch which couldn't pay much. More friends and acquaintances than any one man should have.

He had a great reputation around town. Despite her attraction to him and his seemingly carefree charm, something just didn't sit right with her. Was his search for his daughter a front for illegal activities?

She stepped forward and looked Candice right in the eye. "Anything you wish to talk about before you go back to your cell?"

"Nope. Nothing to tell here." Candice turned toward her brother. "Come on, Justice. Bail me out. Just one last time." Her voice cracked.

Amy had talked to her fellow officers about Candice's arrest record. It was half a mile long. She'd been hauled in over and over again as a teenager. Never for anything serious, just for attending demonstrations and refusing to leave. Until recently, no charges had ever been filed, but notes had been made on her behavior. When she was twenty-one, she'd been arrested. Justice had posted bail every time she called for help. Today, he seemed disinclined to assist her, though he had rushed right over to the station when Candice had called him. The small pot she possessed was nothing. It was legal now. But the ecstasy was a whole different issue. A small amount, obviously for her personal use. But this was Coyote Creek's first instance of ecstasy showing up. Knowing where it came from would help the police keep it in control.

After spending a few months on Regina's drug task force, Amy doubted Candice was using, it seemed more like she was protecting someone. Was she holding out because Justice was a dealer?

"I'm not putting up your bail unless you tell her the truth," Justice growled.

Wow, was his bite as bad as his bark? An image of Justice nibbling her neck flashed into Amy's mind. Crap. She had to keep her mind out of the gutter. This was serious business and she couldn't let him get into her head. Not now. Not ever.

"Okay then," she said. "If there's nothing else to say and he won't post bail, I guess it's back into the cell with you. Come on then."

"Fine," Candice snapped. "The drugs belong to a friend. An acquaintance. My ex-boyfriend."

"Which is it?" Amy queried; her curiosity peaked.

"All of them. Allan and I dated for a few months. We broke up because of his drug use."

"And because he's a big-time loser," Justice interjected.

Amy glared at him and he fell silent. "You can wait in the lobby if you can't keep quiet," she advised even as she wondered what it would be like to have more family members stick up for her like that. She'd always wanted a brother to go along with her sister, Mindy.

"Allan who?" Amy asked.

"Allan Pratt. I met him at a rally to save some wetlands near Camrose. We dated. We went to rallies together. After I broke up with him, I avoided rallies he would likely attend. Lately, he shows up wherever I go. I can't avoid him. We were fighting, arguing, when the gunfire started. He threw me to the ground and the next thing I knew; he was gone." She shivered. "I stayed where I was until the police told me to get up. No way was I risking getting shot." She wrapped her arms around herself and gripped her elbows until her knuckles turned white.

"And the drugs? You said they were Mr. Pratt's?"

"The only thing I can figure is he must have put them in my pocket when we went down. Look, test my blood. Test my hair. I've never used drugs. Not even once. Yah, I drink on occasion, but not drugs. I never felt the need."

"There are plenty of dealers who never touch the stuff." Amy spoke to Candice, but her stare was fixed on Justice. His brows pinched together.

"Are you accusing my sister of being a drug dealer? Are you out of your mind?" His voice was low and threatening, his shoulders bunched together, his back rigid.

She'd definitely touched a nerve there.

"I'm discussing possibilities, not making accusations. Relax, Mr. Flint." She turned to Candice. "Take a seat and I'll get a statement from you regarding the drugs. We'll add it to your initial arrest statement. If your story pans out, I might be able to get the possession charges dropped. No promises. Would you like your brother to leave while we talk?"

Candice looked indecisive for a moment. "No. He can stay. I've got no secrets from him."

"No, just from our parents. You know they'll find out about this, right? They always do." His words were censorious and full of hidden meaning.

"Ugh," Candice groaned. "Promise you won't tell them," she begged.

Justice nodded without speaking. His mouth was turned down at the corners, as if he didn't want to keep her secret.

"Two minutes and I'll get what we need to modify your statement. Take a seat, both of you and I'll be right back." Amy waited until they sat, closed the door and headed for her desk. They'd arrested the shooter, a known paid protester, out to cause trouble. Other officers were dealing with him. Her task was to deal with Candice Flint.

When she returned to the interrogation room, Justice and Candice were in the middle of a heated discussion. Candice sat in the chair; arms crossed over her chest. Justice had both hands on the table and leaned forward, across the table to glare at her.

"You've got to stop all this demonstration crap. Find a way to help that doesn't keep getting you arrested. I get it. I do. I know how important this is to you, but there must be a way to help without landing your ass in jail over and over again. Dad's health won't tolerate the stress."

"Come on. You guys told me to get a job. I got a part time job at the library. I'm doing more online petitions. But sometimes you have to actually be there to help. It takes bodies to stop some of the atrocities. At least now I have a job and I'll be able to pay my own fines. Eventually."

"You almost became a body. A dead body. Stop and think about it. You could have been shot. Think about what it would do to our family if you died," Justice demanded sourly. "I'm just your brother but your foolhardy exploits are going to give me a heart attack or an embolism. Please, for the love of God, just take a step back and think about the rest of us."

"Okay, then. Let's get your statement," Amy declared. The siblings whirled toward him, obviously they hadn't heard her re-enter the room. She'd love to see the outcome of their *discussion*, but she had a job to do. At three a.m. her shift was long over and she was more than ready for bed. Nonetheless, she'd put aside her exhaustion, complete the statement and file a report before leaving for the night. Thank heaven tomorrow was her day off. The only thing she had planned was a trip to the library for something to read.

· ♥ · ♥ · ♥ · ♥ · ♥ ·

Chapter Seven

Amy wandered the stacks in the Coyote Creek's small library. It wasn't big, but it had a large, ever changing collection. She rounded the corner, nearly bumping into Candice Flint.

"Geez," Candice whined. "Are you checking up on me?"

"Guilty conscience?" Amy laughed to show she was joking. "I'm heading into four days off. I've come to stock up on reading material. Something serious, and something light. I was thinking maybe the latest Janet Evanovich book, a cozy mystery, and maybe something to stimulate the mind. Maybe a cookbook or something spiritual."

"Oh, we just received a great book on baking bread. It has some amazing looking sweet bread recipes. It might be what you need."

"Ladies," Justice sauntered up to them.

"Great." Candice groaned. "Are you checking up on me too?"

"Can't a man ask his little sister to lunch?"

"Not without an ulterior motive," Candice quipped. "But if you're buying, I'm eating. Let's get something vegan?" Her words were as much a question as a statement.

"I was thinking more along the lines of Tammy's. I've got a hankering for one of their meat pies. I'm a carnivore, not a vegivore like you."

"A hankering?" Candice rolled her eyes. "Drop the cute cowpoke slang. It's unbecoming and you sound like an idiot."

Amy laughed and Justice glared. "Well," Amy said, "she does have a point." Personally, Amy found his occasional slip into what she called cowboy lingo cute. It lightened his sometimes serious, no-nonsense demeanor and made him more human, like he had been on Halloween. "Mind if I join you?" she blurted. "I'm starving and I hate eating alone."

Candice stared at her with bulged eyes and a slack jaw.

Justice laughed at his sister's expression. "Sure, why not. It's always good to spend time with a neighbor. Especially one who owes me a home cooked meal."

He referred to the meal she'd promised him for helping her put up her Halloween lights. She'd made sure he wasn't around when she took them down even though she'd had some trouble struggling with the ladder through the snow two days after their impromptu Halloween dinner. She had her Christmas lights up now, though she hadn't turned them on despite the temptation to do so.

"Great, I'll buy lunch instead of cooking."

"No, you won't. You owe me a *home cooked* meal," he corrected. "Don't think you can cheat me out of it."

Darn, she'd had an instant of hope she could avoid another intimate dinner with Justice. He was too attractive by half and too secretive. There was something up with him and she wanted to know what it was before she got any closer to him. Not that she had any intention of getting close. Living next door to him was more than relationship enough.

"So much for getting out of cooking." She laughed. No sense fighting the inevitable. She made a promise, and she'd stick by it.

"Are you guys friends, or what?" Candice looked back and forth between them blinking in confusion and looking remarkably like one of the owls in the habitat she'd been arrested defending.

"Neighbors. Amy moved in next door to me. She owes me dinner for helping her move in and she's trying to skip out on her obligation. Come on. It's lunch time and I'm ravenous. I could eat the hind end off a mule."

"Oh, stop with the cowboyisms." Candice complained even as Amy laughed.

Fifteen minutes later, they climbed out of Justice's truck and filed into Tammy's. As always, the small restaurant was nearly full. The decadent aroma of seafood chowder filled the air.

"Can you smell that?" Justice groaned. "Fresh bread and meat pies. Broccoli-chicken unless I miss my guess."

"All I smell is the fish," Candice said with a laugh. "It does smell good, but I think I'll stick to one of their vegan dishes."

"Are you full on vegan?" Amy asked, ever curious to learn more about the people in her new home town.

"Mostly. I think it's a healthy way to live, though I confess to eating eggs and cheese and rarely some fish. Red meat makes me gag. Chicken and pork feel funny on my teeth. I've been lucky, despite the folks being ranchers, they've never forced me to eat anything. As a kid, they made me try everything at least once. Eventually, they realized I wasn't being a pest, I just don't care for meat." She shrugged. "What can I say? I love veggies but I adore chocolate and cake."

"Me too! Although I'll eat just about anything," Amy enthused.

"Hey, everyone," their waitress, Honey, greeted them, skipping up to their table with a jingling of the bells on her anklets. Her blonde spiral curls bounced lightly against her shoulders. "What can I getcha?"

They placed their orders quickly. As predicted, Justice had the chicken broccoli pot pie, Candice a salad with egg, cheese, and fried tofu. Amy went a different way.

"Corned beef hash with sauerkraut?" Justice laughed. "I never would have guessed it."

"Me either," Amy agreed. "I nearly barfed the first time I saw it. One of my foster mothers served it twice a week. It looks disgusting, but to my surprise, when she forced me to eat it, I loved it. I think it's the salt. Besides, it was the only thing she made that was fit to eat. The woman could burn water. She messed up dry cereal, which takes a special skill."

Honey returned with their drinks. "Justice, have you got that thing for me? It's for my cousin and she's only going to be here one more day. She needs it before she goes back to Australia."

"Swing by the house later and I'll give it to you. I just need to finish the packaging. Wouldn't want it to spill out early."

"Awesome-sauce. I'll come by later. I'll text you first." With that normal, though somewhat enigmatic exchange finished, she pranced over to the next table.

"What's she getting?" Candice asked.

Justice reached over and tweaked her nose. "If Honey's order was any of your business, dear sister, I'd tell you. But, since it's not, I won't. Mind your business."

Darn, for a moment, Amy had hoped to learn more about Justice. What did he have for Honey? Money hadn't been mentioned, but it seemed to be implied. The cousin was taking it back to Australia, so it couldn't be drugs could it?

A matronly woman wearing an immaculate linen suit and an inordinate amount of silver jewelry walked past their table and disappeared into the bathroom. The door had barely closed behind her when the man she'd been seated with jumped up and hurried over to their booth and slid in beside Justice.

"Hey, Just. Do you have it? I need it before she comes back. Lord help me if she finds out. She'll kill me," the owner of the local hardware store exclaimed, looking furtively around the restaurant. "Oh, hi officer." He smiled wanly. "Sorry if I'm interrupting, Justice. Call me." He leaped to his feet.

"Wait a minute, Floyd. I've got it here." He dug into his jacket pocket and extracted a small white package and slipped it into the man's palm." I was going to swing by the store later and drop it off. I know your wife helps host the lady's tea at the church today."

"Great. Thanks for keeping my secret." He dug out his wallet, extracted several large bills and handed them to Justice. After a moment's pause, he added an extra twenty. "A tip. Keep this under your hat, if you don't mind."

"Your secret is safe with me," Justice chuckled. "Have a great day, Floyd."

Two minutes later, Floyd was safely back in his seat when his wife returned.

"What was that all about?" Amy asked lightly.

"Oh my gosh!" Candice blurted. "You think my super strait-laced brother is dealing drugs, don't you?" She laughed uproariously. "That's rich. The man doesn't have a moral compass, he's got a moral pointer. For him, there are no gray areas, just black and white. He's the last man on the planet who'd ever sell drugs. I don't think he even speeds." Her laughter got louder and louder and she fell into silent chuckles, tears of mirth streaming down her cheeks.

"Funny." The single word was Justice's only reply.

Amy cheeks flushed. Candice had hit it right on the head. She did think Justice was selling drugs, it would explain so much, but there was no way she'd ever admit it. At least not until she had evidence. She'd bide her time and keep an eye on him. No, she'd keep both eyes on him.

"You have to admit your little exchange did look suspicious. A bundle of money, a small white package. But, I'm no fool. Only an idiot would do a drug deal right in front of a cop and I'm pretty sure your brother isn't an idiot."

Or was he? She might just do a little investigation in her off hours. Tonight.

·♥·♥·♥·♥·♥·

Justice's garage was unattached and sat just off the back alley, beside his shed. Later that evening, his house was dark but light shone through the curtains of his garage. Amy stared at the window, wondering what was going on inside. Had he left the light on and gone out? Was he out there, busy doing something?

Time to find out.

She bundled up her kitchen garbage and recycling and slipped into her coat and boots. She eased out the back door, closing it quietly behind her. Bags in hand, she headed toward her own small garage and the bins sitting alongside it. If anyone saw her out there, they'd assume she was taking out the trash, not snooping on her neighbor. She dropped the garbage into its bin and then wandered in the direction of Justice Flint's garage. Maybe she could get a peek through the window. Luckily Justice's gate was open, allowing un-hindered access to the side window. She stepped carefully through the snow drifts accumulated at the corner of the garage.

Another three steps and she'd be right under the window.

She set her left foot down. It skidded forward. Her arms wind-milled, the bag of recycling she'd held onto as an excuse for being outside flew into the air. Her right foot joined her left and she went down.

Hard.

On her backside. Her head thunked against the ground.

The recycling dropped down on her head just as her breath blast-ed from her chest in an explosive rush. "Ahhg."

She lay there moaning until she opened her eyes to find Justice looking down at her. Caught in the act. Great! Just what she didn't need.

"Good gravy. Are you okay? Why are you in my yard in the middle of the night?"

"I was taking out my garbage, er, recycling, I thought I saw an animal back here. Yeah. I thought I'd check it out. You know, it might have been a skunk." She almost rolled her eyes at her inability to formulate a good excuse, as if she hadn't been planning to come out here for nearly an hour. And she certainly hadn't intended to be spotted, flat on her back, barely able to breathe with a throbbing headache. Sometimes, Karma sucked.

"You were going to take on a skunk armed with recycling? Not the brightest move." He turned on his phone flashlight and shone it around the yard. "No tracks." He shone the light at her, flicking it away when the bright light made her wince. "Are you sure you saw something? Or are you just snooping around?"

"I swear, I saw a skunk." She crossed her heart. "Must have been a shifting shadow."

"Something's shifty." He held out his hand. "Come on Baxter, I'll help you up and make sure you get home safely before you hurt yourself. You aren't hurt. Are you?"

"Shouldn't that have been your first question?" she asked, trying to turn the attention to him. Why did she always get herself into no-win situations? First, she'd trusted her ex which led to her not trusting Justice, or any other man. Now she was caught red-handed snooping in his yard. Were her instincts as a cop so far wrong? Was she a failure? Dread pushed down on her chest stealing her already strained breath. She had to find a way out of this, a rational explanation for why she was in his backyard. A myriad of thoughts scattered through her mind, none of them of any value. She opened her mouth to make an excuse but no words came out.

"Save it, Constable Baxter. You were snooping around. Are you stalking me? Is this professional, or personal?" His hand dropped back to his side as he glared at her laying on the snowy ground.

She could almost see the blending of anger, disappointment and laughter in his voice. "I really was taking out the recycling. I saw the light..."

"And snuck into my yard to spy on me? You know that's insane right? And probably illegal to boot." The hint of laughter disappeared from his voice like a drug dealer from a police cruiser's flashing lights.

"I don't know what's up with you," he stated. "But, I'm tired of having you question my actions. You seem to turn up everywhere I go and you keep sticking your nose in my business. I've seen you eying me up at the school, the post office and grocery store. Frankly, it pisses me off. Enough already! Find yourself another man to irritate and stay out of my yard.

She scrambled to her feet, slipping several times on the ice crusted snow under the eaves. Finally, on firm ground, she straightened her shoulders and looked up to catch his eye. "You might be my neighbor, you might have a sterling reputation in this town, but I know you're up to something. One day, you'll slip up and I'll catch you. I'm going to bring you down, Flint. Mark my words." She scooped up her recycling, pivoted carefully on one foot and marched out of the yard.

Annoyed at herself, she flung her recycling into the bin and stomped up her snow-free sidewalk into the house. It took everything she had not to slam the door behind her.

Darn it. How could she be so stupid? She should have just casually asked him if he worked on cars or did woodworking or something of the sort. If she'd asked him in casual conversation rather than sneaking around his yard, she'd at least have an answer, even if it wasn't the truth.

Now, because of her own stupidity, he realized she was watching him. He'd be extra cautious around her and she might never catch him in the act of doing something illegal, like selling drugs. She hung up her coat and stood rubbing the small bump on her head. It didn't add up. His strange behavior was completely at odds with his reputation. She wasn't imagining things, was she?

She barely slept all night and if she didn't have a date with her foster-sister Mindy for lunch in Edmonton the next day, she'd have stayed in bed. Instead, she climbed into her car and headed for the city to spend a few days with her sister.

· ♥ · ♥ · ♥ · ♥ · ♥ ·

Chapter Eight

Justice paused at the split in his ex-wife's driveway. Straight ahead was her plantation style house. Pristine white with black shutters and ridiculous columns. Two stories tall, it had balconies surrounding both levels. It was boxy and to his mind, ugly. Its only redeeming feature was its enormous yard filled with manicured gardens.

To the left the paved road led past fields of horses, through a valley and up to a series of corrals and an enormous, modern, high-tech barn. Things were hopping at the barn; he saw several trucks and half a dozen ranch hands worked with horses in the training rings. The house, on the other hand, was dark and had an empty, closed-down feel.

Perfect.

He drove to the top of the driveway, turned his truck around so it faced the road in case he had to make a quick getaway, and parked out of sight of the barns. He sat for several minutes, watching and waiting. His heart thundered in his chest. Part of him couldn't believe he was going to do this.

He was breaking into his ex-wife's house.

Anxiety squeezed his guts. For a moment, he thought about driving away. Searching for Hannah, he'd done plenty of things which fell into legal gray areas, but this was the most blatant. He had no right to be here while Ellen was away in Europe. She was gone on her honeymoon trip with her fourth husband. Who needed a six-month long honeymoon? She checked in periodically, but most of his texts went unanswered. It was like she didn't give a shit about their missing daughter. He tried telling himself people grieved in different ways but he didn't believe Ellen grieved. Not for one second.

Straightening his spine, he climbed from the truck and strode to the front door as if he owned the place. Guilty behavior might attract attention, but boldness often went unnoticed. He jogged up the front steps and knocked lightly on the door. He waited. After two minutes he tried the knob. Locked.

With a deep breath, he reached into his pocket and pulled out a couple tools. "Here's hoping," he whispered and set to work on the lock. Last night, after his ridiculous encounter with Amy, he'd watched several videos on lock picking. A few interminable seconds and the lock popped open. He stepped inside and punched four numbers into the alarm keypad. The system disarmed without complaint. One thing he had to say about Ellen was she was consistent; she used her year of birth as her password for everything. Some day, she'd get hacked and lose everything. For now, he was glad she hadn't changed.

Bolder after his success, he eased the door shut, wiped his boots and strode into the house and up to the second floor. He toured quickly, glancing through all ten bedrooms, searching for signs of occupation. Nothing. Drop sheets covered the furniture. There was virtually no dust on the floors, Ellen's cleaning staff must make regular passes through the house.

Back downstairs, he checked the sunroom, library, den, sitting room and kitchen. The walk-in pantry was full of canned and dried goods but the fridge was empty. There wasn't even butter. Ketchup, mustard, barbecue sauce and a nearly empty jar of dill pickles pointed to a house long vacant. He slammed the fridge shut, leaned against the counter and dropped his head to his aching chest.

Hope was all he had left. It seemed his last ray of hope was dimmed. There was nothing here and while he didn't know what he was looking for he'd blindly prayed for a clue. In his crazy moments, he imagined Hannah hiding out here, safe from harm.

"What the hell are you doing?" The female voice came out of nowhere. He stumbled, righted himself and stared at the intruder.

Intruder? He almost laughed. He was the intruder here, not Amy Baxter.

"Baxter, what the hell are you doing here? Are you following me? Isn't that a bit beyond your scope of work?" He went on the offensive rather than admit he was in the wrong.

"A better question is, what are you doing in this house and how did you get in?" she demanded. She stood in front of him, dressed in civilian clothing. Her feet were spread in a ready position, her gun aimed at his chest. "You've got ten seconds to explain yourself before I haul you in."

"Whoa!" He raised his hands. "Aren't you way out of your jurisdiction?" She wouldn't shoot him, would she? He was strangely uncertain and suddenly regretted his actions.

"RCMP. Our jurisdiction is Canada wide. Five seconds." Her stance never shifted, her aim never wavered.

He was in deep trouble. How was he going to talk himself out of it? His mind raced full throttle, going nowhere, like a truck with a broken transmission.

"Listen. I can explain."

"So, you say, and I'm waiting. Three seconds."

"This is my ex-wife's house. I came by hoping to find—I don't know—hoping to find out something, anything. Everyone knows the longer someone is missing, the less chance they'll be found alive. I thought—hell, I don't know what I thought." Slowly, watching for any sign she objected, he lowered his arms.

"You thought you might find your daughter here?" She lowered her gun and slipped it into the waistband of her jeans at the small of her back. "The odds are miniscule. A neighbor would have seen her, or one of those cowboys or jockeys down by the barn. Didn't I warn you not to do anything illegal?" Her voice was strong with censure and her eyes chastised him.

"You did. I just thought, maybe if I came by there'd be something here. I don't know, a clue. I wasn't planning on taking anything or damaging anything."

"It's still breaking and entering. I saw you pick the lock. How'd you disarm the security system?"

"Ellen uses the same pin code for everything. I warned her about it a thousand times. Look," he gestured vaguely, "Can we just pretend this didn't happen. I'll leave and promise not to come back." An idea hit him smack dab in the middle of the chest. "You *are* stalking me. You followed me from Coyote Creek. Didn't you?" He glared at her, wishing his stare could cut her down in her tracks. "I can't believe you don't trust me."

"First, you're right, I don't trust you; despite your reputation. Second, I didn't follow you, I was on my way into the city when I saw you shoot past me going well over the speed limit. Third, I was right to be suspicious, I caught you red handed."

He huffed out a resigned sigh. "You were right to distrust me. Believe me, if I had any other options, I wouldn't have let myself in here. I'm just hoping to find a clue. I don't know, maybe a letter, an email. Something. It makes me sick that Ellen is off in Europe while our child is missing." Shame battled with anger and disappointment. His guts churned and he swallowed back bile. He never should have given in to the urge to come here. But how could he stop searching for Hannah?

"How much searching have you done?" Amy demanded, clearly in full cop mode.

"A quick walk through. Everything's covered up, but there's barely any dust. Nothing to eat in the fridge unless you've got a hankering for pickles dipped in ketchup."

"Gross. Did you touch the stack of mail on the table by the front door?" she asked, her voice not quite accusatory.

"No, I missed it. I swear, I didn't touch it."

"Well then, I suggest we start there." She grinned at him.

"W-what?" he stammered.

"Look, I don't know you well, but I do know you're one of the most stubborn and persistent men I've ever met. You'll just come back again. I'll help you search." She paused. "I can't believe I'm twisting the law like this. I could lose my job." Her smile was half frown.

"You're going to help me look? That's incredible!" He raced across the kitchen, picked her up, swung her in a circle and kissed her on the cheek. "Thank you. Thank you."

She pushed herself free of his arms and stepped back, her arm going behind her back to where she'd put her gun. "Don't make me shoot you."

Something in her voice told him she was teasing.

He held his hands up in surrender. "Tell me, Constable Baxter, where do we begin?"

"Amy will do fine. We'll search the mail. Then, if we can get beyond the password, we'll check the laptop I saw on the coffee table."

"Nothing here but fliers, junk mail and bills," Justice complained after sifting through the mail on the table. "I was hoping for a letter, or something. Maybe I should open up her credit card bill and search it."

"For information on Hannah, or to see what your ex is doing? Are you still hung up on your wife?" There was something in her eyes Justice couldn't quite identify, so he chalked it up to professional curiosity.

"Definitely not mooning over Ellen. We're long since done. But what if Hannah has a credit card? Ellen always talked about giving her one, despite my objections." He raised one eyebrow beseechingly.

"I'm in deep enough trouble as it is, I can't let you perpetrate mail fraud. The bill stays unopened. I'm sure your ex checks her bill every month and would notice unusual charges."

He snorted. Fat lot Amy knew. Ellen never cared about her bills. Raised by wealthy parents until she inherited their wealth, Ellen spent whatever she wanted without care.

"Let's try the laptop instead," Amy suggested.

How he had missed both the mail and the laptop, Justice didn't understand. Probably because he was so wrapped up in looking for Hannah rather than other clues. He dreamed of walking in and finding her on the couch watching television. "Yeah, let's fire up the computer. You want to do it, or shall I?"

"I better do it. At least I can fabricate a legal reason for checking it. You on the other hand have no right to be here and snooping on the computer only makes it worse." She sighed heavily. "I can't believe the crap I'm doing. Don't you dare tell anyone I was even here." She shook her finger warningly.

"Your secret, our secret, is safe with me." He mimed zipping his lips.

His nerves twitched and he battled the urge to push her aside when she hesitated after opening the laptop. "Try this," he rattled off Ellen's birthday.

"Nope. What else? What's Hannah's birthday?" she asked.

She typed in the numbers and gave a crow of success.

"I can't believe anyone, in this day and age, uses birthdays for security codes." She shook her head. "Hang tight and I'll check her email. She keeps logged into her email? Good grief. This woman needs a lesson in cyber security. Un-fricken-believable."

Justice watched nervously as she searched around. She drove the trackpad like a pro. "Hurry up. Is there anything?"

"Sh. I'm scrolling through her emails. The woman doesn't open or delete anything."

He paced back and forth staring at Amy, willing her to hurry. His hands fisted and opened. Fisted and opened. Bunching and unbunching until he thought they'd cramp closed.

"Wait."

"This one's weird. Hang on, I'll open it."

He froze, afraid to move a muscle, as if moving would make the email vanish. Finally, Amy read the message aloud.

Mom

I've been calling the house and your cell. Where are you? I need money.

Can you come get me? I want to come home.

Hannah

"Where is it from? What account? Can we find out where she is?"

"Hang tight. It's three months old. Give me a second to find out where it was sent from."

"Is that legal?" he asked, wishing he didn't feel guilty about having her break more rules.

"Probably not. I learned a bit about tracing IP addresses. I'll see where it's from. And if I get fired, you're supporting me for the rest of my life." Her tone was half joking.

"If you find Hannah, I'll gladly support you forever. Hurry."

"Give it a rest," she joked. "This takes time."

He resumed pacing. His heart thundered in his chest and his mouth went dry. Where the hell was it from? Couldn't she hurry up? The waiting was killing him. He'd already waited nearly two years; he was out of patience.

"Got it." She leaned back, a self-satisfied smile on her face. "I am going to rock cyber-crime when I get out of Coyote Creek."

"Where is she?"

"She *was* in Montana, three months ago."

· ♥ · ♥ · ♥ · ♥ · ♥ ·

Chapter Nine

This might be the stupidest thing she'd ever done and she'd done her fair share of foolish things. What it was, for sure, was the most impulsive action of her life and she hoped she didn't end up regretting it. Helping him search the house was wrong on so many levels. It was potentially career-ending stupid. But this was above and beyond that.

"I can't believe you agreed to this; but I do appreciate it." Justice stated as he shut off his truck. He turned to look at her.

"I can't believe I agreed." They'd spent the last six hours in the vehicle, almost eight if you counted rest and food stops. Finally, they sat outside the public library in Shelby, Montana. "This is probably the most insane thing I've ever done in my life. I should have turned the email over to the city police rather than follow it here."

The building sat atop a small slope. It was long and low, and surrounded by a large snow-covered expanse, perhaps grass.

"You're right, we probably should have. Look at it this way, you are the police. Doesn't that give you the right to investigate the clue?"

If only it were so easy. She had no jurisdiction in Montana and definitely no right to ask for email records or question people. She should have stopped him while she had the chance rather than helping him on this wild goose chase. She was, however, impressed he was trying to help her find a way to justify participating in this fool's errand.

"You know, the email was dated over three months ago. It is highly unlikely anyone will remember a teenage girl in the library at all. Especially after all this time. We've probably wasted our time, and your money on this fool's errand." This fool's errand was beyond a mistake. It was asinine, ridiculous and foolhardy at best. Still, here she was following a long-cold lead in an unsolved case. Worst of all, it was her idea to be here. She wasn't under any illusions he'd have stayed home if she hadn't suggested coming. He'd be here without her potentially stabilizing influence. She was doing this to protect him, not because she wanted to spend time with him.

Somewhere during the endless drive from Edmonton to Shelby, she'd started trusting him. Certain things still bothered her and left her a touch uneasy, but for some inexplicable reason, she trusted him. Trust and unease shouldn't work together but, in this case, they did. It wasn't just because she'd searched his truck from floor boards to visors, including the back seat, when he was in the gas station washroom either. She'd searched repeatedly, she'd done everything short of tearing the truck apart with a screwdriver. He'd nearly caught her too. She'd been on her hands and knees on the floor looking under the seat when he'd caught her red-handed. Thinking fast, she'd pulled an earring out and claimed to be looking for it. She wasn't certain he'd bought it, but he'd let the matter drop.

She stared at the library, wishing for a moment she was somewhere else. Steeling her nerves, she unbuckled her seatbelt. "Let's do this." She jumped out of the truck before she changed her mind and demanded he take her home. She hurried past the low stone wall up a short flight of cement steps, across a flat sidewalk and up a second set of stairs. She opened the front door and stepped into the foyer.

The library was toasty warm inside, a nice change from the icy winter wind blowing outside. It had the reverent, near-silence all libraries seemed to possess. It felt like the books were waiting in anticipation of being taken home by a lucky reader. As an avid reader, she spent plenty of time in libraries and bookstores. To her fanciful mind, these havens smelled like knowledge and refuge.

The library was spotless. She paused for a moment to admire a glass-fronted display of fossils. Two patrons sat in front of computers, their fingers flying over the keyboards. Books, DVDs and CD filled the shelves, their edges lining up perfectly. Clearly the staff here cared about their job. The entire room had an inviting feel.

"Let me take the lead here," she suggested.

His brow wrinkled and he shifted from foot to foot. After a moment of apparent indecision, he nodded. "After you," he said and waved toward the help desk.

"Good afternoon," she greeted the impeccably dressed brunette manning the desk. "I was wondering if you could help us." They'd been lucky to arrive before the library closed for the day.

The woman looked up from her computer and smiled. "Certainly. I'd be happy to assist in any way I can."

"I'm Constable Amy Baxter, of the Royal Canadian Mounted Police, and I have a few questions, if you have time." Hopefully, giving her credentials would make asking questions and eliciting answers easier.

The woman looked at her and raised one eyebrow. "Is this official business? If so, perhaps you might want to talk to the local law enforcement. I can call them for you."

"Frankly," Amy answered. "It is, and it isn't, official business. This is Mr. Flint. We're here about his daughter."

Flint took the hint and slid Hannah's most recent picture onto the counter.

"His daughter ran away nearly two years ago. Recently, our investigations turned up an email from Hannah to her mother. The email originated here, in your library." Her heart thundered at the small lies. Okay, more stretching the truth than outright lies. The churning in her stomach was enough to make her wince.

"What can I tell you?" the woman answered, picking up the photograph.

"Do you recall seeing this girl?"

"She doesn't look familiar. Perhaps we could check with the other staff? When, exactly, was she here?"

Amy gave her the date of the email. "I know it was months ago. Still, this is the only clue we currently have and Hannah said she was out of money and needed funds to get home."

The librarian called the other staff members together. Initially, none of them admitted recognizing Hannah, though one young woman studied the photo carefully. She stared at Justice and back at the photograph.

"You know, I might recognize her. If you cut her hair shorter, like up to her shoulders and greased it up with dirt, this could be a girl who spent most of a day here. She was off and on the computer all day. She only left when we were closing. I talked to her a bit. She was reading about horses and famous jockeys. I noticed because I've always wanted to learn to ride. That's all I remember." She fixed her stare on Justice's sheepskin lined leather jacket. "What's that logo?"

"It's for our family ranch. Why?"

The eager tone of his voice told Amy he was getting ahead of himself and their investigation.

"It looks familiar. I can't tell if I've just seen something similar or if the girl had it on something." She sighed and blinked heavily. "I wish I'd known she was in trouble. I might have been able to help her. I could have helped her call home—or something. She was a bit dirty, but she seemed healthy, if it's any consolation."

"Thank you," Justice blurted. "I'm glad Hannah ran into some friendly faces. It's good to know there are still kind people out there." He handed the woman a business card. "If she comes in again, or if you think of anything else, could you please, please, call me? Collect if you need to."

Amy passed her own card to the first woman they'd talked to, and addressed the small group. "Please, don't hesitate to call our office if she shows up again. Our detachment would like nothing more than reuniting this family and helping them get past their problems." She thanked everyone and they headed out.

"Well, that was damned disappointing," Justice grumbled as they walked down the sidewalk.

Amy had to hurry to keep up with him. "Justice, slow down. I know you're upset. I told you it was unlikely we'd learn anything. We can ask around town and see if anyone else saw her or talked to her."

"It's just so—dammit." He winced. "I knew not to get my hopes up. I couldn't help it. I'm so worried. I'd hoped for a clue. Something, even something tiny might help."

She clasped his elbow and held him in place. "I understand, I swear I do. The next step is to ask around. Maybe someone talked to her. We can start at a local eating place. Kill two birds with one stone. Get a bite to eat and talk to the staff."

They spent the rest of the day talking to people in public places, shops, restaurants. They took a moment to admire the displays and quilts in Marias Museum of History and Art. After that, they made a quick stop at the Sheriff's office and asked the officers to keep an eye out for Hannah. In the end, their search came up dry. After a sleepless night at a local hotel, they headed, bleary-eyed, for home.

They rode in silence for several hours and were back in Canada before Justice finally found the words to speak. "What I don't get is why she didn't call me. Or her grandparents. She could have called anyone. Why didn't she? It doesn't make sense. Why email? And why didn't she email me?" He slammed his palm against the steering wheel in frustration. He turned toward Amy. "Explain that to me."

He was grasping at straws. Desperate to understand his daughter's reasoning. It hurt so much to learn she'd been alive just months ago. It should have brought him comfort, not this aching sense of despair. Why didn't it make him feel better?

"I feel so helpless. I can't even help my own child."

"You know," Amy interrupted his self-flagellation. "If Hannah was reading about jockeys, maybe we can send her picture out to racing stables and see if anyone has heard of her or seen her. It's a long shot."

"Jockeys. She was always on about being a jockey." It hit him like lightning to the heart; being a jockey hadn't just been a passing fad for Hannah, it wasn't just the reason she'd left. It was why she hadn't contacted him. She knew he'd be upset that their disagreement had separated them.

This was his fault. Every single moment of fear, loss and agony could be placed smack dab at his feet. This wasn't because of his selfish ex-wife or a careless child. This mistake, the breaking up of his family, fell entirely on his shoulders. If he'd bent and let her test her wings, this would never have happened.

"I need a drink." He swerved off the highway into a small town boasting only a gas station, grocery store and a hotel with a bar.

"Won't it wait until we get home?" Her words sent irritation jolting down his spine, threatening to disrupt the last vestiges of his self-control.

"No. It won't. I need a drink now." He jumped out of the truck and stormed into the bar without waiting for her. He'd downed a shot of whiskey and started swilling a beer by the time she caught up with him.

"I guess I'm driving home then?" She fixed him with the female, parental stare that terrified men and children alike. God, he hated that look.

He almost caved. Instead he took another deep swallow of beer and dropped the mug heavily on the bar. "Amy, I like you, and I appreciate all the help, but mind your own damned business. I need to think. Go sit over there and leave me be." He waved to the other side of the dingy bar.

"Screw you, Flint. If you're drinking, I'm drinking. You dragged me halfway across the continent. I skipped spending time with my sister to help you. I deserve a break too." She climbed onto the stool beside his. "I'll have a pint of Canadian, please," she addressed the bartender.

"And she'll drink it over there." He gestured again and glared when the bartender laughed.

"Buddy, one thing I've learned in this job is not to try to argue with a woman who has her mind made up about something and this one seems to be determined to be the fly in your ointment." He dispensed a pint and slid it in front of her. "I'll put it on his tab." He winked at Amy and sauntered from behind the bar toward a table of four men in work clothing.

Justice spun his glass on its cardboard beer coaster. Annoyance warred with admiration that Amy had stood up to him. She had more facets than a diamond. Rough and tumble cop, helper, friendly neighbor, good cook, friend and yeah, he had to admit it, a very attractive woman. But dammit, right now she was annoying as hell.

She sat beside him, slowly sipping her beer without saying a word. She dashed off a couple text messages and received replies before tucking her phone into her purse and ordering another beer.

The classic rock love ballads playing in the background only made the lack of conversation worse. "Aren't you going to pester me to talk?" he asked, unable to deal with the endless silence.

"Would it do me any good?" She nudged him with her elbow.

He grunted. Women. She wouldn't go away, but she wasn't talking to him either. Go figure. She ordered herself a burger and fries and a third beer. She didn't even ask if he wanted anything. She ate and made small talk with the bartender.

"It's my fault," Justice declared when the bartender walked away.

"I doubt that, he's got work to do." She shrugged.

"Not him walking away. Hannah."

"Oh?" Her tone was bland and barely interested.

Typical woman, feigning disinterest to get him talking. How did women do that? Make one syllable sound like an entire conversation of questions. Every woman he knew could do it. It annoyed the hell out of him because it worked. Every time.

"I figured it out. Hannah wanted to be a jockey. She was crazy about horses. Her mother kept horses at the ranch until she moved back to her own spread. You know, where you caught me busting in." He expected Amy to offer a word, or dissent, or encouragement, but she remained mute, wordlessly forcing him to continue.

"Hannah was small, very slight. She only weighed about ninety pounds. Much too small to control a massive race horse. I said no. I refused to allow her to learn to race professionally. Against 4H kids was one thing, for a career, against seasoned pros? No way. I wouldn't even consider letting her train for it. One of Ellen's friends owns a famous riding outfit. They race thoroughbreds. He wanted to train Hannah to ride professionally. I refused."

"She was just a kid," Amy offered.

"And he was a rich son-of-a--. Living the high life. Doing drugs and drinking. Every time he visited Ellen; he brought an entourage of groupies. I didn't want my daughter mixed up in that lifestyle. The parade of men through Ellen's life was bad enough. She's on her fourth husband for Pete's sake."

"I'm surprised the judge gave her custody."

"She wasn't a serial dater when we divorced. It started later. When it did, Hannah was well established in her new school and didn't want to leave her friends, so I let her stay with Ellen." He massaged his thigh with one hand. "I should have known better."

"Did you know Hannah was unhappy?"

Amy's logic annoyed him. "Do you think I'd have left her there if I'd known?" The glare he gave her had withered bigger, stronger men. Amy didn't even flinch. His anger and self-loathing ratcheted up a notch. Great, now he was taking a strip off his neighbor, the one who helped him out when she should have, by all rights, arrested him and hauled him to jail.

"I thought we'd worked it all out. Ellen agreed with me; Hannah was too young to be a jockey. Ellen had grander dreams for Hannah. Doctor, lawyer, engineer. I just wanted her to find a career that made her happy. The way ranching makes me happy. We made an agreement, the three of us, she'd wait and reconsider being a jockey once she graduated high school, if she was still interested. Until then, she was welcome to ride horses as much as she wanted. Just no racing. I thought that was the end of it."

He tossed his Stetson onto the bar beside him and raked his fingers through his hair. Life shouldn't be this hard. Having kids was tough, but he'd been so naïve about how difficult it really was.

"Now, Hannah is gone and it's all my fault. If I'd broken into Ellen's sooner, I'd have seen the email and I might have caught up with her. If I'd let her do what she wanted, this never would have happened." He guzzled the last of his fourth beer and it hit his stomach like lead, and his veins like pure grain alcohol. Great, now he was getting drunk.

"You should eat," Amy advised and called the bartender over.

A few minutes later an enormous steak with a baked potato and fresh asparagus appeared in front of him. Suddenly famished, he flashed Amy a grateful smile and dug in.

"I've contacted the precinct and they've started the ball rolling to be able to monitor the email account, in case Hannah logs in again, even though you and I saw no other emails since that last one, and the staff didn't seem to recall her being back."

"Thank you. I didn't think of that."

"It's my job." She shrugged off his praise. "I had the bartender book us a room at the hotel while you were in the bathroom. We can chill for a bit and head home tomorrow."

"I thought you wanted to get home today?"

"I did. I do. I've had three beer; you've had more than that. Even though we've been here for hours, neither one of us should be driving. We'll stay over."

She made a motion with her fingers and fresh beer appeared in front of each of them. The woman was magic.

"Thanks." He was expressing more than the single word implied. He couldn't seem to find a way to express his gratitude to Amy for listening, helping, looking after him. She'd done so much for a near stranger. Was it the woman, or the cop? He posed the question aloud.

"Honestly, I'd go with neither, or both. I did what a friend does. Supported you in your quest. The detachment needs to think I was acting on my own, I came across the email legally. I warn you, if anyone hears what happened and that I didn't arrest you, I'll end you."

He laughed. "You will not. You're too much of a good girl for that. I'll bet you've never done anything in the gray zone in your life. You've probably never even had a speeding ticket."

Her expression changed in a flicker. From semi-serious teasing to flat and expressionless. He'd hit the nail on the head. Somehow. Time for more digging. "What secrets does your past hold, Amy Baxter?"

"I'm not an angel by any stretch. I've never been arrested, but I've done my share of inappropriate things." Her words sounded like a shameful confession.

He rested his fingers on her hand comfortingly. "Somehow, I doubt it. I don't know much about you, but I know you're a good person."

"Go with that." She swilled a quarter of her beer.

"Slow down, Amy. Don't get drunk over a simple conversation. You don't have to talk about it. We'll call it one of those never-bring-it-up-again topics. Right?" He lifted his glass in a toast.

She clinked her glass against his, glad for the reprieve and agreement. "I had an affair with a married man," she blurted without thinking.

"Whoa! No way."

"Sad but true," she said. No sense in denying it now since she'd let the cat out of the bag. Nor was she going to explain. Let him think the worst of her. It didn't matter, she was leaving Coyote Creek in a couple years and she trusted him to be discrete with her accidental revelation.

"There had to be extenuating circumstances."

The certainty in his voice surprised Amy. "I didn't know he was married. We worked together, he said he was separated and had filed for divorce. Turns out while we were *dating*, they reconciled and everyone in the precinct knew. Except me. I guess they assumed I knew and didn't care."

"What the devil? You worked with him and your friends didn't tell you? Those aren't friends and he's an asshat."

"I'm a cop, I should have seen the signs he was lying. You can bet the ranch I ended it the second my sister told me. She saw them cuddling in a restaurant. It sickens me." She bit back a gag and a sense of worthlessness. Every time she thought about what happened, she started a backslide into depression.

"The guy is a tool. A jerk. Somebody needs to take him down a peg. I could run him over with my truck."

He looked like he was joking. At least she hoped he was. "Funny. Tempting, too. But no, thanks. I'll just get on with my life and eventually, in a couple years, I'll leave Coyote Creek and move on with my career."

"Can't you do that here?" He looked as bewildered as he sounded. He shoveled the last bite of steak into his mouth and pushed his plate away.

"Does it matter? Really?" He seemed to be driving at something, but for the life of her, she couldn't determine what. For a moment, it was as if she was back in high school, wondering if the cool guy liked her. Ugh. She didn't want to live those uncertain years again. She was thirty-four, not sixteen. She was done with teenage angst, where every little thing seemed life or death.

"Oh gosh. That makes so much sense," she exclaimed.

"It does? What does?" He wiped his lips with a napkin and stared at her.

For half a minute, she was distracted by how kissable his lips looked. "Teenage angst explains it all!"

"Wait, weren't we talking about your ex? You weren't exactly a teen if you were already a cop. I think I missed something. You're talking in riddles, or code. This simple ranch boy doesn't get it."

She swatted him lightly on the arm. "Simple ranch boy, my ass. You're a lot of things, and I'm not sure all of them are on the up and up, but I'm giving you the benefit of the doubt. One thing you definitely aren't is simple." She shook her head. The man was unbelievable. For certain he was doing things under the radar. Sooner or later, she'd figure out what it was, and if it was legal. Weirdly, despite her doubts and the suspicious activities, she was beginning to think whatever he was up to was a secret but not illegal. He had her instincts off kilter.

"I was talking about Hannah. Boys are different, so this might not have occurred to you. Teenage girls can get into total snits over little things. The smallest dream crushed leads to great angst and perceived wrongs. It makes them vulnerable. Suppose, and I'm guessing here, suppose one of your wife's friends went behind Ellen's back and offered Hannah her dream. If she was upset and angry enough at you guys, she might take them up on the offer." She paused. "I'm surprised the police didn't follow up on the idea, or did they?"

"They asked a few questions, but nothing came of it. You're brilliant."

He threw his arms around Amy and drew her into his embrace. His hug was warm and inviting. For a moment, before she recalled her career plans, she wished she could stay in his arms forever. She eased away from him and picked up her glass. "If you give me a list, I can call up some of Ellen's old contacts and push things. Maybe someone will spill the beans."

He looked crestfallen. "Wait, that won't work. She was in Montana, maybe working her way home. That line is dead."

"Maybe, maybe not. We can put some officers on it and maybe get some inter-agency, cross-border cooperation going. You never know what'll come to light if we rattle a few horse stalls." Impulsively, she grabbed him by the lapels and kissed him on the cheek. "Closer to home, we'll investigate ranches and riding venues and start a fresh search of hostels and shelters. Who knows what we'll find?"

· ♥ · ♥ · ♥ · ♥ · ♥ ·

Chapter Ten

Two days later and weary to the bone, Justice climbed out of his truck and trudged across the snow dusted sidewalk to his house. Today had been a day from—well, suffice it to say he couldn't wait for it to be over. He'd fought with his father over ranch chores. Robert Flint was one stubborn man and refused to see what was right in front of him. If he'd just adopt some of the methods Justice's brother, Ken, used on his own ranch, they could up their efficiency and take some of the strain off everyone. His father's health was failing. He grew frailer and paler every day. He had a doctor's appointment coming up soon, but not soon enough to suit Justice.

If that wasn't bad enough, one of the goats had chewed a hole in his favorite jacket. Yeah, it was his fault entirely, he'd left it hanging on a post while dunging out their pen. He knew better. Goats would eat anything.

The straw which broke the proverbial camel's back was the skunk. Skunks were a pain in the backside, plain and simple; and when they wandered too close to the house, they had to be dealt with. Few people realized female skunks stayed close to their birthplace. They set up what amounted to skunk hotels with ever increasing numbers of them living together. They could, if space allowed it, grow colonies numbering in the dozens, or hundreds, all living together.

While the family believed in leaving mother nature alone as much as possible, skunks nesting in a hollow they'd dug under the ranch's front porch was an issue. It wasn't safe for the dogs and cats and they couldn't risk any of the kids getting sprayed. With Robert being unwell, Justice had been elected to deal with the problem. He'd dealt with the first two quickly and efficiently. The third, not so much.

He'd startled it and it sprayed him in the face. Now, even after a shower, washing with skunk removal spray, baking soda, peroxide, and tomato juice, he still reeked. His eyes burned and his favorite hat was ruined. He was wearing his father's clothing and he'd have to leave his boots outside to air and it could take days. Or longer before he'd smell anything but skunk. He wanted another shower, supper, and an evening of relaxation. And probably an enormous tumbler of whiskey.

A car door slammed and he pivoted toward the sound. Amy. He called out a greeting. Her answering smile and warm hello was a balm on his stretched nerves. Rather than analyze the feeling, he invited her to dinner. Spending time with her could be just the thing to turn this crappy day into something pleasant.

"Good to see you. I'm just about to shower and make dinner. I've got some chicken breasts out. I'm making homemade chicken fingers and fries. There'll be lots, why don't you join me?" he asked.

She seemed startled he could cook but accepted readily enough.

"Give me half an hour to shower before you come over. I'll leave the door unlocked, just let yourself in."

He showered, lingering as long as he dared, shampooing repeatedly. He rinsed his eyes with the solution the pharmacist recommended. By the time he was dressed and back downstairs, Amy sat at his kitchen table, feet up on a second chair. She set her phone on the table and looked up at him, her blue eyes shining. She was beautiful in dark blue jeans, and a soft, fuzzy, cardinal red sweater. She'd pulled her long hair up in some kind of messy bun with stray strands hanging down brushing her cheeks and neck. He clenched his fists to keep from touching them or taking her into his arms.

Something about her called to him. It wasn't just physical. Nor was it about the way she'd stood by him and helped him search for his daughter, even when they were disagreeing. He barely knew her and every time he saw her, he wanted more time with her. He'd been sexually attracted to women before and that was part of what he felt for Amy, but only a small part. His compulsion to be with her worried him, even as he found it comforting. Being with her reminded him of the love which flowed endlessly between his parents.

"Hi, sorry I took so long. I was trying to get rid of the stench." He stepped past her to reach into the fridge for the chicken.

"Yuck. What the hell, you smell like bad pot."

"Skunk, it's skunk. I got sprayed out at the ranch today. I feel like I'll never be clean again. It doesn't matter what I do, I can't get the burn out of my nose."

She wrinkled her nose and stared at him. She seemed to doubt his story but didn't say anything else. He took the safe road and ignored her dubious expression, making small talk while he prepped the chicken.

He sliced it into long thin strips, dredged them in egg, then flour, repeated the action, and after a final dip in the egg mixture, coated them in a mixture of seasoned bread crumbs, parmesan cheese and flour. Each strip went onto a baking sheet. The chicken went into the oven along with a small tray of French fries. As they cooked, he whipped up a salad and set the table.

They talked movies, books and a bit of gossip while they ate. The conversation was stilted and awkward. Justice concluded she must have something on her mind. With every minute that passed, Amy grew increasingly antsy. Justice watched her fidget and avoid his gaze. So much for their friendship resembling the fond feelings of his parents. Uncomfortable dinner complete, he loaded the dishwasher, refilled their wine glasses and settled into his chair. He leaned back, crossed his arms over his chest and studied her. After a moment, he stated, "Out with it."

"I beg your pardon?" She blinked owlishly. "I said thank you for supper, but thanks again. It was delicious. It's nice to meet a man who can cook. So many guys at the station rely fully on take out."

"No, not that. What's up your backside? You're twitchier than a squirrel in a fox's den. I thought we were over being awkward with each other. Didn't our trip to Montana and back break the ice?"

"It did but..." She looked away, jerked to her feet and paced the small kitchen, arms wrapped around her middle.

"But, what?" he prodded.

"Look, I'd rather not talk about it, but since you insist. Something's bothering me."

There was no doubt about it, her unease was why he started this conversation. They couldn't create or maintain a friendship if she wasn't honest with him. After her confession in Montana and him revealing so much about his past, he'd thought...he pushed his mental musings away. "I can see you're uncomfortable. Spill the beans."

"Everything about you screams respectable. Yet, at the same time, there are things setting off warning bells. I'm looking at all those packages on the dining room table. Packages coming in, packages set for mailing. What's up with that? Is it related to the pot smell pervading this place? I mean, come on, it reeks. I can't have a friendship with someone who uses and sells drugs. You're not licensed to sell, I checked. Your sister was arrested on drug charges for drugs she could have gotten from you, though she claims otherwise. You spend way too much time hanging out around the school. Are you dealing to kids?"

He leaped to his feet; his chair crashed to the floor behind him. "Are you nuts? Where the hell did you get an idea like that? I don't use drugs; I don't sell drugs. I wouldn't. Ever!"

"So, explain it. Make it make sense." She stood, hands on her hips glaring at him.

How could she not trust him after all they'd shared? She was privy to more of his life than most people. She knew the shame of his marriage and failure with his daughter. She'd been the one to figure out the most likely cause of Hannah's disappearance, which should have been obvious. "Ask me anything," he demanded. "I'll answer every question until you are satisfied."

"I don't think that's necessary. I'll just go."

He stepped between her and the door. "I'd rather clear this up."

Amy sighed. He was going to be a jerk about this. "And if I say I want to leave? Then what?" she asked.

"I can't keep you here if you want to go. But, for the sake of our friendship, and my reputation, I'd rather straighten this out. You want to know what's in the packages? Open them. Open them all."

"I don't need to go through your mail," she hedged, double thinking her doubts about him. He was so adamant. Was it all bluster to defuse her suspicions or was he telling the truth?

He strode through the doorway to the dining area and grabbing a package, tossed it to her. She barely caught it. "Open it," he ordered. "Open it or I will."

She inspected the package. It was about four inches square. Professionally wrapped, it came from someone in Winnipeg, identified only by JGG and a return address. She looked up at Justice. He met her gaze with a stare and a brisk nod. She fumbled with the package, turned it over and opened it. Inside was a stack of four white jewelry boxes. She peeked into the top one. It contained a broach shaped like a horse with sparkling diamond eyes.

Shoot. She'd messed up.

"That one's for Sue. There's a different one for each sister. It's almost Christmas. I ordered them from an artisan friend in Winnipeg. I met her at an art show when I was married."

"Justice..."

He flipped her another package. She barely got the small boxes onto the table in time to catch it. This one was from him, addressed to someone in New Brunswick. "Go on, open it. Though I know you'll be disappointed."

She wasn't sure what that meant, but she slid a fingernail under the edge and opened it. Inside was a sleek black jewelry box with a Flint Designs logo. What the devil? She flipped the lid of the hinged box open and stared inside. "Wow!" the exclamation slipped out accidentally.

"Yeah, wow." Sarcasm dripped from his voice. "It's not drugs. Hope you're satisfied."

"It's beautiful." She stared down at the pendant. A hexagonal piece of tiger's eye stone with a rounded top was nestled into a silver filigree pendant, suspended from a silver box chain. "It's lovely and the box says Flint Designs. Does one of your sisters make jewelry?"

"Oh. My. God." He raked his finger through his hair. "No. One of my sisters does not make jewelry. I do. I'm a silversmith. I make the jewelry and I cut the stones to fit. Sometimes I do the stones first. Every one of those packages is a sale going out or a gift coming in. Would you like to see my financial records, maybe my income tax returns? We can open every package if it'll ease your mind and convince you I'm not a drug dealer. Oh yeah," he went on without allowing her time to speak. "I talk to the kids at school. A lot of them have friends and relatives in nearby towns. I check in regularly and they keep an ear open for rumors about my daughter or other missing kids."

Jeepers, she'd been so wrong. Her knees wobbled and her guts lurched. She was going to be sick. Where had her cop instincts gone? Dizzy, she grabbed the back of a kitchen chair and dropped into it. Swallowing hard, she mustered her courage and ignored the roiling in her stomach. She breathed deeply and spoke. "I'm so sorry. I misjudged you. Totally. But from my perspective—never mind; it doesn't matter what it looked like. I'm a cop. I should know better than to jump to conclusions. I can't apologize enough. I believe you and I'm sorry I ever doubted you. The guys at the station told me I was nuts."

"Damn. You talked to the guys about me? Wow, if that isn't adding insult to injury." His icy glare could have cut steel. "I can't believe you. I'm surprised you didn't bring out the drug dogs."

Her face burned with shame. "Actually, I debated it, but Coyote Creek doesn't have its own dog and I couldn't justify bringing one in on a gut feel. I'd need more evidence." She cringed knowing how damning her words were. His laughter came out of nowhere.

"That's rich," he choked out between deep chuckles. "I've got a sexy new neighbor I'm attracted to and she's busy snooping around trying to convict me of a crime I didn't commit. All I want is to find my daughter. Man, the universe is out to get me. I can't fricken win."

She didn't know which part of his statement to focus on. He was attracted to her? A shiver of excitement raced down her spine. She pushed it away. She was not interested in a relationship, not even with him. Even if he was the most alluring man she'd met in ages. When she looked at him, she wondered how she could have ever been attracted to her ex. Justice Flint was handsome, kind and caring. He was helpful, generous and had strong family values. Come to think of it, when she added his actions all together with his concern for his daughter, she couldn't imagine how she'd come to the conclusion he was a criminal.

"Man, I feel like such a jerk. I misjudged you in so many ways. I'd like to blame my cop instincts, but I don't think that was it." She picked up the packages, wrapped them and returned them to the dining room table. "Sorry for doubting you. But with all the odd bits and the smell. Oh gosh, the smell, it's killing me."

He chuckled. "Try being inside my nose. Skunk oil is pervasive and impossible to get rid of. I even rinsed with peroxide which isn't pleasant to say the least. I can't get rid of it. You should have smelled me before two showers and a bath in tomato juice. Nothing cuts skunk odor, except time. And, I admit, to the untrained nose, one unfamiliar with skunk, it does smell a bit like pot. You do know pot is legal in Canada, right?"

"Selling it without a license isn't," she countered, not sure why she was arguing. "The pendant was lovely. Can I see more?"

"After all this, you want to see more? I suppose you want a tour of my jewelry studio too?"

"You'd do that? Even after I was a jerk?"

"That was sarcasm," he drawled. "I was being facetious. But, come on. Grab your jacket and boots. It's in the garage." He sighed heavily and walked to the door. "You might as well have the full tour to ease the rest of your doubts."

Outside, the smell of skunk re-doubled.

"Gross," she choked out.

"Tell me about it. It's up my nose, and those were my favorite boots. My favorite Stetson is ruined. You can't launder a felt hat. I had to pitch it in the burn pit." He shook his head sadly and unlocked the garage door. He flipped on the light and they stepped inside.

A low rumbling filled the air.

"What's that sound?" she asked heading toward it.

"Rock tumbler. I do a lot of work with random shaped tumbled stones. Mostly wire wrapping, but some casting as well."

She stopped in front of a slowly rotating rubber drum about eight inches across. Yup, it looked like the rock tumbler she'd had as a kid. All around her were saws, polishers and other miscellaneous lapidary equipment. When she was young, she'd wanted to be a geologist and work with stones. She'd been disappointed to learn they did more than play with pretty rocks.

"This is where I do my casting," he said and flicked on another light. "I've got an air to air exchanger to pull out the fumes. I work with wax and carve pieces for casting. I work in silver rather than gold. I prefer it, and when I was starting out, in my early twenties, there was no way I could afford to mess around with gold."

She walked up to the bench he leaned on. Beside it was a glass fronted display cabinet filled with jewelry. Necklaces, rings, bracelets, earrings. You name it, it was in there. There was even an elegant scrolled tiara. "Wow! Just wow," she whispered in awe. "You should have a shop."

"No way. I don't have time for that. Or the ambition. This is a hobby. Something to pass the time. If I make money good, if not, so be it. I do have a few pieces in craft shops and galleries. I don't make a living; ranching pays the bills. This is my fun, my relaxation. I haven't done nearly enough since Hannah disappeared. I'm caught up in looking for her. The night you were snooping around outside was the first time in almost a year I'd been out here puttering."

She flushed and ducked her head. "Sorry."

"Water under the bridge." He shrugged her apology off. "Let's move beyond our mistakes and back to friendship. Deal?" He offered his hand.

She shook with him, sealing the deal.

Her gaze went back to the display. "Oh, look at that ring. Is it topaz and rubies?" She asked. The piece was glorious.

"Topaz and garnets, actually. You like it?"

He seemed surprised, like he didn't understand why she would.

"I do. I love it. Can I see it?"

He opened the display and handed her the ring.

She slid it onto her finger and held it up to the light and twisted her hand back and forth. "It looks like a dragon, if you hold it just right," she exclaimed. "It's lovely." It fit her finger perfectly.

"I was going for a dragon, or rather the feel of a dragon. You're the first person to notice. Thank you."

"Is it for sale? I need this ring."

He looked from her face to her hand and back. "No, that one's not for sale. The rest of the jewelry is. This one's special. I'm keeping it. Sorry."

Something about his words struck her as false, but she didn't doubt for a moment the ring was special to him. Maybe he just wasn't ready to part with it. Some artisans were fussy about parting with their creations. She slipped it off and handed it back to him. She'd only worn it for a moment, but she missed it.

"You, Justice Flint, are a genius. Every piece is beautiful. You could get rich doing this." He could, she could see it. The world would clamor for his designs. He'd have more orders than he could handle.

"Maybe. I don't want to do custom work. I want to create what inspires me and I pride myself on the fact that each piece is one of a kind. No mass reproductions here. I never make the same piece twice. Not even the same setting with a different stone. I've only been out here a few times since Hannah disappeared. I lack inspiration right now, but I do try to produce new ideas."

She reached out and touched his shoulder. "That's admirable. Thank you for showing me your passion. And thank you for forgiving me for being an ass and jumping to conclusions."

"It's okay, we all make mistakes. Let's go back inside. There's wine left to drink."

She followed him inside. He was so strong. So vulnerable, and incredibly creative. If she didn't watch herself, she'd fall for him and mess up her plans to leave town and advance in her career. Besides, once they found Hannah, he'd be wrapped up in family and she'd be pushed aside. Her heart ached at the thought.

She was not going to let herself get attached to Justice Flint. Not now. Not ever.

·♥·♥·♥·♥·♥·

Chapter Eleven

After a late night of talking with Amy, Justice drove out to the ranch, trying to ignore the lingering scent of skunk in his truck. He loaded his horse in a trailer and headed toward Smoky Lake where he had intended to go the day Amy moved in. It was only days ago, but felt like years.

He travelled north on the highway, turned west and took a well-maintained gravel road into a heavily wooded area. He was deep in sour gas country. The oil companies kept the roads in good shape for the operators who checked each well daily. Snow covered the ditches and capped fences and trees. He turned again and again, the road growing increasingly small until he reached his destination.

He parked on an oil and gas lease, out of the way of any field workers who might come to the site, and saddled Buttercup, an aging mare named by his step-sister, Beth. Buttercup was older, but strong and fit. She wouldn't win any races, but she was the perfect mount for travelling slowly and searching for Hannah. Races, damn it. All Hannah had wanted to do was race horses. Being a jockey was her dream and he hadn't approved of it.

Sometimes, in the dark hours before dawn, he regretted his refusal to let her train as a jockey. Especially since their journey south. He still hated the idea but knowing it might have led her to run away bothered him. What if he'd let her try? Maybe she'd have failed, though he doubted it, she was too skilled a rider for that and with her small physique, she likely would have made a perfect jockey. His biggest objection had been her age and her need to finish high school. After that, who knows what he would have agreed to.

He locked his truck, secured the horse trailer-camper combination, slipped his keys into his pocket and snapped it shut. He secured his .303 rifle in its scabbard alongside the saddle. After double checking his saddle bags for his thermos of coffee and lunch, he mounted up and rode down a lightly travelled game trail. Though he was only a few miles from town, it hadn't snowed nearly as heavily here. He was thankful for the inconsistency of nature.

He'd chosen a spot about four miles from where the teen had been found. The police had scoured the area and search and rescue and covered every inch of forest close to where she'd been found. He had no special reason for choosing the spot, aside from once having ridden nearby with Hannah. Today, he felt drawn here, as if he had unfinished business. Perhaps because he'd been away when the teen had been found and the search was conducted. He hadn't been part of it. The girl had perished and he couldn't help but wonder if she'd been out here, in the back of beyond, alone. The possible answers didn't sit well with him.

Why would one teenage girl be out here alone? Rumor said she wasn't dressed for camping and she was dirty. The details were being kept from the press, but in Coyote Creek, nothing was faster than the rumor mill fueled by the local twenty-somethings who had stumbled on the body during a night of drunken camping. The girl had been identified as a missing teen from Edmonton and her family notified.

Terror stabbed at him. That could have been his daughter. Could he handle it if she turned up dead? He'd lose his mind. It would break him. He pushed the thoughts away. Sympathy for the dead girl's parents washed over him, but at least they had the peace of knowing her fate. Living in limbo wasn't a life at all. Without closure you could never move on. You were trapped in a terrible place between life and death. Not living, not dying. Torn between dread and hope. Locked in a nightmare you couldn't escape.

Buttercup paused, as if sensing Justice wasn't paying attention. She always had been an unusually sensitive horse with a knack for reading his moods.

"Dammit." How was he going to find anything if he wasn't focused on the task at hand? Searching was why he was out here. Getting lost in despair and self-recrimination wasn't. He patted his mount on the neck. "Sorry, girl. Thanks for hauling me back from the abyss."

He sat and pondered his options. Weather was turning colder by the day. Soon these paths would be impassable by anything but the fleetest deer or moose. He'd search physically until the going got too tough, then he'd turn his attention to the internet again. Maybe the enquiries the police sent out after his trip to Montana with Amy would produce a new lead.

Anger and helplessness thundered through his veins.

Buttercup made a sound of protest and shifted under him. With great effort, he forced his body to relax, his thighs unclenched and Buttercup nickered in relief. He patted her again and clucked his tongue and she started forward.

For an hour, she followed faint game trails without his guidance. He kept his eyes and ears open as they wandered through the bush. He munched on his lunch and sipped at his coffee as they went. He was about ready to pack it in for the day when Buttercup abruptly turned onto a wider trail and trotted eagerly forward into a wide clearing.

Her actions jostled him unexpectedly and he cursed to the sky, startling a flock of crows into flight. Buttercup shied and stood motionless.

Midway across the clearing, a dark shape lay in the snow. The snow that hadn't melted in the warmth of the past two days was packed and marked with crow tracks around the object.

"Shit." He cursed under his breath and leaped off the horse, tethering her to a bush. He strode toward the dark shape, shooing away the returning crows as he approached.

Closer he could see a coyote tangled in rope and what appeared to be a purple backpack. The crows had ravaged the coyote's corpse, clearly enjoying the easy meal. On a normal day, he'd leave them to enjoy their feast; but the backpack could be important. Or, it could be nothing.

It could belong to the girl who'd been found out here, or to someone else. Jesus, what if it was someone else's? It could belong to anyone. Hell, it could be Hannah's. What if she'd teamed up with another teen and had gotten lost heading home? Dread lodged in his stomach like lead.

Someone had to investigate the backpack. Tempted though he was to do it himself, he knew better. It could contain evidence related to the girl who'd been found. Or, it could be nothing. This was a matter for the police. Trying to convince himself the chances of the pack belonging to Hannah was slim to none, he pulled out his cell phone. Full service. Thank heaven for technology and cell towers. He punched in the number for Coyote Creek's RCMP office and listened to it ring.

"Coyote Creek RCMP, Constable Baxter, how can I help you?"

"Amy? This is Justice Flint," he responded. "I'm out west of Smoky Lake. I've stumbled across a flock of crows eating a coyote."

"You're calling me because a murder of crows is eating a coyote?" Confusion rippled through her voice.

"I'm calling you because the coyote is all tangled up in rope and there's what looks like a purple backpack in the mix. It's probably nothing, but I thought someone might want to check it out."

"Send your GPS coordinates to my cell. We're on the way. Don't touch anything and try to keep the crows away." She rattled off her cell number and disconnected.

"Keep the crows away? How the hell am I supposed to do that?" Shaking his head, he texted his coordinates to the number she'd given him. Thank heaven he had a good memory. She responded with a smiley-face emoji and he braced himself to wait.

One by one, the crows returned to the body and not wanting to step too close and ruin any potential tracks, he jogged back to Buttercup. He pulled his rifle from the scabbard and slid a round into the chamber. Checking his surroundings, he fired into the decaying stump of a spruce tree. The thump-boom of the shot scattered the crows in all directions. Moments later, they began settling cautiously near the coyote again.

"Damn. This is going to take a lot of ammo." He reloaded, checked the area and fired again. Splinters of wood exploded from the stump and the birds scattered.

Much sooner than he expected, Constable Baxter and two other officers arrived on foot.

"You didn't take long," Justice greeted them.

"Thankfully, Jeff here knows these lease roads like the back of his hand. We took the shortest route here. The nearest lease is only half a mile that way," Amy informed him. "You're going to want to put the gun away now."

"Yes, ma'am. Mind if I unload it first?" She nodded her agreement and he carefully checked the firearm and stowed it back in its scabbard. Buttercup, like all the ranch horses, was gun trained. She was accustomed to the sound of rifle fire and stood steady when one was in use. It was handy in hunting season, and when shooting predatory animals plaguing the ranch.

"You got a firearm possession license?" she asked with a nod at the gun.

"I do, and a valid hunting license. Would you like to see them?" he asked, wondering why she wasn't more concerned with the coyote and the returning crows.

"Later. How close did you get to the body?" She strode from the edge of the tree line to stand in front of him, legs spread shoulder width apart, arms hanging loosely at her sides.

She was the picture of relaxed power and control. The confidence looked damned good on her. Somehow, he could tell she didn't want to be talking to him, she wanted to be right in the thick of the action around the coyote.

"I stayed back as far as I could." He waved toward his tracks. "That's as close as I got before I called. I never went closer. I used my rifle to scatter the crows. I only fired into that stump." He waved toward the shattered tree remains. "I fired nineteen rounds before you arrived. My empty brass is in my jacket pocket."

"Baxter," Jeff called from beside the coyote, "I need you over here to keep these damned birds off."

After warning Justice not to leave, she hurried over to her coworkers and started to work. He poured the last of his coffee into his thermos cup and paced.

· ♥ · ♥ · ♥ · ♥ · ♥ ·

"This is ridiculous," she muttered under her breath, waving her hands to keep the crows away. It was nearly impossible to photograph the scene with the birds swooping in every few seconds. They had very little fear of humans, which was unusual. No wonder Flint had used up so many shots.

"Flint," she shouted. "Do something about these birds."

"Yes, ma'am."

She winced. Did he have to call her ma'am. It made her feel like she was a hundred and seven years old. Jeepers, she was barely thirty-four. He was probably only a year or two older than she was.

"Fire in the hole," Flint shouted, half a second before he fired into the stump again.

They worked for a few moments and as the birds settled again, she called, "Flint!" Obediently, he took another shot. The routine continued for nearly ten minutes until they had enough photographs and were ready to handle the coyote and the backpack. They made short work of checking the animal for tracking tags. Amy and her fellow officer slipped on fresh latex gloves, and after untangling the rope from the pack and coyote's body, they slid the rope into an enormous evidence bag.

The backpack was covered in blood. Amy shuddered. The lost teen they'd rescued before hadn't had any major injuries. Nothing which would leave this much blood. Was this blood hers, or the coyotes? Or from someone or something else entirely. Only forensics would tell them for sure. Amy spread a piece of plastic on the snow. Holding her breath, she opened the bag. Jeff kept busy with his camera, photographing every step of her emptying the pack onto the plastic and searching the items she found inside. Food wrappers, a pair of filthy socks, a brush, lip gloss and two school notebooks. Deep in the bottom of the bag, she found a tattered child's wallet.

Her heart thundered in her ears. Inside the gloves, her palms grew damp and cold. Cautiously, she opened the wallet. It contained $1.85 and a junior high school ID card.

It belonged to the girl who had been found out here last month. The information opened up more questions than it answered. They raced through her mind, one after the other. Finally, the whirlwind of questions in her mind stopped at the most important one. Why was this bag so far from where they'd found the body?

"Danny," she called to the third officer in their small group. "This wallet belongs to last month's victim. How far are we from that location?" She watched as he punched something into his phone.

"Four point two miles as the crow flies. Further by road. Shortest route by road is about seven miles. Way outside the initial search parameters."

"Something's not sitting right with me. This is weird. We'll send the coyote to the lab. I think the coyote being tangled in the rope is a coincidence but I need to be sure. I'll call Sergeant Pfeiffer and organize another search and rescue mission. The odds of her being out here alone are astronomical." If she had been here with someone else, they could be long gone. Or injured. Or dead. This part of her job sucked.

Everything was packed up in short order and Amy turned to Flint. "Okay, Flint. You can stand down. No need to chase the birds off. I'll want an invoice for the rounds you spent. You'll be reimbursed. Thanks for the help."

"Thanks for the help?" He gawked at her. "That pack could have belonged to my daughter. I'm thrilled it didn't. But if there's a search and rescue mission going on, I'm part of it. I'm on Coyote Creek's search and rescue team. My family provides the food truck. I'm helping."

"You've been out all day. I saw you leave your house at four-thirty this morning. It's pushing two in the afternoon. Go home. Rest."

He looked at her like she'd flipped her lid; like she was nuts.

"Are you seriously telling a man with a missing daughter to back away from the search for clues to another missing child? Are you off your fricken rocker? I'm here. I'll stay. Besides, if you saw me leave, you've been awake just as long as I have."

"Will your own loss affect your search? Will the search make your loss worse?" She hated to ask the questions but she had no choice. He was in an awkward position, and if he wasn't up to this, she needed to know. Now. Before it became an issue for her, the case, or God forbid, her career. She was trying to keep their friendship from affecting her job. She waited, hands on her hips, her stare never leaving his face.

"I'm staying," he repeated. "As for your questions—my loss will make me work harder and more meticulously."

"Are you sure?" she probed. "You need to be one hundred percent committed."

"I'm hoping that helping bring another family closure will lighten my own guilt at losing my child." He stepped closer to her and mimicked her stance. It could have felt confrontational, instead it felt like he was pleading with her.

She looked into his eyes. Those deep pools of Flint green. Emotions deepened their color. For a moment she thought she saw anger and wondered if he was angry at her, himself, or something else entirely. His mouth dipped down at the corner, and his eyes turned sad.

"Please, Amy. I need this." His words were barely audible though she stood only three feet from him. He lifted his Stetson to run his fingers through his hair, like he was pulling it out, resettled his hat and met her gaze.

At that moment, reading the pain in his eyes, she'd have given him anything he asked for. She nodded once and turned away. She paused and looked back at him. "Don't mess this up," she warned in a low voice.

"I won't. I'll do exactly what you tell me to do, as long as I'm allowed to help."

"Call your family. We'll need soup, sandwiches and plenty of coffee. Get the lease coordinates from Jeff, we'll set up there and search until dark. If needed, we'll start again in the morning. And have someone come and get your horse." There weren't many search and rescue missions in the Coyote Creek area, but when there was, the Flint family provided the portable kitchen they used for roundups, parties and public events. They were always at Spring Fling, cooking and selling food and donating all the profits to charity. Food for rescue missions was at the Flint family's expense. Their small contribution to the community.

She wasn't more than five steps away when she heard him asking someone to prep the food truck and get it out to them. She listened carefully. He didn't say anything other than the police were doing a search and rescue and they were needed. She nodded to herself, pleased he could be trusted...at least so far. She still wasn't certain why he thought he'd find his daughter out here in the back of beyond. She was impressed he had called in the backpack without touching anything.

Still, deep in the back of her mind, in a place she didn't like to go, doubts plagued her. Had he driven away his ex-wife and subsequently done the same to his daughter? Was his grief as real as it seemed? She pushed the thoughts away. They'd made their peace;

she was just letting her experiences with her ex color her vision of her handsome neighbor.

Chapter Twelve

Justice watched his brother Carl climb out of his truck at the muster point before anyone else even arrived.

Carl waved. "Mom called. I closed up the garage and came out." Justice embraced his brother, unafraid of anyone seeing the strength of their relationship.

"I left my truck and trailer a few miles back." Justice described the location. "Can you run me over to pick it up? I thought we might trade vehicles and you could take Buttercup back to the ranch for me."

"Are you sure you're up to this?" Carl's gaze was serious and unrelenting, as if he could see right into Justice's heart and soul. "I know there's not a chance in hell that anything, or anyone, will be found, but this cuts close for you. It has to be killing you." He patted Justice comfortingly on the back.

Justice sighed and nodded his reassurance, despite being uncertain. "I know. But as a father, there's no way I can sit by and not help. The pack belonged to the girl they found, but there could be someone else out there. Or, this could turn out to be nothing. I pray it does. It could be Hannah. I need to do this." They climbed into the truck and headed toward his trailer. "I'd hope that in the same circumstances, people would pitch in for my family, so I can do nothing less."

"And the nightmares?" Carl flicked a quick glance at him.

"What nightmares?" Justice feigned ignorance. He hadn't realized anyone took note of his nightly wanderings.

"Dude," Carl drew the word into two extended syllables. "You walk the streets at odd hours. I've lost track of the times I've seen you wander past my place, your face all stony, your eyes glum and your head hung down in misery. You trudge down the street oblivious to everything but your inner demons. You don't even hear me when I call out to you. Something's keeping you up. I figured bad dreams."

"You don't know crap," Justice growled. He turned to stare out the window. He lied. Carl had it dead to rights. Nightmares, worry, panic, fear. Any given night could find him awake and restless. He'd walked through three pairs of top of the line Alberta Boots since Hannah disappeared, but there was no way he'd admit it. He probably put on six or seven miles every night. Rain, shine or snow. "What were you doing up so late anyway? Hot dates?"

"Something like that," Carl grumbled clearly disinclined to discuss his own reasons for being awake.

Justice reached out and clapped his brother on the shoulder. "Anytime you want to talk about it, I'm here."

"Ain't gonna happen, but same to you. I've got ears and an open door."

They nodded in unison and fell silent for the remainder of the drive. The muster point lay between Justice's truck and town and by the time they arrived back at the muster point to pick up the horse, people swarmed around like ants. Two school busses of volunteers had arrived and Amy was issuing search orders and assigning grids. Robert, Sue, and Justice's youngest sister, Jennifer, scurried about in the portable kitchen and the heavenly scent of coffee filled the air. Justice and Carl loaded Buttercup into the stock trailer and grabbed coffees.

"Thanks for doing this," Justice smiled gratefully at his brother. "It means a lot." Probably more than Carl would ever realize. If Justice had been forced to abandon the search it would tear another hole in his heart; even as it added another brick to the wall he'd created to protect himself from being hurt again.

"Never forget; I've got your back, bro. Tell Dad I'll take care of the ranch and the chores while you guys search." Another manly clap on the back and Carl strode to the truck and headed back to the ranch. Justice watched the tail lights disappear around a bend and sent a silent thank you to heaven he had such a supportive family. They were there for him and for the community. The tougher the times, the stronger they stood together.

Sipping blessedly welcome, fresh coffee, he stood near the makeshift kitchen and searched for Amy so he could report for duty. He found her alongside a bus, head down, staring at the clipboard clutched between her gloveless hands. She looked cold.

"Hey, Dad." Justice called to his father. "Can I get a half coffee, half hot chocolate with whipped cream for Constable Baxter?"

Robert Flint turned toward him and grinned. "What makes you think we brought whipped topping to a search and rescue?"

"Just hoping. I guess." His father's grin set Justice's nerves on edge. The man acted like he knew something secret, like he could read his son's mind and was amused by what he saw there. Guilt washed over Justice making him pause, mid-step, on his way to the counter. What did he have to feel remorseful over? His over-developed guilt gene whispered he shouldn't be attracted to Amy, or any other women, while his daughter was missing. Sure, life went on, but he had his priorities, at least he should have them. Ruthlessly, he pushed the guilt aside. What he felt was nothing more than concern for a cold neighbor and public official. That was it.

"Everyone knows Mom loves whipped cream, especially on her cocoa," Justice said.

"Yes, she does; at home too. Though the infernal woman won't let me have any. No marshmallows either."

Justice studied his father in the late afternoon light. His skin was pale, but not as pale as it had been in recent weeks. He wasn't the picture of health but he didn't look like death warmed over anymore. Getting those medical tests done and the results back couldn't happen soon enough. Alberta's free medical care was a blessing, but wait times for limited resources could be horrendous and you had to travel to the city for specialized tests. What Coyote Creek needed was a major fundraiser for the hospital. They needed a better medical facility or at least more equipment. He'd have to mention the idea to the festival planning committee. There was a celebration of some sort virtually every month; maybe it was time for the hospital to be the beneficiary of local generosity. He tabled the idea for later consideration.

First things first.

They had a search to run.

"Here you go, son. Take this to your lady friend, and don't let the guilt get to you. She's a good woman and you deserve to be happy. Hannah would want you to move on."

"Hannah would want me to keep looking for her and I will." He snatched the cup out of his hand, sloshing hot liquid over his hand. "Dammit."

"Take it easy, I didn't mean for you to get all riled up. We'll find our girl, somehow, someway. But the good lord wouldn't want us to stop living in the meantime." He reached across the counter and sprayed more topping into the cup in Justice's hand.

A dozen arguments ran through Justice's mind but in the end, after a split second of indecision, he decided to keep quiet. This was neither the time, nor the place to start a family feud. His father was only trying to help.

"Thanks, Dad." He wiped the slopped coffee of his hand, and strode across the well-site to Amy's side. She looked up as he approached, her brows furrowed and lips pursed together. Was it worry or anger creating the lines on her pretty face? The slow squeak-squeal of the site's lone pumpjack as it pumped up and down set his nerves on edge.

"I brought you a hot drink, you look like you could use it." He held the cup out like an offering. Just in case she was peeved with him. Her mouth opened and snapped shut, but the lines between her brows lessened, just a fraction.

"Thanks. I could use something to warm me." She tucked her clipboard under one arm and clasped the offered cup between her hands.

"Where are your gloves?" Justice asked. Didn't the danged woman know she needed gloves in this weather?

"I forgot them on my desk in my rush to leave the office," she confessed, her cheeks turning pink.

"Hold tight. I'll find you some." He pivoted on a booted heel and strode back toward the food truck. She called out for him to wait and he pretended he didn't hear. He was back in under a minute with a pair of thick gloves. He held them out with one hand and reached for the steaming paper cup with the other.

"Thanks, but I was fine."

"Sure, you were." He winked. "But this could be a long, cold evening and there's no sense in getting frostbite. Mom keeps a box of gloves in the trailer. She buys them up in the after-winter sales every year. Her motto, or at least one of them is, *you can never have too many mittens*. She carries them in the pockets of all her jackets, even her summer wind breaker. In the summer, the box of mitts is replaced with a box of ball caps." He chuckled, hoping to lighten the mood. The situation wasn't the place for levity, but her frown left him—disconcerted. He held her coffee while she slipped on her gloves. "So, where do you want me?"

"I've got the volunteers split into groups, or rather the head of the search and rescue team has." She waved toward Garth Gunderson, owner of the local guide shop. Garth ran most of the local rescues and was often called in to assist in rescues province wide. "He said to put you in charge of a group."

Her gaze met his, silently challenging Justice to man up and bow out if he couldn't handle the responsibility. For a moment, he considered backing down. Instead he took a quick mental stock of his emotions and decided participating was the best thing to do. For him, and for anyone who might be out here.

"I'm good to go. You can count on me." He sketched a salute and gave her a serious nod. Her sigh told him she was hoping he'd bow out. "I know you have your doubts, but I promise, on my daughter's life, I'm up for this. No matter what the outcome." He paused. "Do you honestly think I can do anything less?"

"Go see Garth. He'll set you up. It looks like he's waiting for you. Some of the other groups have already left." She gave a general wave toward the suddenly clear area.

Justice looked around, surprised the groups had dispatched while they were talking. He saluted Amy and jogged over to Garth. "Reporting and ready for duty," he claimed, coming to a stop in front of the six-foot two giant of a man. Dressed in heavy canvas pants and a thick flannel shirt, Garth didn't seem to feel the increasing chill. Of course, he was used to spending endless hours outside. He was owner of the local guide shop and spent most of his time giving wilderness or hunting tours, leaving his store in the care of well-trained employees.

Being six feet tall himself, Justice didn't feel diminished by Garth's heavily muscled physique, but he knew he'd never take the man in a fight. Thankfully, while not close friends, they were on good terms.

"I've given you this group. You'll search this section." He handed Justice a map, with a highlighted area, and a walkie talkie. "We're looking for disturbances in the snow, anything out of the ordinary. You know the drill; this isn't your first search. Call in if you see something." He dropped his voice low enough that Justice had to lean in to hear. "We don't expect to find anything. I believe the pack was lost when the girl was. Most likely she was alone or abandoned but keep your eyes open."

A wave of dizziness passed over Justice as his heart plummeted and all the blood rushed from his head. Shoot. Maybe he wasn't cut out to help with this search.

Garth's hand shot out and clapped him on the shoulder. "You've got this, man."

Justice nodded, straightened his spine and turned to gather his troops. They set off in the proper direction and set to work.

·♥·♥·♥·♥·♥·

Amy watched the interplay between Justice and Garth. She wondered again at the logic of letting a heart-hurt man lead a group of searchers. His family troubles might interfere with his concentration causing him to miss something, perhaps a vital clue or sign someone else was out here.

"He's up for this," a female voice said close behind her.

She whirled around to find Sue Flint, Justice's salt and pepper haired stepmother, standing behind her with a sad, yet reassuring, smile on her face.

"In fact, I'm hoping this will help him heal. My boy needs to move on with his life." She held up her left hand in a stop motion. "Don't get me wrong, we'll never stop searching for Hannah and neither will he, but life goes on. Even after mistakes or tragedies."

"I suppose so." She winced at the uncertainty in her voice. What was Sue getting at? Did she know more than she was letting on, or was she on a fishing expedition? Either way, Amy wasn't going to give away any clues about her past. It was unlikely that most of Coyote Creek, including this woman, knew about Amy's past. Amy suspected her new supervisor was aware of her indiscretions, despite them not being part of the official record, though he'd never mentioned it to Amy. Cops were discreet if nothing else, so she trusted him to keep it to himself.

"I see the shadows in your eyes and the way you stand back from the Creekers. You were hurt in the past. Don't fret, you hide it well, only those of us who also bear the burden of loss would ever see it and most of us wouldn't mention it or pry." She laughed lightly, no doubt recognizing the irony of her actions against her words.

"I have no idea what you are talking about, but I do hope Flint is up to this."

"Flint? We're all Flints, but I love how you've given him a pet name. Flint really suits my hard-headed son. Not that Justice doesn't. He'll get justice for his daughter, he'll find her, and he'll get through this search without trouble. You mark my words. Justice is a good man; you could do worse. Much worse. You done with that?" Sue nodded toward Amy's empty cup. "I can take it to the trash for you while you work." She turned to walk away and called over her shoulder, "Oh yeah, the kitchen has a bathroom, if you need it."

Amy couldn't stop the chuckle which bubbled up inside of her. Sue Flint was a force to be reckoned with and Amy suspected if Sue had you in her crosshairs, for good or bad, she wouldn't miss. Still, it was nice to know there was a bathroom, she wasn't looking forward to sneaking into the dense coniferous forest and tramping through the snow to relieve herself if this thing lasted late into the night.

Two of Garth's professional guides were tracking the coyote's movements to see where he'd come from, although they weren't optimistic they'd get far. Snow continued to drift down, small white flakes intermingled with an increasing number of thick, intricate ones, their size growing as the afternoon faded to evening. It would be too dark to search before long, and they'd have to call the volunteers back.

The city had been so different. Loss of daylight was a bigger issue out here in the wilds of Alberta. In Regina, with its streetlights, searches could, and did, go on well into the night, often continuing until morning. Surprisingly though, Coyote Creek residents had turned up just as many, if not more volunteers than Regina. The camaraderie and community spirit here were unmatched by any place Amy had lived. Coyote Creekers pulled together.

Her walkie-talkie crackled with periodic updates from the team leaders. Nothing so far. No tracks, no signs of life besides animals and birds. Her spirits began to slump. She hadn't expected anything, not since they'd already found the owner of the backpack. For the life of her, she couldn't tell if she wanted something found or not. Finding something could mean more teens out here. Finding nothing would leave too many unanswered questions.

· ♥ · ♥ · ♥ · ♥ · ♥ ·

Chapter Thirteen

Justice and his crew traversed the forest in as straight a trajectory as possible, swerving around trees and natural barriers which prevented them from maintaining a straight line. They walked within sight of one another, strung out side by side. Despite the ominous nature of their task, the light snow made their journey pleasant, if he ignored the occasional gust of wind. Cold weather was moving in. Fast. The radio was calling for another snowstorm and no doubt the snow would be here to stay for the rest of winter.

Occasionally, he called out suggestions and reminders to the group. Twice, he had to request they keep quiet and remember to listen for sounds of human activity.

"Mr. Flint? Sir? I think I have something." A teenage boy called from the eastern end of their line.

"Hold up!" Justice called and when the line fell stationary, he jogged over to Marley Chowdry, the mayor's seventeen-year-old son. "What have you got?"

"I don't know, it could be nothing, but that kind of looks like a shoe print?" His voice echoed his uncertainty. "But I only see one." He shrugged and waved vaguely around the area. "I don't see anything else."

Justice squatted beside the faint imprint. "It is a print. Don't move. Everybody stay right where you are," he called loudly. "I'm going to try and track this." He wouldn't call it in until he was certain it wasn't just an oddity left behind from hikers. The print could be old, it was under the thick overhang of a towering blue spruce. Carefully watching where he put his feet, he searched under the tree, his heart pounding.

There.

On the far side of the tree, just beyond easy sight, another partial footprint, more a scuff than anything else, and once again under a tree. He turned back toward Marley. "There are more tracks. Good catch. Stay put I won't go far." He unclipped a flashlight from his belt and stepped forward. The tracks seemed to be sticking close under the trees and headed east.

He radioed the track in. "Flint here. I've got small shoe prints under the trees. Teenage size. Looks like sneakers. I can't tell how old the tracks are. There are none in the snow. They could be nothing, but I'm going to follow them if I can. Likely they're leftovers from fall hikers."

"What are your coordinates?" Amy's voice came back through the radio.

He checked and recited them to her. "I'll put my team on hold until another leader arrives. I'll keep you posted as I search."

He scrambled under the branches, crawling from tree to tree, his eyes searching every inch of ground and every crevice for signs of overturned dirt, scuffing or footprints. He continued crawling until he was about a hundred yards away from his group. In the distance he could barely hear the quiet talking of the group he'd left behind. As the light dimmed, it became increasingly difficult to find signs of human activity.

His heart thundered and blood pounded in his ears. What if this *was* someone lost out here? Or hiding? They could be injured. He couldn't afford to lose them now. He had to know where this went.

If someone was still out here. Panic clutched at his heart. He had to do this, had to find this person. For him. For Hannah. For whoever might be out here in this frigid weather. Jesus, it could be Hannah! His daughter was friendly and outgoing. She could have befriended the missing girl. They could have been trying to get home. No! He wasn't going to go there. He'd follow the trail to wherever it led.

He closed his eyes, cast a prayer for his daughter's safety heavenward. He whispered a second prayer for whoever left the track and opened his eyes. Squatting motionless, he searched the ground carefully.

There!

Another tiny scuff. He scuttled forward. And again. Another twenty feet of progress.

A twig snapped to his right. He paused without turning and waited. The light breeze ruffled the trees, showering him with snow and sending icy tendrils of moisture down his back. He'd have worn a scarf if he'd known he'd be outside this long. He tugged his collar closed.

He rested, motionless, and caught a glimpse of something moving. He squatted down, scared of frightening whatever was in the spruce tree's shadow. He inched forward until he had a better view. His instincts had been right, that was no animal.

Matted hair, so dirty it could be any color, hung below what seemed to be a shirt wrapped turban style around a youth's head. Her delicate features told him it was a girl. She wore holey jeans and a battered hoodie of some dark indeterminable color. Clearly, she'd been surviving out here for a while. Thin and visibly shivering she pressed back against the rough bark of the spruce she huddled under. Piles of leaves and branches surrounded her, like she'd tried using them for warmth and cover.

"I can tell you're there," he called out softly. Silently he hoped this was Hannah. Maybe he'd found his daughter.

A soft whimper reached his ears and crushed his heart. Deftly, he pushed the button on his radio and spoke.

·♥·♥·♥·♥·♥·

A my's radio crackled to life.

"I'm not going to hurt you." She stared at the radio for a second until it occurred to her, she knew the voice. It was Justice. Her breath seized in her throat and the people around her gasped.

"I don't know who you are," he continued. "My name's Justice. Justice Flint. I'm not going to hurt you. I just want to talk."

The radio fell quiet. She couldn't tell if he'd released the button, or just stopped speaking. The only thing she knew for sure was the radio's battery was fully charged. The thought brought a measure of relief.

The searchers who had returned gathered around Amy and crowded forward, trying to hear what was going on. She waved them back but they only moved a few inches.

"I have a daughter. She's going to be sixteen soon." Even through the crackle of the radio, the emotion in his voice raked across Amy's heart.

Faintly, Amy heard a reply but couldn't make out the words.

"Well then," Flint replied. "If you have a gun, I guess you don't need any help getting out of here. Though, frankly, I'm darn near lost myself and I'm in charge of part of this search and rescue unit. Next thing you know, they'll be searching for me too." His laugh was low and Amy recognized it as fake but doubted the girl would pick up on it.

Again, the faint sounds of a response she couldn't understand.

"I won't come any closer. Let me tell you about my daughter." Amy heard something in his voice. Relief? Disappointment? Had he been hoping this was his daughter? It had occurred to her earlier that this could be Hannah. If it were his daughter, Justice would have recognized her voice. Disappointment must be killing him.

Justice spoke again. "My daughter, Hannah, ran away from her mother's place. We're divorced. She left nearly two years ago. She was fourteen. I haven't seen her since. She's good and gone." He paused and cleared his throat. "There isn't a day goes by when I don't look for her. In person or on the internet. We had some fights. Some big ones and some small ones. All families have them. But I want her back. I need to know she's safe. My heart breaks every single day."

Although Amy had heard Hannah's story a dozen times, the pain in his voice echoed the pain and loss she'd felt when she found out the truth about her ex. Why did people always hurt the ones they loved?

"My family hates me!" The voice was louder now. Either Flint had edged closer or the girl was getting braver.

"Well, that's downright unfortunate. Still, my daughter wouldn't want me to leave you here. So, I'll just settle in and get comfortable while you get to know me."

Amy waved Garth toward her and whispered instructions to take an officer and find Flint. They couldn't let this girl run. They had to help her out before weather or wildlife took its toll.

"I'm a rancher, most of the time. Sometimes, I hunt, or spend time with my nieces and nephews. My brother, Riley, just found out he has a kid. Funny thing is he didn't even know about her and she's five."

"That sucks. He shoulda been there for her."

"Darn right, he should have. But her Mama didn't tell him about her. He only found out when her Mama died. But Riley took that wee girl in and made her his own."

"I don't have a family."

Well, that contradicted with her statement that her family hated her. Amy wondered which was true and shoved the thought aside. It didn't matter. Getting this child out of the elements was their first and only task.

After a moment of silence, Amy's radio crackled to life again. "I'll bet you have friends. I heard the police found a girl around here a while back. Was she your friend?"

"Maryanne?" The girl's voice rose in alarm. "Where is she?"

Amy sucked in a breath and prayed Flint wouldn't tell this terrified girl her friend was dead. She was fragile enough she didn't need a bigger burden to shoulder.

"I don't know what her name is. But if you come along with me, I can take you to town and we'll find out." The lift in his voice changed the suggestion to a question.

"No."

"Come on sweetheart. I'm one of the good guys. I don't know how you ended up here, but you can't stay out in the cold any longer. You must be frozen and probably hungry." He paused and a rustling sound came over the radio. "I've got a Mars bar right here. I'll toss it over. Here you go. Have a bite or two of that. It'll help you feel better. Then, when you're up to it, you can come on out."

Amy smiled. Flint should be a hostage negotiator. He was great with this girl. Calming, reassuring and authoritarian all at the same time. He might just pull this off. More than anything, she wanted to be there helping him, but her job was to organize and supervise the volunteers and the officers she'd sent in to help out. Before they left, she'd cautioned them to stay back and not interfere without instruction. More than ever, she was grateful for the technology that allowed her to talk directly into their ears rather than over the walkie-talkies.

· ❤ · ❤ · ❤ · ❤ · ❤ ·

Flint didn't move after he carefully tossed the chocolate bar toward the girl. His legs shook with the stain of squatting, his thumb ached from holding the radio button so the police could monitor his interaction with the girl. Hopefully Amy, Constable Baxter, he corrected himself, was smart enough to let him handle this. Admittedly, he wasn't the best with teenagers, he'd failed his own daughter epically, but he was certain he could help this girl.

Thank God this wasn't his daughter. Or maybe not. He sighed inwardly. His life would be easier in so many ways if this was Hannah. They'd be out of here in no time. Of course, that meant that he'd have to begin repairing his relationship with Hannah. Still, it would be better than sleepless nights and nightmares about her whereabouts.

Focus!

He needed to focus on this child and worry about his own later.

"How about if you tell me your name, in exchange for the Mars bar, which was supposed to be my midnight snack. I was camping a few miles from here with my horse, Buttercup."

"Your horse's name is Buttercup? That's dumb." Her voice was petulant and he recognized the tone for the relaxing it implied. She was less wary.

"My sister, Beth, named her. I'm just going to sit down over here. My legs are killing me from squatting so long." He plopped gracelessly down and suppressed a groan as the blood flooded back into his legs and feet. He'd be lucky if he didn't have frozen toes after this. "How about your name?"

"Casey," she mumbled around a mouthful of candy.

Progress!

"So, Casey, my folks are close by, they have their portable kitchen with them. How about we head over there and get ourselves some hot chocolate and some sandwiches? Peanut butter and jam? Ham and cheese? Egg salad? They might even have some soup."

"I can't." Her voice was so low it barely reached him.

"Why is that? Your family will be so pleased to see you you won't catch trouble."

"I told you, I don't have a family."

Perhaps she told the truth; but what dire circumstances had led to Casey and her friend being lost in the woods in the back of nowhere? "Okay then, we'll find you a safe place to stay. All you have to do is come out of there."

"Can I stay with you?" Her voice trembled.

His breath exploded out before he could stop it. Talk about a sucker punch to the gut. Memories of a much younger Hannah crying to stay with him and not return to her mother's house played through his mind. Chills, unrelated to the falling temperature, chased through him. Had wanting to be with him prompted Hannah to run away or was it the jockey thing?

"I can't promise that, but I can promise to try. You've been out here a while. You may need time in the hospital, probably at least a checkup. I promise, I'll stay with you at the hospital." Again, he went with his gut and reacted without thinking. "Why don't you come on out of there?"

"I can't." Tears filled her voice.

He pulled off his hat and raked his fingers through his hair. Why were teenagers so stubborn? She had to be injured, it was the only explanation.

"Casey, are you hurt?"

"My leg. I think I broke my ankle. I can't walk."

Shoot! Now what?

"Tell you what, Casey. If it's okay with you, I'm going to stand up and come over there and check it out."

When she didn't answer, he stood and stepped slowly forward. He had to crouch to scoot below the branches and every movement sent more snow cascading over him. The poor girl had to be nearly frozen solid. It was a wonder she was even alive after all this time. She must have a guardian angel watching over her.

Kneeling in front of her, he smiled his most reassuring smile and offered his hand. "Justice Flint. Pleased to meet you, Casey." She ignored his hand. "Which leg is hurt?" He already knew, she had her left shoe off and held it in her hand like a weapon and the foot was bent at an unnatural angle. Compound fracture for sure. "That looks mighty painful. I don't think I could handle a bad break without pain medication. This is what we're going to do," he said in a no-nonsense voice. "I'm going to put a splint on your ankle and carry you out of here. But first, I'm going to wrap you in my jacket. Your hoodie doesn't offer much protection from the cold. Once we're all splinted up, we'll head back. The police will be there, and probably an ambulance, but I promise not to leave your side. Are you okay with that?"

She nodded nervously. "Promise?"

"Cross my heart." He sketched an X over his heart with one finger.

He couldn't even fathom how she was still alive in this weather. She'd been out here for weeks, injured and dressed for a warm autumn day. She had to be in shock from the injury and nearly hypothermic. People had died from less.

It was time for action. He released the button on the radio, confident Amy would know what was happening and would set the right chain of events into action. He slipped out of his coat and leaned in to wrap it around Casey's shoulders and helped her slide her arms into the sleeves. He was no medic, but he'd taken first aid and knew the basics. He needed to immobilize her foot before he moved her. A quick search of the underbrush provided two stout, broken-off limbs. Bracing himself for the cold to come, he shed his thick flannel shirt, and used it to hold the limbs in place against her ankle.

She groaned in agony with each motion, but finally, he had her ankle secured.

"You ready?"

"No." She laughed weakly. "Maybe."

"Okay then. I'm going to pick you up. It's going to hurt. I won't lie to you. It'll hurt until we get some pain meds into you. I'll carry you until we meet up with the paramedics. They'll take over, but I won't leave you. Are you ready?"

She wiggled around and grabbed a filthy navy-blue backpack from behind her and nodded. "Ready."

She didn't sound ready, but he knew she was choosing the less terrifying of two options. Go with a total stranger or freeze to death in the woods. "Here we go," he exclaimed, sliding one arm under her legs and the other around her back. He almost recoiled at the smell of her. Dirt, sweat, urine and fear commingled in a breath stealing stench.

She screamed in agony, the shrill sound pounding against his eardrums and carving a groove into his heart. He forgot about the ripe aroma and tugged her close, holding her securely to his chest.

"Okay then, that's the worst." He reassured her. "There'll be some jostling, but it won't be so bad. Wrap your arms around my neck and hold on tight."

She obeyed and he started retracing his steps, back toward the search team he'd left standing in the cold. She groaned with each jostling step, but he knew she was trying to keep quiet. In less than three minutes, he met up with two paramedics with a foldaway portable stretcher. Amy must have sent them in while he was talking to Casey. The rest of his search team was nowhere in sight.

"Hi, guys." He nodded to the paramedics, both of whom he'd known in high school. Garth and a police officer stood nearby. Garth looked comfortable, the officer huddled into himself, trying to keep warm. "This is Casey. She's in a bit of a pickle." He looked down at her. "I'm going to set you on the stretcher and they'll carry you out. I'll be with you the entire time."

"Don't leave." She panicked and tightened her arms around his neck.

He looked her right in the eye. "I promise not to leave you but you have to go with the guys. I'll be with you all the way."

"Swear. On your daughter." Her voice was weak but determined.

"I swear on Hannah's life I won't leave you."

He took her hesitant nod as agreement and lowered her gently onto the canvas and aluminum-bar stretcher. The paramedics covered her in blankets, took a quick set of vitals, gave her a shot of pain medication, and hefted the stretcher up. They managed to quick-march back to the muster point without jostling her too badly. Exhausted from the stress of the ordeal, it was all Justice could do to keep up with them and chat what he hoped were reassuring words to Casey as they went.

"Were you alone?" he asked at one point.

"Just me and Maryanne."

Justice radioed the new information to Amy. Her friend was found two weeks ago. There was no reason to keep searching the area.

Disappointment that this wasn't Hannah pounded him, but was tempered by the knowing he'd done a good thing in rescuing Casey.

·♥·♥·♥·♥·♥·

Chapter Fourteen

Amy stood in the doorway of Casey's hospital room. Hands in her front pockets, she leaned against the jam for support. Midnight had long since come and gone. The afternoon and evening had been interminable, she wanted nothing more than to head home, have a shower, and sleep for two years. The doctors had finally given her permission to question Casey, only the girl was now fast asleep in her bed. Flint slept in the chair beside her, their hands wrapped together.

His face was dirty, his hair adorably disheveled and he'd acquired a fresh shirt from somewhere. His hat lay discarded on the bedside table. He looked as exhausted as she felt.

Casey's face and hands were clean but her hair was still filthy. Her sodden, grimy clothing had been replaced by hospital pajamas which barely peeked out from under the pile of blankets she was burrowed into. Her leg was elevated slightly. The doctors had decided food, liquids, and rest were more critical than immediate surgery to pin her ankle. They'd have to deal with the swelling before they attempted to piece her ankle back together anyway. Earlier, they'd taken care of her basic needs, medicated her and put her to bed.

The only questions Amy had been permitted before now were to ensure Casey was indeed without family and that she and her friend had been the only teens out there. Details of their ordeal would have to wait until morning. Amy was dying to know what led to them being alone in the woods to start with.

Her attention turned back to Flint. His eyes were open and those Flint green eyes bored into her soul.

"Hi," he whispered. "Shouldn't you be at home?"

"Shouldn't you?" she countered with a shrug, wondering why his comfort mattered to her.

"This is right where I need to be. Casey needs me. I promised her I'd stay with her."

"Can I get you anything?" She offered, knowing she lied to herself that she was only offering to be polite and she didn't care about him, even if she had to admit she'd been wrong about him.

"I'm good now; Mom and Dad brought me dry clothing." He smiled. "But I would kill for a cup of coffee and a donut."

"Won't the caffeine keep you awake?" She could use a coffee herself and a donut didn't sound bad at all. "The cafeteria is closed but if you don't mind waiting, I can run by Tim Hortons and get you something. I made the mistake of trying hospital dispenser coffee once. I wouldn't touch it again with a ten-foot pole." She shuddered just thinking about the pathetic excuse for coffee from the hospital's vending machines.

"Don't go to any trouble."

She smiled because his words said one thing and his voice cried the opposite. "No problem. I doubt I'll sleep until after we have a chance to question Casey. I'm exhausted, wired and half twitchy. I don't know what to do with myself. Rather than figure it out, I'll get us coffee."

"Make mine a double-double. Please, and thank you."

Timmy's was only five minutes away, yet by the time she returned, Flint was asleep again. She tiptoed into the room and set the coffee on the table beside his hat.

"Is that all I get?" he whispered. "Just coffee?"

"Oh, I thought you were asleep. I didn't want to wake you." She handed him one of the two bags she carried. "Sausage and egg breakfast sandwich. Orange juice, a donut and a bran muffin with butter. I figured you'd be hungry. You burned a lot of energy out there in the cold today. Yesterday. Whatever it was." He'd been a hero out there while she waited helplessly with the rest of the search and rescue team. She'd have given anything to be right in the thick of the rescue, but she knew her duty and she'd followed protocol. Along with her disappointment was a sense of satisfaction in knowing she'd done her job and done it right.

"I'm a light sleeper," he confessed. "I'm up and down all night and this isn't the most comfortable place to sleep. I never realized how noisy a hospital is at night."

His shrug of unconcern didn't fool her. He was here keeping an eye on Casey as he'd promised and he was one hundred percent alert in case she even whimpered. The man was honorable beyond anything else.

"Mind if I join you?"

"Sure. Why aren't you at home asleep?"

"I wanted to get started questioning Casey. I hung around until I had the doctor's permission. Her falling asleep never occurred to me, which is ridiculous because I doubt she slept much in the last couple weeks. I can't believe she survived alone for over two weeks with a broken ankle." She picked up the second guest chair and placed it where she could watch both Flint and Casey. Settling into it, she popped the top on her coffee and took a bracing sip before unzipping her heavy police jacket.

She was still cold from the time spent outside. It didn't make sense; she'd been in the hospital more than long enough to warm up and she'd had the heater of her squad car blasting on full all the way to Timmy's and back. She should be warm by now. She wasn't.

"Something's bothering me about this whole situation with Casey and Maryanne," she blurted. The words seemed to startle Flint as much as they did Amy. Instead of dropping the subject, she kept talking, her voice barely a whisper. "Why were two teenage girls in the bush in the back of beyond? Maryanne was from Calgary and I expect Casey is too. How did they get here, nearly seven hours north?"

"I've wondered that myself."

Amy watched him take a bite of his sandwich, chew it thoughtfully and swallow.

Dang.

Even dirty, disheveled and exhausted, he managed to make eating look sexy and strong. She stuffed her libido back in its box and nibbled her own sandwich. It could have been filet mignon or it could have been cardboard, she was so caught up in her neighbor's good looks she barely tasted it. Her ability to focus sucked right now.

"During the ambulance ride back to town, Casey mentioned knowing Maryanne through foster care."

"I assumed that's where they met. Maryanne's dad is dying of cancer, her mother died in a car accident years ago. With no other relatives, she'd been put into foster care. Maybe they were in the same home. I sure wish Casey was awake I have a million questions for her."

"Go ahead and ask," Casey said quietly from the bed. "It's not like I can sleep with you guys yammering away." She waved her hand for them to ask, but didn't open her eyes.

Flint patted her hand. "Go back to sleep. Constable Baxter's questions will wait until morning. You need rest more than we need answers. We'll shut up."

Amy glared at him. She could have gotten her investigation started. Flint shook his finger at her in a no-no gesture. He was right. This wasn't the time or place for their discussion, and Casey needed rest after her ordeal. It might be for the best if Amy went home for a nap. She could get up early, formulate a list of questions and be back before the doctor even made his rounds.

Wordlessly, they finished their late-night snack and coffee. The silence between them was surprisingly comfortable, almost amiable. She stood and returned her chair to the corner and saluted him. With a nod, she whispered, "I'll be back in a few hours. Try and get some sleep."

As exhausted as she was, Amy found sleep elusive. Notebook and pen in hand, she dragged a chair closer to the fire she'd lit in her tiny fireplace, sat down and covered herself with her comfort quilt. Patterned with golden stars on a deep purply-blue background, it was one of her last remnants of her birth mother. It had brought her comfort since she was six. It was growing tattered, despite her caution with it. She no longer used it except in the most stressful times. Perhaps she should learn to repair it.

Tonight, she needed its warmth and memories. She had so many questions. Too many. About Casey and about Flint. She pushed Flint aside and focused on what she wanted to ask Casey.

·❤·❤·❤·❤·❤·

Chapter Fifteen

"I'm not talking to you if he leaves." Casey glared at Amy.

Great, just what she needed after last night. She'd been awake twenty-six hours before finally catching a nap and wasn't even close to rested. This case was hers and she had to do what needed done. Sure, she could have passed the case to one of her fellow officers. Any one of them would be happy to take over. Coyote Creek didn't have much serious crime; but she decided to stick it out. She'd dealt with runaways in the past and had more experience than her coworkers. Thus, this baby, or rather teenager, was hers.

"He's not your guardian. You don't have to answer my questions, but I'm asking you to."

"And if Justice stays, I'll talk to you. I don't need a guardian. I'm sixteen. You can send her away." She gestured to the legal advocate from child services who had been appointed to protect her rights.

"I stay. It's the law," the woman declared kindly. "I know this is tough, but we need to straighten all this out. I'm okay with Mr. Flint staying if he has no objection and it helps you feel better."

"I'm in." He strolled to the bedside chair and settled in, grasping Casey's hand in his.

"Tell me what happened," Tricia instructed.

Casey seemed to shrink into herself. She stared off into space, not meeting anyone's eyes. Casey squeezed Justice's hand until they were both white knuckled.

"Maryanne and I had the same foster family. At first, it was good. Not great, but good. We had food. We shared a room. They were nice."

She stopped talking. Amy knew to let her gather her thoughts. She'd need to wait the girl out. Pushing would only drive her into herself.

"What happened then?" Justice asked.

"Our foster dad lost his job. He started drinking. He started staring at us." Tears slipped down her cheeks. "You know—creepy-like."

Amy knew where this was going; it was a story she'd heard all too often. The majority of foster parents were exceptional people, but a few bad seeds slipped in. Occasionally, difficult circumstances could break people, make them do things they wouldn't ordinarily do. The lawyer shook her head sadly and Justice went pale. His shoulders bunched and his other hand fisted against his thigh.

"A couple times, he walked in when we were showering." She shuddered. "At first, we thought it was an accident. But it wasn't," she shouted. "He was just a pig." She broke into tears. "How could he do that to us? He was supposed to look after us!"

"What did he do?" Justice demanded, his tone both angry and comforting.

"He...he...he touched her. He grabbed Maryanne by the," her voice dropped to a whisper. "He grabbed her boob. She told him no and he hit her. But he stopped."

"Did you tell your case worker?" the lawyer asked.

"She didn't believe us. She said we were telling lies. She was friends with them. She'd put kids in their house for years."

Amy and the lawyer scratched down notes as the conversation progressed. Details of the abuse haltingly came out. It never went beyond touching which was bad enough. But eventually, the girls reached their limit. They ran away to protect themselves, to protect their innocence.

"We didn't think it would be so hard." Casey sobbed.

Justice leaned in and stroked her back. Amy thought Casey might rebel, but it seemed by saving her from freezing to death, he'd earned Casey's trust.

"It wasn't bad, living on the streets when it was warm, but it started to get cold. The shelters filled up. 'Tough economic times,' one old cow said when she refused to let us into the shelter because it was full. It was too cold to live outside so we decided to try and find Maryanne's cousin in Grande Prairie. We thought she could help. We caught a ride with a trucker as far as Edmonton. We spent a few nights in a shelter there. We stole some money before we ran away from our foster home but it wasn't much. We were running out of cash so we tried hitch hiking. Finally, we got a ride with this guy. He was bald and dirty and drove this old, disgusting car. It had to be a hundred years old. But he said he was going to Grande Prairie and we went with him."

She broke down and sobbed uncontrollably for several minutes. Amy's heart pounded and her eyes ached. A product of the foster system herself, she'd been blessed with a loving family, one she'd come to call her own. She couldn't even fathom how tough it must have been on the two teens.

Slowly the details came out. He'd driven north and stopped to feed them. He'd even purchased a large bag of snacks. As they neared Coyote Creek, he'd claimed he had a stop to make. After driving further and further into the bush, the girls knew he was up to no good and they were in danger.

"I said I needed to pee. He stopped and let me out, he tied Maryanne up with a rope. When he wasn't looking, I bashed him on the head with a rock and we ran. I was so scared." Her voice shook with tears but she went on. "We hid until the next day. When we went back to where we thought the car was, it was gone. Maybe we didn't have the right spot. We didn't kill him, did we?" She paled and hunkered closer to Justice.

"We never found anyone. He must have woken up and driven away," Amy reassured her. How terrible to be so afraid for your safety and to worry about having killed someone intent on harming you. No wonder they'd hidden in the bush.

"I hurt my leg and Maryanne went for help. She was going to follow the gravel roads until she found someone. Where is she?"

"Finish your story, we can talk about Maryanne later," the lawyer advised.

"Oh my God. She's dead. I killed her. I killed my best friend because I hurt myself tripping over a stupid rock."

"You guys can leave now," Justice demanded. "Casey needs time to adjust, to process. You can resume questioning later."

"I'm sorry, Mr. Flint. You have no right to make demands. You are here as Casey's friend, not a guardian. The questioning continues." Again, the lawyer spoke.

"Amy. Constable Baxter, please. Just give her some time." His eyes pleaded with Amy. She knew he was right. Casey needed a few minutes to adjust. There was no rush with the questions. Their abductor was gone, nobody else was missing.

"We'll take a break. I need coffee. We'll be back in a few minutes. Come on, let's leave them alone."

"You expect me to leave a child alone with a strange man?"

Amy cussed silently about the stubbornness of outsiders. The lawyer was from Whitecourt not Coyote Creek. She couldn't know about the Flint family and how trusted they were in town. Even Amy had come to trust Justice and knew Casey was safe with him.

"Mr. Flint is an upstanding citizen. Ask anyone in town. As an officer of the law, I am ordering you to step back and give them a few minutes to recoup. Casey has bonded with her rescuer and he hasn't left her side for a moment. I give you my word; she'll be fine in his care."

The lawyer looked skeptical but followed Amy from the room. A short time later, they returned and finished questioning Casey.

"I can't believe they didn't tell you I ran away with Maryanne," Casey griped. "She's dead and they didn't even care what happened to me."

"There will be a full investigation," the advocate stated firmly.

Casey had lived off puddle water, eating snow, and the odd berry after she used up all the food they'd stashed from soup kitchens in Edmonton and the snacks they'd stolen from their abductor. Though she didn't know what kind of car it was, just that it was dark blue and had four doors, she recalled part of the license plate.

Amy immediately put out an APB on the vehicle.

At the doctor's insistence, the questioning was brought to a halt and Casey was taken in for the surgery to repair her foot.

After three days of recovery, Casey stood proudly at the end of her bed, her unsteady stance stabilized by crutches. She glared at the representative from child services.

"Why can't I stay with Justice?" she demanded. "He's been here for me since he saved me. He'll look after me."

Justice blanched and Amy knew he wasn't ready to take on a new teenager with his own daughter missing.

"I don't want to leave here. I like it here. I won't go. If you make me leave, I'll run away. I know how, I've done it before." She backed unsteadily away from the adults in the room.

"Yeah, that didn't turn out so well," Justice stated. "Maybe we can find another solution. Aren't there any foster families available in Coyote Creek?" Perhaps she could stay with his family. He kept the idea to himself for the moment. No sense getting her hopes up for nothing.

"Everyone is full. Nobody has space," the advocate declared.

"Maybe not," Amy injected, wincing as the words came out. "I'm a registered foster parent. I'm registered in Saskatchewan, not Alberta. I'm not sure what the jurisdictions are."

"Can I stay with you? Please, please, please. I'll be good. I won't run away. I like you." Casey wobbled, almost toppling over, in her excitement.

Amy stifled a groan. So much for not getting attached to this town. Coyote Creek was pulling her in. Bit by bit.

"I'll have to confirm your credentials, Miss Baxter."

"It's Constable Baxter and please do." Taking in a child isn't what she'd planned, but she'd put it out there and nothing in the world would make her snatch the brief moment of happiness from Casey. The girl had been through too much already.

Three hours later, as they walked up the front walk to Amy's house, she delivered more good news to Casey. "We found your abductor. He's already in jail. He was caught in the act of kidnapping another girl. It is unlikely he'll ever get out of jail."

Casey whooped in excitement.

"Fabulous. He deserves to rot in hell," Justice declared.

"Language," Amy chided him without heat.

She held the door open for Casey and for Justice who obediently trailed behind them, laden down with bags of necessities Casey would need. As always, his family had come through. They'd rounded up clothing and gift certificates for Coyote Creek's newest resident. After a quick shopping trip Casey had enough clothing and toiletries to get her through her first week at school. She'd need more in the long term, but she had enough to get started.

·❤·❤·❤·❤·❤·

Chapter Sixteen

After a good night's sleep, Justice, his brother Riley and Riley's newly discovered, six-year-old daughter, Daisy pulled into the yard of the Bar Three, the Flint family's ranch, just as a tan Jeep Wrangler pulled out.

"Hey," Daisy called out, "that's the guy that looks like Daddy."

"Who is?" Justice asked.

"The guy in the jeep. I sawed him in the restaurant on my birthday." She pivoted in her seat to follow the Jeep's exit. "He looks like Daddy and like you too Uncle Justice."

"Interesting," Justice replied. "I don't recognize the vehicle. I wonder who he is. I'll ask Dad."

They pulled to a stop in front of the house, Sue hurried down the front steps to meet them. "Your father is in the barn. Kettle Corn is whelping. She's having trouble. Can you see if you can help? Daisy, come inside with me, we'll make some cookies."

"Is she going to be okay?" Daisy asked, a slight tremor of worry in her voice.

"Certainly. Dogs have puppies all the time. Today, she just needs help. Good thing your daddy is a veterinarian." Justice looked at

Sue for confirmation as he comforted his niece. She nodded, hurried them along and led Daisy inside.

"I'll make sure Corn and the puppies are all fine," Riley stated, giving his daughter a quick hug.

Their visit wasn't meant to be a vet call, they were here to discuss the future of the ranch and how things were done. Justice, Riley and their brother, Kendrick, wanted to stop making their own hay and buy it instead. The land could be used for grazing and they could sell the equipment. Buying hay in the cold months would be costly, but it would reduce the workload, especially when it came to maintaining the haying equipment. The tractor and bailer were aging and required constant repair. Carl, their brother the mechanic, helped with the maintenance, but his garage business was booming and he was finding it difficult to keep up with the dual workload.

"Hey, Dad," Justice greeted their father, Robert, who sat on a small square bale of straw in the corner, petting Kettle Corn's head. The dog was a mixed breed. Part Australian Shepherd, part husky and part something else. She was a rescue, but still a great cattle dog. "How's Corn doing?"

"She's okay. I think. My gut tells me Riley better have a look at her. I was just about to call him. Glad you boys showed up."

Justice and Robert leaned against the wall, out of the way, while Riley examined Corn. "Who named her anyway?" Justice asked. "I forget."

"Beth," Riley groaned. "She's named most of the animals and she's got this thing for crazy names. Frankly, I was glad to get my own place so I could start naming my own critters." They laughed together. "Of course, I didn't have a pet until Daisy got her kitten."

Justice watched Kettle Corn squirm in discomfort. Why was watching an animal in pain as bad as watching a family member hurting? Likely because he'd always loved the ranch animals like family. It was part of the reason he didn't have any house pets. They took a lot of time and effort. While he missed having a companion to come home to at the end of a hard day, he was so busy with the ranch and looking for Hannah, he couldn't give an animal the love and attention it deserved. When Hannah came home, he'd get her, them, any pet she wanted. Even a lap dog. Yeah, he'd like a small dog who fit on his lap. His brothers would laugh themselves silly but a lap dog would suit him just fine.

"Dad, whose jeep was leaving?" Justice asked.

"Name's Ira. He's new in town. Retired soldier looking for work, I guess." He paced away from them and wandered around the bar doing what their stepmother called busy work. Small things which didn't need done, just to look busy. He straightened things already in their proper place, rearranged feed bags, closed empty stalls. Shuffled the tack and tools hanging on wall pegs.

The brothers shared a questioning glance. Something was up. Why would their father avoid talking about a stranger? What was he hiding? Maybe he was just nervous about Kettle Corn and her pups.

"Been thinking about your foolish plan to stop haying." He pivoted to stare at them. "I've decided your plan is a no-go. Been doing it this way since I took this ranch over from my father, we'll keep doing it that way. End of discussion."

"Then we're going to need to replace the tractor. We're spending more on parts than the hay would cost us," Justice informed him, straightening up from the wall. "A new tractor and baling system could run into hundreds of thousands of dollars. Carl's right when he says the one we've got is a relic and likely won't last another year before failing catastrophically. What'll we do then? The ranch is yours, not ours. I work here, I get paid, but I also know with this economy, beef prices are down. At least to the rancher, not so much in the grocery store." He snorted at the irony of that. "I think we need to seriously reconsider how things are done around here."

Robert stomped over and shook his finger under Justice's nose. "Mind your manners boy. You've got it right; this place is mine."

His cheeks turned red and he gasped for air. Justice toed his brother in the leg to pull his attention from the dog.

"When I die, you kids get this ranch, until then you can either do things my way, or you can hit the highway." His declaration was spoiled by his wheezing. "I'll hire that Ira guy and you can find your own way instead of relying on me for a living."

His words were unusually harsh. Something, beyond changing their way of ranching, had to be bothering him. Sweat rolled down his brow and he gasped. Justice raced over to him. "Are you okay, Dad?" He couldn't keep the panic from his voice, he didn't even try.

Riley abandoned the dog, leaped to his feet and was at his father's side in seconds. One on each side of their father, they lowered him to the floor. He writhed in agony, clutching his chest.

"Call an ambulance and get Mom," Riley demanded. "Heart attack."

Justice called emergency dispatch, barely remaining calm enough to relay the needed information. Thank heaven the entire department knew the family ranch. He raced toward the house to get Sue, and dialed Riley's business partner. He paused on the front step and explained the situation and Houston agreed to hurry over and take care of the dog.

Hands trembling, Justice reached for the door handle. Shit. He was terrified. He couldn't lose his father. Not like this. Robert was only sixty!

Dammit! His daughter was missing, his father was ill, maybe dying. He did not need this shit. This was bullshit! The universe was handing him a shitty deal, again. Hadn't saving Casey earned him some good Karma?

"Okay, suck it up, Flint. You've got this. Mom needs you to be calm." Half a dozen deep breaths and he stepped into the house, relatively calm. "Mom, got a minute?" he called toward the farm house's enormous kitchen.

"Coming," she shouted back. She said something he couldn't hear and came out of the kitchen.

He pitched his voice too low to hear from the kitchen and got straight to the meat of the matter. "Mom, Dad's ill. We've called an ambulance. Riley thinks it might be a heart attack. Dad's breathing and conscious."

Sue swooned a bit and then straightened her spine. "Turn off the oven. Put the cookie dough in the fridge. Take Daisy to Tricia's apartment. Thank heaven today isn't a school day. Or maybe it would be better if it was, then she wouldn't be here." She turned toward the kitchen and pivoted back. She yanked her apron over her head and tossed it at him. "I'll go with the ambulance. You follow when you can. How's the dog?"

She was babbling. Sue never babbled. He wrapped her in his arms and pulled her close. "Breathe, Mom. We were right there, he didn't fall. Riley's watching him. Listen. I hear the ambulance already. Get your coat and shoes." He helped her into her jacket, handed her her purse and steadied her while she slipped into cowboy boots. He hugged her once more and kissed her cheek. "He'll be okay, Mom. I swear."

He watched through the screen door until she entered the barn just as the ambulance pulled into the yard. They must have broken more than one speed limit to get here that quickly. It was a fifteen-minute drive and they'd made it in under ten. Impressive. Scary impressive.

"Hiya, Daisy," he greeted his niece as he entered the kitchen. There would be hell to pay later for not removing his dirty boots. "We're just going to clean up the cookie stuff and take you to see Tricia. Grandma has to go with Grampa right now."

"I heard a siren?" Her voice quivered. "Is Grampa hurt?"

"His heart hurts, he has to go to the hospital and Grandma is going with him. He's going to be okay." His words were probably not comforting. Heaven knew Daisy had spent more than her share of time in the hospital watching her mother die of cancer. Her mother's father was battling health issues as well. She was probably terrified.

"I want Grampa to be okay." She sniffed and wiped away a tear.

"He will be. He just needs to visit the doctor. I promise. Your dad is with him, and now the ambulance is here. They'll take him to the hospital and get him fixed up, right as rain, in no time. What we need to do to help is tidy up a bit. Later, when Grampa feels better, you can finish baking. Okay?"

She nodded solemnly and put the lid on the flour container. Quickly, working together, they put everything away and loaded the used dishes into the dishwasher. They stepped outside just as Riley strode up the steps.

"Time to go little one. Uncle Justice and I have to go to the hospital and check on Grampa. Grandma might need company. We'll drop you with Tricia and we'll call you and tell you how Grampa is doing."

She nodded, somewhat mollified but still obviously worried. She adored her teacher who was Riley's fiancée, Tricia. Engaged, they hadn't yet set a date but the entire family loved Riley's future wife. Riley's life was still in upheaval; he'd only discovered he had a daughter in September. Here it was, early November and they were beginning to settle in nicely. Tricia had been instrumental in helping Daisy and Riley solidify their burgeoning relationship and had become part of the family in the process.

Justice already loved his new niece as much as he did his younger brother Kendrick's brood of three children and he knew when Hannah finally found her way home, she would love Daisy too.

They stopped briefly at Riley's place which was adjacent to the Bar Three. He grabbed a few things for Daisy and they split up. Justice and Riley took separate vehicles to the hospital to avoid leaving anyone stranded.

Justice found Sue pacing the emergency waiting room. She rushed into his arms. "They've taken him for testing. I'm so worried. I can't lose another husband."

"It's okay, Mom. We got him here quickly. If, and I stress if, there's something wrong with his heart, it might explain his health issues. This could, in a weird way, be a good thing." He held her tight and rubbed her back. He hadn't considered how difficult this would be for her. She'd lost her first husband twenty-three years ago. She'd married into the Flint family five years later. She'd been part of the family for eighteen years. Long enough that she'd become their mother, rather than stepmother.

He'd been twenty and still living at home when Sue and Robert married. He married Ellen and started his own family not long after Sue and Robert married.

Living with an enormous family had been claustrophobic on occasion. It seemed like someone was always in a crisis of some sort. As the eldest child, he was the go-to for fixing problems better kept from parents.

"You know it's going to be okay. I called everyone on my way over. I used my Bluetooth," he advised before she could chide him for using the phone while driving. "I told them I'd keep them updated and that they don't need to come right now. And, I brought your phone and charger. I saw them on the counter while Daisy and I tidied up." He passed her the items. "I locked up the house and Houston is watching the dog. "He texted a minute ago, just before I came in, Corn is fine. She's delivered two healthy pups, both of which share her adorable husky looks. She's having an easier time of it now, but he'll stay until she's finished whelping."

He led her over to a bank of molded chairs. Bright orange and dingy blue, they looked supremely uncomfortable but he settled her into one anyway. "Rest, Mom. You'll need energy for keeping Dad in bed once this is over."

She blushed.

"Gross." He laughed. "Not that way." He knew they shared an active sex life but he sure didn't need to hear about it. Talk about TMI. He shuddered. "He'll be a cranky patient. It'll be all boots on the floor to keep him roped down."

"This better not be serious. You know how he is when he gets a man-cold. He doubles down on all the grief you boys ever gave me."

The automatic doors swooshed open. Kendrick, Carl and Riley strode in with Jennifer and Candy hot on their heels. Only two of his siblings were missing.

"Oh my," Sue exclaimed. "They didn't all need to come."

"As if we'd leave you alone in this, Mom," Candy exclaimed. "Jason can't get away until help shows up at the butcher shop. Beth's writing midterms. She'll be out when her tests are done."

"I had to promise to keep her updated," Kendrick added.

"Okay guys, why don't you head to the cafeteria? I'll sit with Mom. Jen, can you go get me a coffee, please? Mom needs tea, something soothing. The rest of you better make yourself scarce. The nurse at the desk is giving us the evil eye." He gave the nurse a nod of acknowledgement.

After a brief chat they scattered, leaving Justice and Sue alone in the corner, impatiently waiting for Robert's return or news of his condition. Jennifer popped back with hot drinks for them. They sipped slowly, passing time, trying for patience. Doctor Brown, the family's physician, finally came out to them, forty-five minutes later. Sue stiffened and gasped at the frown on his face.

"Oh my God, he's dead, isn't he?" Tears rolled down her cheek.

Justice grasped her hand. "Don't jump to conclusions."

"He's fine," the doctor stated. "But it is his heart. I'm airlifting him to the Mazankowski Alberta Heart Institute at the University of Alberta Hospital. The STARS chopper is on its way. A cardiologist will see him immediately. I don't like to scare people, but it looks like he might need surgery. What or how involved, I don't know. He needs more tests than we can provide here. Just be prepared for anything."

"Oh no." Sue wilted in her seat.

"Why airlift?" Justice asked. "Isn't that just for life and death emergencies?"

"It's mostly precautionary. It's all about expediency so we'll airlift. If there's a blockage, the sooner it's cleared the less likely there'll be permanent damage. Unfortunately, your father minimized his symptoms during our office visits. We should have been dealing with this months ago. Water under the bridge now. We'll get this taken care of. Immediately. He'll be back on his feet in no time."

"What do we need to do?" Justice asked.

"They'll need any medications he's on. Bring a list and the meds themselves. Robert might prefer his own pajamas and slippers. He may want a book or two. His phone. Anything he'll need for a short hospital stay. We can't send anyone with him in the chopper. You'll have to follow. I'll tell the cardiac unit to expect you. Sue, you can visit with him until the ambulance comes to take him to the airstrip."

Being small, Coyote Creek's hospital didn't have its own helipad. Instead patients were transported to the airstrip less than two miles away. It was a short run with little traffic and the ambulance often arrived before the chopper.

"Go on in, Mom. I'll find the others and tell them the plan. Once Dad is in the air, I'll take you home to get your things and we'll head to the city." He hugged her tightly. "Dad's going to be fine. The doctors have this in hand."

He had no idea if his words were true. He wasn't much for lying, or even stretching the truth, but in this case, he easily made an exception. His mom was an intelligent woman and knew there were no guaranties; but in times of stress, comforting words meant a heck of a lot more than cold facts or uncertainty.

She nodded, brushed the tears from her eyes, blew her nose and smoothed her hair. "Okay, I'm on." She plastered a cheery, though clearly fake, smile on and followed the doctor into the treatment area.

Justice's siblings stood when he entered the cafeteria. He slid into an empty chair at the large table they occupied. "Dad's stable, but they're airlifting him to Edmonton to see a cardiologist." Everyone started asking questions all at once. He waved a hand and shushed them. "I don't know much. There's the possibility of surgery." He repeated everything the doctor had told them.

They all wanted to be in the city, at the hospital for their father but it wasn't feasible. They'd drive the staff crazy. With nothing to focus on besides their father's illness, they'd overstress. Sometimes, distraction from troubles was a good thing. Besides, somebody had to be home to take care of the ranch. Justice and his siblings organized themselves quickly. Justice would go to the city with Sue, his brothers would shoulder the burden of running the ranch and their own businesses and the girls would help. It wouldn't be an easy transition. Juggling jobs with chores might be difficult, but they'd been raised on the ranch and all of them knew what needed doing without instructions. If their father's stay became extended, they'd take turns driving to the city for a visit.

Justice booked a hotel room a reasonable distance from the hospital and went to gas up his truck and pack while he waited for his father to depart. He bumped into Amy at the service station.

Her golden blonde hair shone in the muted daylight filtering through the clouds. She wore a bright red, thigh length, wool jacket, and knee-high black boots. She looked cozy and warm and entirely too good for his overtired, stressed eyes. Until that moment, he hadn't realized how much toll the events in his life had taken. He was beat down and ready for life to turn around. He needed something positive in his life. He needed...her. She stepped between the pumps so she was close enough to talk to him without anyone else hearing.

"Justice, hi. How's Robert?"

"Coyote Creek's gossip hotline must be working overtime." He tried to laugh. He managed a smile for Casey who sat in Amy's car. "Dad's stable, but they're sending him to the city. Mom and I will follow. Can you keep an eye on my place?"

"You know I will. It's what friends do." She smiled warmly at him. "I know you'll be stressed and busy, but please let me know how he's doing. If you need to talk, call or text. I'm here for you." She placed a hand on his arm. "I mean it. Please call."

Her light touch through his heavy, fleece lined, denim jacket eased the chill in his heart. He nodded, unable to speak through the lump in his throat. Days ago, she barely trusted him, now she was offering her help. Rescuing Casey and searching for Hannah had brought them closer together. Amy Baxter was a very special lady. He swallowed hard.

"I appreciate the offer, thanks. Any word on the notifications you sent out to those ranches?" His focus should be on his father, but the ever-present worry about Hannah intruded.

"Nothing yet. I'll let you know the minute we hear anything, good or bad." She slipped her arms around his waist, hugged him quickly, and stepped back. "Don't worry about her for now, or at least try not to. One worry at a time. If you can. Otherwise, you'll burn yourself out and won't be any good to either of them."

"Good advice," he admitted. "I'll try." They finished pumping their gas in silence, said goodbye and departed.

He only paid partial attention on the short drive back to the hospital. Amy had hugged him. In public. Sure, it was nothing but a display of comfort and friendship. Did she realize that in Coyote Creek her action could be construed as a public display of relationship? People would think they were a thing now. Despite all the stress, a flicker of happiness landed in his heart at the thought. He had way too much on his plate and didn't have time for a relationship, but having Amy in his camp, backing him, felt good. Really good.

·❤·❤·❤·❤·❤·

Chapter Seventeen

There was, Justice decided, nothing worse than waiting for bad news. After two years of waiting for any news of his daughter's whereabouts, he was sick of it. Now, with his father ill, he was just plain angry. It was time for the universe to cut him a break and give him good news for a change.

The drive to Edmonton had been interminable. Delayed by bad weather, snow, and icy roads, it felt like they'd never arrive in the city. But, hours after their departure they entered the city only to land smack dab in the middle of rush hour. The University of Alberta hospital, where Robert was sent, was inconvenient to get to at the best of times. Add in rush hour, and frustration became the word of the day.

"Can't you drive any faster?" Sue nagged. "I need to be there. I need to be with your father. Robert needs me." She twisted a tissue between her hands until it was nothing but fluff and dust.

"Come on, Mom. I'm doing my best. Rush hour sucks. This isn't Coyote Creek. We'll get there. Probably just in time to get Dad's test results. Try and relax." God, if that was even possible. He couldn't relax and traffic had nothing to do with it.

She threw the tissue in the trash and stared at her cell phone. "Why don't they call?"

"They know we're on the way and tests take time to run. Can you pour me some coffee?" The last thing he wanted was more caffeine, but Sue needed to be distracted. As she poured from the thermos, he said, "I hear Daisy is thrilled with her kitten. It was a mean trick, offering to give her one. I don't think Riley really wanted a pet."

"The man is a veterinarian," Sue declared. "He should have a pet. And every child needs someone to love them unconditionally. Someone they can talk to. Daisy has been through entirely too much in her short life. She needed that cat." She thrust the cup into his hand and crossed her arms over her chest. "I think you need a pet too. I don't know why you never let Hannah have one."

Really? She was going to start questioning his parenting? As if he didn't doubt himself enough. "Maybe I should have, but she was at the ranch every day when she was home. She adored the dogs and cats out there. Ellen has barn cats too. One thing Hannah didn't lack was animal companionship. She was surrounded by horses too." He winced at his harsh tone. "But you might be right. I've been debating getting a dog myself."

"Marvelous. Someone to help at the ranch and keep you company."

"I was thinking more about a house dog. A lap dog to come home to." He confessed.

"Oh, Hannah will love that," Sue exclaimed. "She always wanted a pet."

"After Christmas, I think I'll start looking for something. A rescue probably." They delved into a discussion of the merits of different breeds. He was thinking small and one who didn't shed too badly. Housework wasn't his favorite thing, no sense adding dog hair to the problem.

Before he knew it, they'd arrived, found a parking spot and made their way to the Cardiology department where the real waiting began. Robert was undergoing a balloon angioplasty for the blocked veins in his heart. The doctor's insistence on airlifting him to a specialist had been spot on. If the blockage was cleared in under three hours, there was less chance of permanent damage. According to the charge nurse, he'd been in the operating room for close to two hours. The procedure lasted anywhere from thirty minutes to two hours, which didn't include preparation time and recovery. And that was barring any complications.

"How long does this thing take anyway?" Sue asked Justice for the tenth time. "Can't they just fix him and get it over with." Tears rolled down her cheeks. "I love him. I can't live without him. Dammit. He better not die."

Justice winced. His mother never swore. Ever. He could recall maybe half a dozen cuss words leaving her lips in his entire life. The most memorable was when she crashed her car into his father's truck the day Candy got arrested at a protest. Right now, she had to be beyond stressed worrying about her husband. Justice struggled to find comforting words.

"It'll be okay, Mom. Dad'll be fine. We were there, we caught it in time. Medicine has come a long way since you lost your first husband. We'll get through this."

"I'll kill him for not telling me he was having chest pains. I swear that man needs a solid kick in the pants."

"Mrs. Flint?" A woman in scrubs popped her head into their waiting room.

"Yes, that's me." Sue bolted out of her seat and flew to the nurse's side.

Justice followed and grasped her elbow in case it was bad news.

"Your husband is out of surgery and in recovery. His stay there will be relatively short. Only a couple hours. You should take this time to unwind, if you can. Maybe take a walk and get some food." She explained the recovery process and later visitation.

"Thank God," Sue said through tears.

"Thank you," Justice said to the nurse. "I'll make sure she eats while we wait." He handed the nurse his business card. "Please call me if anything changes."

"I'll do that, sir."

· ♥ · ♥ · ♥ · ♥ · ♥ ·

"Robert Adam Flint, if you ever pull a stunt like this again, I'll kill you!" Sue hurried through the doorway into her husband's room and threw her arms around him.

Justice stifled a laugh. You knew you were in big trouble when his mother broke out all of your names. It was the one sure sign you'd done the inexcusable. She wasn't finished her reprimand though.

"You do realize we have eight children dependent on us? And five grandchildren? And how about me? How do you think I felt when I heard you were collapsed on the barn floor? Who's going to feed Kettle Corn's puppies? She had six. Six babies to look after? Dammit, Robert, don't you ever do such a stupid thing again." She flopped into the chair beside the bed, dug a tissue out of her sweater pocket and wiped her eyes before launching into her next tirade.

"I'm not leaving this room until I talk to your doctor, your physiotherapist and whatever or whoever else comes in. You'll abide by every single one of their rules or so help me God, I'll divorce you."

Robert, a kind man at heart, but not one who tolerated criticism well, nodded his head and mumbled, "Yes, dear. As you wish."

"Mom, take it easy on him, he's just had surgery."

"You, mind your own business." She gave Justice the evil eye and poked her finger out at him in what the kids had not-so-affectionately dubbed 'the boney finger'. "He'll do as I say. I didn't marry him just for him to kick off the next week."

"Darling, we've been married almost eighteen years. I'd hardly call that the next week."

She stood up, towering over the bed and glared. "I intend to be married to you until my dying day. I'm only fifty-eight years old and don't plan on dying until I'm a hundred and two. When we go, together, we'll go peacefully, sitting on the porch in the rockers you promised to build me. Don't be screwing up my plans or I will end you."

A bubble of laughter burst out of Justice and he slapped a hand over his mouth. "How's he going to die alongside you if you 'end him'?" He made air quotes around the last words.

Sue blinked at him. Her blue eyes turned from stormy to laughing and she chuckled. "Okay, I may not have thought that one through." She clutched her chest dramatically. "I swear I've never been so worried in my life. I was so frightened I didn't even reprimand Justice for his foolhardy driving. He was doing well over the speed limit until we hit a snow storm."

Accustomed to winter driving conditions, he hadn't bee worried, but he wasn't about to correct her.

Robert grasped her hand and pulled her toward him, urging her to sit on the edge of the bed. "My darling wife, I was petrified. I thought I'd die without saying goodbye. I didn't stop being afraid until you started screeching at me like an old harpy. I knew I was going to be fine then. You wouldn't shout at me if I was at death's door." He winked and leaned up just enough to kiss her.

She giggled like a school girl and drew him into her arms. "I swear...," she whispered and kissed him back.

Justice's recognized the cue to disappear for a while. "I'm out. I'm going to hit the hotel. I'll be back with food later. After you call me and tell me what to bring. I won't mess with the rules they have for Dad, but I'll bring you anything you want. I'll call the family and update them."

Robert was released four days later with instructions on eating, exercise and stress management. With a handful of informative papers in hand and his follow up appointment booked, they climbed into the truck and headed home.

In cahoots with his sisters and brothers, Justice planned a small welcome home party for their father. Family only. Nothing fancy, very low key. A light supper, heavy on the veggies, fresh fruit for dessert. There was no element of surprise. If there had been, the lineup of vehicles in the driveway and lights on in the house would have been a dead giveaway.

"Why is everyone here?" Robert asked gruffly as he entered the living room.

"Because we love you, Dad," Jennifer exclaimed.

Glancing around the room, Justice saw all of his siblings and their children as well as Riley's fiancé, Tricia. Casey sat, over in the corner, seated on the edge of the couch, her foot up on a stool. She looked good. The scratches on her face were healing. Her hair was washed and cut, brushing her shoulders in a mass of blonde waves. She wasn't tall, nor was she short. But she was still a bit on the thin side after her ordeal. Green eyes sparkled at him and she sketched a tiny wave.

Whoa! Wait! This was family only. Someone was playing match-maker. If Casey was here, Amy must be here somewhere too.

The soft clatter of dishes came from the kitchen. He followed the sound and the delicious aroma of roasted chicken to the back of the house. Amy stood, her back to him, stirring something on the stove. He must have made a sound, she turned to look at him.

Glory, he'd missed her. He couldn't decide if seeing her again thrilled him or scared him to death. This was not good.

"Amy."

"Hi, Flint. Er, Justice. Sorry if we're intruding. Riley invited us, although I'm not sure why." She blushed and turned to glance out the window. "I hope it's okay."

"It's fine. I'm glad you're here." He reached out and snagged her sweater, pulling her into his arms. "Do you mind?" He smiled down at her. "I could use a hug. These past few days have been brutal. I haven't slept a wink. Hotel beds are uncomfortable and Mom snores." He closed his eyes, savoring the feel of her in his arms. She fit perfectly. In his arms and in his heart. "I missed you. That chicken smells heavenly."

"I see. I rank right up there with chicken. Nice," she teased. "And it's chickens. I thought with this gaggle of people, three might be better. There'll be leftovers for sandwiches." She leaned into his shoulder, pulling away when something spattered on the stove.

"That'll be my spuds. I'm making them with less butter and low-fat milk to keep them more in line with a heart healthy diet."

"Fabulous. But why are you cooking?" He didn't understand why she was even here, not that he wasn't glad to see her. His confusion doubled when he realized she seemed to be in charge of the meal.

"I offered. Jennifer and Candy were doing their best. Neither one is much in the kitchen, which surprises me. Sue's such a good cook. The guys were doing chores, I just stepped in and helped. Sometime along the way the girls vanished." She waved around the kitchen and gestured at herself. "Here I am, getting it done. I don't mind."

"I do. You are not my sisters' maid."

"I think you mean chef," she teased. "And it's really no bother. I love cooking and if I recall correctly, I am still indebted to you for helping me move in. Consider this your payback meal." She flipped off the burner and lifted the heavy potato pot off the burner.

"Here." He nudged her with his hip. "I'll drain those for you. Squeak over."

She set the pot down and let him drain the potatoes.

"The masher's in the middle drawer beside the fridge. I'll carve the meat while you mash." He shouted for his sisters who scurried in. "Come on brats, set the table so we can eat. I'll bet Dad's starved after eating hospital food."

"Darn right I am," Robert declared entering the kitchen. "That stuff will kill you faster than a heart attack." Everyone fell silent. He looked around the room. "Oh, get over it. I had a heart attack. I'm on the mend. I'll be good. A little joking is good for the soul."

"It's stress relief too," Tricia exclaimed from the doorway. "What can I do to help?"

·♥·♥·♥·♥·♥·

After dinner, Justice watched Casey study the photographs on the living room wall. She pointed at a family picture.

"That's your daughter, with you, and the brown-haired woman. She's the one who disappeared, right?" Casey asked Justice.

The innocent question exploded within him; shards of pain lanced his heart. For a fraction of a second, he wondered if this was how his father felt in the throes of a heart attack. If so, he never wanted to have one. He stared at the picture. It was identical to the one he had at home. Ellen and Hannah stood with him in Disneyland. It was a great shot of them. "Yes, that's Hannah and her mother, my ex-wife, Ellen." He tried to keep his voice neutral but knew his anger, and disappointment showed. Self-loathing and sorrow boiled through him, setting his teeth on edge and his heart pounding in a sad and depressing way.

"Wow, that totally sucks. You must be devastated. You talking about her made me trust you. You know, the other day, in the woods. Being homeless sucked. I never met one homeless kid who didn't hate it and I met a lot of them. In Calgary and in Edmonton. But sometimes, you have no other choice. Running away turned out to be kind of a good thing Except I miss Maryanne. I did find a new foster mom and got away from the abuse. That's a good thing."

"I'm glad for you." He really was. Hopefully somewhere out there, someone would show the same kindness to his daughter.

"Sorry about Hannah, you're a good guy and she's lucky to have you. You'll find her, I know you will."

Her impulsive embrace broke his melancholy. "You're a sweet kid, Casey. I'm glad I know you." He flung his arm around her shoulder. "Come with me, I know where Mom hides the cookies."

Riley, Kendrick and their kids must have had the same thought. They were hiding in the walk-in pantry, scarfing down cookies while the rest of the adults had fresh fruit salad for dessert. They squished inside with the others and grabbed their own cookies. Justice took oatmeal raisin; Casey took a layered chocolate mint one.

"This is kind of like a good deed, right? Casey asked. "You know, eating the cookies before your dad does. Cookies aren't good after a heart attack."

Justice laughed and they bumped their cookies together in a toast.

·♥·♥·♥·♥·♥·

Chapter Eighteen

Justice fell into bed, glad to be home at last but exhausted from the past few days. He rolled onto his side, bunched up his pillow and settled in. A few moments later, he switched sides and tried again. No go. Something was digging at the back of his mind. He couldn't quite put his finger on it. He sat up and leaned back against the headboard. He grabbed the remote control for the bedroom drapes. It was a luxury; a costly one he and Ellen had installed when they first married. It let them stare out the floor to ceiling windows without having to get up and open the drapes. With the house being near the edge of town and on a slight hill, the view was invigorating and relaxing.

The heavy drapes parted and what little there was of the moon shone through, lighting the dark room. Stargazing and moon watching was a favorite camping pastime for him and Hannah. In colder weather, they'd spent more than one night in this bed, leaning against each other, talking and staring at the moon. There was something about the stars and the depths of night which made sharing the details of their lives and small problems easier. Lord, he missed those days. He couldn't wait to do it again. Hope battled despair, making his chest ache. Suddenly, his dinner sat too heavily even though he'd eaten it hours ago.

With every passing day, hope grew dimmer and frustration grew. How would he ever cope if this went on? Even knowing she was dead, God forbid, would be better than endless waiting with barely any hope. Not knowing was pure hell. With every passing week, the walls around his heart grew higher. He found himself fighting the urge to push his family and friends away.

He needed a drink or two. Maybe three or four.

He shoved the thought aside. He rarely drank alone and he certainly wasn't going to let depression and fear for her safety push him over the edge into alcoholism. She'd need a clean and sober father when she returned. He leaned back, closed his eyes and hoped.

The quiet jingle of his cell phone startled him awake. A glance at the bedside clock and the kink in his neck told him he'd slept just over an hour. Who'd be calling him this time of night? He leaned over and glanced at the phone display.

Amy?

He picked it up and accepted the call. "Amy?"

"Justice?" A whisper came over the line.

"Casey?" Why on earth would she be calling in the middle of the night? Why was she whispering? "What's up?"

"I need to talk to you. I was going to wait until morning..."

"Will it wait?" No, she'd called. Best get whatever it was out now. "Never mind, go ahead. Talk to me. I'm listening." In the background he heard Amy talking.

"Shoot. Gotta go." The phone went dead in his ear. He stared at it for a moment. There was no going back to sleep now. He pulled on some sweats and went downstairs to start coffee. Maybe after a cup or two he could create a new jewelry design while he waited for Casey to call him back. Creating something new might help deal with tension. He could design a piece for Hannah.

Someone knocked on his back door. Perhaps he wouldn't have to wait after all. He pulled the T-shirt he'd grabbed over his head and opened the door. Casey and Amy stood on his back porch, shivering in the early morning cold.

"Come in, ladies. To what do I owe the pleasure of your visit? At this ridiculous hour of the morning?"

"You're up anyway." Amy laughed.

"I'm up because someone called me." He looked at Casey and smiled. "What's so important it won't wait until decent people are out of bed?"

She twisted her hands together and stared at the floor. Sure, now she's shy. He banked his impatience. She didn't know him well, yet she was willing to sneak Amy's cell phone and call him when the entire world was asleep. She'd been through a lot and was a serious girl which added strength to the feeling that this was important. At the very least, she felt it warranted a late-night call.

"Hot chocolate?" He asked and plugged in the kettle after she nodded. He poured coffee for himself and Amy, grateful for his fast brew pot, and settled at the table to wait. He was half a cup down and Casey had her drink before she spoke.

"I know this sounds crazy. Really crazy. But after I saw that picture of Hannah. I remembered a girl who looked like her. At least I think I did. It was weeks ago. In Calgary." She gulped some of her drink.

Try as he might, Justice couldn't stop hope from blooming. Logically, it was a long shot. Ridiculously long. The odds were impossible, which didn't mean he'd let it go. He was all over this, like a dog on a pork chop. Amy stared at Casey.

"This could have waited, sweetheart," Amy chided softly.

"No! I lived on the streets. I know what it's like. If this is her, Justice needs to find her. Lots of kids are runaways, but some are just lost. Maybe she's lost. She needs him. Besides, he'd want to know, now." She thumped her mug onto the table for emphasis.

Amy grimaced. Justice suppressed any visible sign of admiration for Casey's spirit.

"Tell me more. Please." Justice sipped his coffee, feigning relaxation but dying to hear what she had to say. *This could be the break he'd been waiting for.*

"We stayed at this one place, for a couple days, before we hitched a ride to Edmonton. It was okay, but crowded. We wanted to get on with the trip and get to Grande Prairie to Maryanne's cousin's place before it got too cold."

Tears filled her eyes and stole Justice's breath. She'd gone through so much and here she sat, trying to help his daughter, a girl she didn't even know. Her compassion was incredible.

He reached out and grasped her left hand in his, Amy grasped her right. They waited until she collected herself. She shook her hands free and dashed tears off her cheeks. After a moment of visibly trying to regain control, she swallowed hard and spoke.

"I didn't see it right away. She looks different now. I remember her hair. It was weird. Long on one side, jaggedy on the other. She said she'd burned it." Casey's shrug indicated she wasn't sure she'd been told the truth. "We didn't talk much, she mostly kept to herself. But I think she said something about her parents being mad about the horses." She shrugged. "I don't know. I just thought it might be important. I probably should have waited until tomorrow."

"No, you did the right thing," Justice reassured her. Amy agreed. "I'm glad you called. Tell me everything you remember."

Mixed emotions battered him. Fear for his daughter, pride in Casey for braving Amy's wrath to call him. Elation that they had a fresh clue. Panic because he might be too late. And guilt. Oh, the guilt. It was massive, a ten-ton weight bearing down on him. He should have pushed for custody and failing that, he should have kept a closer eye on Hannah. He cursed his ex for getting wrapped up in another man and ignoring their daughter. Strong though the emotion was, it had nothing on his own self-recriminations.

Forcing an outward calm, he said, "I guess a road trip is in order."

· ♥ · ♥ · ♥ · ♥ · ♥ ·

Chapter Nineteen

A my called the school and left a message explaining Casey would be away for a few days. She also notified the office she needed some personal time. Fortunately, her boss answered the call and after a brief explanation, immediately granted her request. She sat and waited as Justice called his family and let them know he was taking off for a few days. He asked his mother not to tell everyone, and privately groused to Amy that he knew she'd share. He just prayed they didn't end up disappointing his entire family.

It was a six-hour drive to Calgary. They debated taking Amy's car to save fuel and, in the end, took Justice's truck. A four-wheel drive, it was better on bad roads and had a larger backseat where Casey could sit and put her injured foot up.

"How's it going between you two?" Justice asked once Casey fell asleep.

"Pretty well, I think. She talks to me a lot. She's trying hard at school, though it's only been a few days. I hate taking her out already because she's missed a lot of the year. The guidance counselor felt she should be able to catch up. I hope he's right. She is smart." She paused and whipped her phone out of her purse. "I have to call her case worker and let her know what we're doing. I hope it's okay."

"Good thinking. Although sometimes it's easier to apologize later than to get permission first."

"I'll pretend I didn't hear that." She chuckled and dialed the phone. Well, Justice was right, the case worker wasn't impressed they were taking Casey back to the shelter. She felt it better to cut those ties and move forward. She lightened her stance once she learned they were in search of Justice's daughter.

Justice and Amy chatted amicably until Casey tapped him on the shoulder. "I need to go," she groaned.

"Again?" Justice groaned. "We stopped less than an hour ago. I'd have done this drive in a straight shot if I was alone. I'd only stop for fuel."

"I need to go to the bathroom," Casey insisted. "And I'm hungry."

Amy leaned over and checked the gas gauge. "And a bit of extra gas wouldn't hurt. It's a good plan to keep your tank topped up in the winter, in case something happens."

Justice raised his hands in defeat before placing them back on the wheel. "Fine. You win. But this is the last stop. We need to get there."

Amy glanced at him. His tone was light, but the words were serious. He was doing his best to be accommodating when he wished he was already at their destination. She patted his arm. "Thank you. I know you want to arrive as quickly as we can. We'll grab some take-out and hit the road right away."

"We'll eat in. I don't eat and drive in the winter. Too risky. I prefer my full attention on the wheel."

They stopped at a pizza place, grabbed a fast meal, gassed up and were back on the road in forty-five minutes. "That was great, thanks for the break. Maybe we can make it all the way without another stop," Amy enthused.

"She sleeps so much," Amy whispered a short time later. "I worry about it."

"Perhaps she feels safe. She lived hard and rough for a long time. I've never stayed in a shelter or hostel, but I expect you have to keep one eye open and guard the few possessions you have. She sure didn't hesitate to grab her backpack when I found her. When you have almost nothing, what you do have must be important."

"Still, I worry." Fret, panic, and obsess were more accurate labels for what she did. She kept the thought to herself. She checked on Casey several times every night. Not because she was afraid the girl would leave, more because she wanted to be sure she was comfortable and didn't need anything. Parenting was turning out to be a tough gig. Having a teenager, long-term, was much more difficult than the occasional emergency overnighter with a child waiting to move into a proper foster home.

She'd always wanted a family, after her career settled. That might be part of what drove her into her ex's arms. He represented the future she wanted for herself. Too bad she couldn't see past her rose colored glasses and recognize the signs of his dishonesty. She turned her mind back to the conversation with Justice.

She cleared her throat and spoke. "We're getting along well. I think. She doesn't complain. She's very easy to live with. I hope she knows she can be honest with me and talk about her needs and fears. Why didn't she talk to me instead of sneaking around and stealing my phone?" Casey's lack of trust was a burr under her skin, digging in, nagging and making Amy uncomfortable.

"You're new. She doesn't have a lot of trust for adults. Give it time."

"She trusts you," Amy whined. She was being petulant. She couldn't help herself. She'd offered Casey a home, perhaps a forever home if things worked out, Yet Casey still trusted Justice more than Amy.

"Ah, but I saved her life. That counts for a lot. I also put my heart on the line with her. I bared my soul to her, and half the town through the walkie talkie, I might add. I've given her a piece of myself. That builds trust."

The man had an uncanny knack for getting to the crux of the matter. She needed to find ways to connect with Casey. Their relationship needed a foundation. Something more than just foster parent and child. Casey knew she'd grown up in the system, not how she'd gotten there or how she'd lost two sets of parents to tragic accidents. Sharing her past might be a good place to start building the foundation of their relationship.

It was rather like her and Justice. They knew a little bit about each other's pasts. They grew increasingly close as they spent more time together. He didn't mind Casey being around; which was important if they were to build a relationship.

A relationship?

Where had that idea come from? She wasn't building relationships, except with Casey. She was doing her job, letting her past fade from memory, and moving on. She'd like to be transferred to a major drug crimes unit, or perhaps be involved in combatting internet crime. City work, not small-town beans. She was destined for bigger and better things.

The little voice in the back of her head gave her a poke. Wasn't keeping a small town safe while you raised a family enough? Motherhood was a lofty goal. Good parenting wasn't just something you pulled out of the air, you had to work on it, like you did a relationship. Part of her wondered if, maybe, just maybe, Coyote Creek could provide her with everything she needed.

It didn't matter. With the RCMP, you went where they transferred you. It was rare to spend your entire career in one place. Change kept you alert. If she stayed here and built strong relationships, permanent ones, she'd have to leave them eventually. Or give up police work for something else. Maybe she could take some online university classes. Take whatever she'd need to become a social worker. Coyote Creek needed its own foster care placement worker. She could do that. Helping kids find the right place would be a rewarding career. Maybe it would allow her to have kids of her own. Of course, she could have kids while working with the RCMP.

Justice patted her leg. She turned at looked at him.

"What's going on inside that pretty little head? A million expressions have passed over your face, not all of them good."

"Pretty little head? Seriously? Shouldn't you focus on driving?" she chided, hoping to turn the conversation away from herself. Was that all he thought of her, a pretty face? He better realize she was much more. There was no way she'd share her thoughts. They were too new and she really didn't understand where they originated.

"Well, you are pretty. I'd say beautiful and you haven't said a word for a hundred kilometers. You've grunted and sighed. Frowned and smiled. Once, you chuckled. I'd like to be part of your internal dialogue." He paused. "If you let me. I'd love to talk about whatever plagues you."

"I don't know if it's talk-about-able." She groaned at the made-up word. "See, I can't even not talk about it."

"Kids will do that to you. Steal your words, confuse your mind. Make you rethink your entire life. My world changed when I fell in love with Ellen. Everything went topsy-turvy. After a while we settled into something less turbulently sexual and more comfortable. It turns out she was bored by comfortable, but that's another story altogether. When Hannah came along, I was shell shocked. It's crazy how such a tiny thing can make your heart come alive."

He smiled broadly. Love and parental confusion lit his face. She responded with a grin of her own. Knowing he understood her feelings was comforting.

"Then, as she got bigger, she learned to play with my heart. The right smile. A sappy I love you. Tears, God the tears. She had me wrapped around her finger and she knew it. It's all the usual stuff. Men and their daughters, women and their sons. Or so my friends tell me. Kendrick is a total wimp when it comes to his daughter. Jane's got him under her thumb, and my Dad too. I already see it with Riley and Daisy. It seems—inevitable."

"You know you make a good case against becoming a parent." She shook her head and laughed. "I want to make a difference."

"You do. A police officer has a huge positive impact on the community. Keeping people safe, helping them, battling crime. Inspiring children. And now, a foster parent? I don't know that I could handle looking after other people's kids. Caring for a child who has been beat down by the system; or has emotional problems from losing their family; or is wounded mentally, or physically by abuse."

He paused thoughtfully. "It's a wonder Casey's not a total basket case after all she's been through. It didn't matter to you. She needed help and you stepped in without hesitation. That makes you a hero. It does," he insisted, "even if you did nothing heroic for the rest of your life, and I know that won't be the case. If you did nothing special from here on out, you're already a hero. You've made an enormous difference in one person's life. You've helped save her and given her a safe place to regain her footing. That's amazing."

Casey's hand landed on Amy's shoulder and she let out a gasp.

"He's right you know." She unbuckled her seatbelt and slid forward to embrace Amy. "You're my hero. Both of you. Justice saved me and brought me to you. My life's been shit for a long time. From here on out, it only gets better."

"Don't cuss," Amy ordered in perfect unison with Justice. "And put your seatbelt on." The trio shared a quick laugh, Casey put her belt back on and they fell into a comfortable silence as they rolled down the highway.

· ❤ · ❤ · ❤ · ❤ · ❤ ·

"I'm telling you. This is the best way," Casey declared.

Amy winced but held her tongue.

"I doubt it," Justice disagreed.

"I'm a kid. I stayed here before. Some of the same kids might be here. I can talk to them. I know the lingo." They sat in the truck, half a block away from the shelter Casey remembered seeing Hannah in.

"By that logic," Amy said, "Justice is the logical candidate. He'd know Hannah better than anyone else."

"And, if she's upset at him, she might bolt. Kids do weird things, I know. I've been there." She looked pleadingly from adult to adult, clearly hoping they'd see her side of it.

"We'll go together. Amy and I can talk to the staff while you chat with the girls. Okay?"

Casey agreed to the compromise and they went inside.

Ten minutes later, Justice sat in front of the manager's desk, clutching Amy's hand in a death grip. "What do you mean there's been nobody here by that name?" he demanded.

"I'm sorry," the middle-aged woman said. "We can't make them give their real names. Some have ID, some don't. Many of them have secured fake or stolen IDs. We go with what they give us. If this were an urgent police matter, I could show you footage of the front door. But we only keep two weeks of door footage on the computer. We archive the files every Friday. I'd need a court order to produce it. I'm sure you understand."

Justice growled.

"I'm with the Coyote Creek RCMP," Amy informed her. "I'll be getting you a court order as quickly as I can. Now, I'd like to go talk to the girls."

"Hey guys." Casey stood in the doorway beside a tall, thin girl with dark brown, almost black hair. "This is Potts. I think she knows something about Hannah."

"I don't know no Hannah. But the girl in the picture. Yeah, I saw her." She folded her arms over her chest belligerently. "But I'm not talking."

"Come on," Casey urged. "I told you. These are the good guys. This dude saved my life. Rescued me and my broken leg from freezing to death in the forest. She's my foster mom. You can trust them. I swear on my life. I wouldn't be here if I didn't know they were on the level."

"Not talking."

"Girl, you promised." Casey looked at the manager. "Can we have two minutes alone?"

She looked puzzled, but rose from her desk. "I'll be right outside the door." She walked out and eased the door shut behind her.

"You know she's got her big fat ear pressed against the door listening," Potts said in a raised voice. "She's probably got a camera recording this room."

"Hey, respect her. She gave you a place to sleep." Casey turned to Justice. "I need money."

To his credit, and Amy's surprise, he didn't bat an eye, just handed over his wallet. Casey extracted forty dollars, handed back the wallet and gave the money to Potts.

As a cop, Amy knew sometimes giving a homeless person large sums of money could be a mistake as it often went to drugs or booze. She studied Potts, the girl was clean and neat. Her eyes shone with a healthy glow. She had a few bruises on her face and arms, she wore them like badges of honor. Okay, maybe Casey was right to think this girl wasn't a risk. Either way, it was too late to take the money back.

"Look, she didn't go by Hannah," Potts blurted. "She used something generic. Like Rose or Lily. Something flowery. Her hair ain't like the picture but it never is. Hack it off with scissors, some cheap dye and wham! A new look. Nobody'd even see you."

"And," Justice urged.

"She was here a few nights. Lit out of here one day. Like last week. Said she was going home. I never believed her. People say crap they don't mean. Throws the keepers off your trail in case the cops are looking for you." She pinned Amy with a stare. "Ya. Cops like you."

"Going home? When was this?" Amy asked, trying not to take offense at being labelled a bad guy. She'd been in the system. She knew how it worked and where it failed.

"Not long. Maybe a couple days? I mean she was here a while. Then she left and came back. It happens. I only noticed because she wouldn't shut up about horses. Like street kids can afford horses." She snorted in derision.

Justice stood and shook her hand. "Thank you, Potts." He handed her a business card. "My name is Justice. If you hear anything else, please call me. I won't make her come home if she doesn't want to.

I just need to know she's okay. If you ever need anything, maybe a helping hand, call me. Collect."

She stared at the card in her hand and nodded. The card disappeared into the pocket of her oversized jeans.

Casey gave the girl a quick hug. "See, told you they didn't suck."

Amy hid her smile. She didn't suck. High praise from a teenager. She'd take it and by the look on Justice's face, he'd take it too. "Thank you, Potts. We appreciate your candor," Amy said.

A brisk nod and Potts disappeared out the door.

"So, Edmonton?" Casey suggested. "It is on the way home."

Home. The word sounded amazing, like it had new meaning, coming from Casey's mouth.

"Come on girl," Amy urged Casey forward. "We've got an obstinent teenager to catch."

"Takes one to catch one," Casey laughed.

Amy and Justice groaned.

·❤·❤·❤·❤·❤·

Chapter Twenty

The first thing they did in Edmonton was check Ellen's house for signs of occupation. Nothing looked disturbed and the ranch hands hadn't seen anyone. It was too late to hit the shelters to talk to people so they had a late dinner and found a hotel.

Morning couldn't come soon enough for Justice, even though it fell hot on the heels of a completely sleepless night. He'd spent the night on the fold out sofa in the two-bedroom suite they'd rented. Casey had one room; Amy had the other. He barely slept. He should be tired, make that exhausted. He wasn't. However, he was terrified. Enthusiastic. Hopeful. He'd waited and searched so long; it was frightening to be this close. He didn't know if he was afraid he'd find her; or afraid he'd fail. Finding a daughter who didn't want him would kill him, but it would be less painful than agonizing over her unknown fate.

While he waited in the sitting area, he texted his family the day's plan. The beauty of texting was he could do a group text and inform everyone all at once. It also allowed him the luxury of not responding if he was busy or inclined to avoid them.

Casey had only spent a couple nights in the Edmonton shelter but they had generated a list of places to check. With her along, perhaps some of the teens would open up to them. He was cautiously optimistic. It was exhilarating to know they were only days behind Hannah, if indeed the girl they followed was his daughter. He buried the doubts plaguing him and focused on the positive. It might not be her at all. Why wouldn't she be at the house if she was on her way home. Spending the night in a shelter didn't make sense.

Impatience pulled on his nerves as he waited for his cohorts to get out of bed. Then they could hit the first shelter before the residents and guests departed for the day.

The day's weather was slated for minus forty. Life on the streets would be brutal at those temperatures. On the plus side, the girls might hang around the shelter longer, giving him more time to talk to them. Great. Now he felt guilty. This emotional rollercoaster was wearing him down. How long could a body survive this crap without falling apart or going insane? Some days he was fine, today he was stretched to the point of breaking. Tension coiled in his guts, threatening to explode and destroy his sanity.

A slight tick sound alerted him to Amy's arrival from her room. "Good morning," she greeted him with a smile. "I didn't expect to see you up already."

"Ha. I slept maybe half an hour. I'm too nervous to sleep. How about you?"

"I tossed and turned a lot. I'm nervous about today, but my cop-gut tells me we're on to something. I had an idea during the night. I know a few guys in the city police department. Former RCMP. I could call on one of them, see if he'd accompany us. Make it more official." She scratched below her neck nervously.

"It's a thought. Would they do that? Won't it scare away the girls?"

"The guy I have in mind, Perry Moorey, he works with street people. His beat is downtown. He's got something about him which opens people up. They talk to him. I can call him." Her voice put a positive spin on her words, but they left him wondering if she was hiding something.

An hour later, he had his answer. Holy hound dog. Perry Moorey was something else. Six foot three, brown hair, brown eyes, broad shoulders, he was the most attractive man Justice had ever seen.

"Sweet!" Casey whispered when the cop climbed out of his cruiser. "He's delicious."

Amy leaped out of the truck and hurried to meet Perry. He yanked her into a tight embrace, swung her in a circle and planted a huge kiss on her mouth.

Justice saw red. He was out of the truck and beside them before he knew he'd moved. Crap on a biscuit. "Hi," he blurted and thrust out his hand. "Justice Flint. Nice to meet you."

Perry shook his hand, gripping it a little too tight for comfort. Justice squeezed back. Their eyes met in a battle as old as time. Male dominance for the right of the female. They stared into each others eyes, daring their opponent to admit defeat and loosen the grip.

"Give it a rest guys," Amy demanded. "Get real. We're here on business. Put the testosterone away. You can punch it out another day. Men!"

"Yeah, dudes. You're, like, redonkulous." Casey hobbled up on her cast, frowned at Justice, and smiled at Perry. "Hi, I'm Casey."

"Nice to meet you Casey," Perry smiled at her. "I was thrilled when notification came through that you'd been found. Sorry I never had the chance to meet you while you were here."

"You know about me?" Her eyelashes fluttered.

Great. Did all women fawn over this guy? Yesterday, Justice had been Casey's hero. Now he rated as low as chopped liver. How fickle a woman's heart? He almost laughed at his own jealousy.

"It's my job to know about you. I watch all the lost and missing people notifications. Helps me do my job, keeping people safe." He smiling winningly.

Justice's fists clenched. Gag. How was he going to keep a straight face all day with this guy oozing bull crap? They walked toward the shelter. Perry ambled ahead with Amy, his arm companionably around her shoulder. Casey tottered eagerly behind them. Justice paused to take stock of what he was feeling.

Lord love a duck. He was jealous. This ridiculously good-looking cop was honing in on Justice's girls. Ha. His girls. Right. Amy was his neighbor and Casey was her charge. They weren't his, not even close. But they could be. They should be.

He stumbled over a tiny lip in the sidewalk.

Holy hell! He was in love with Amy. When had that happened?

"Dude, you coming?" Amy called to him.

He scrambled to catch up. "Just bracing myself. This isn't easy for me you know."

"I can't imagine the pain and anguish you're going through," Perry said, clapping him on the back. "I deal with family and runaways every day and it still baffles and pains me. The hurt, the agony, the love and regret. Kudos to you, man. You've got balls to stick with this and not leave it in the hands of overworked officials."

"Thanks, man. It's been a rough ride for me. I shudder to think how it's been for my daughter." He handed over the picture they'd brought and let Perry take the lead. He knew many of these kids and he certainly had a way with women.

The night staff was gone, and the day shift didn't recognize Hannah's picture but agreed to let them question the girls left in the shelter. They talked and questioned until they'd spent a few minutes with everyone. If anyone had seen her, they weren't about to confess. Admitting defeat at this shelter, they were about to leave when a new face walked in.

"Pst," Casey hissed. "I recognize that one. I'm going to talk to her." She eased away from the table they were sitting at and hobbled toward the coffee pot, without her crutches, her cast thumping with every step. She joined the girl at the drink table.

"Hey, you look frozen. It's colder than hell out there," Casey poured two cups and passed one over. "You've gotta try one of these little pastry things. I ate three before they cut me off. The sugar'll give you a boost and warm you up." She loaded half a dozen pastries on a plate and held them out. "Come on, let's sit over here, away from those guys," she semi-sneered.

The girl didn't speak, she just grabbed the pastries and followed Casey to a table within earshot where they quickly fell into trivial small talk. After what felt like an eternity to Justice, Casey started in on the real questions, her voice just loud enough to hear.

"She's good," Perry whispered. "The girl has no idea she's being interrogated. Casey'll rock a career in law enforcement if she follows your lead." He winked at Amy across the table.

Amy leaned subtly closer to Justice. "She's in my care temporarily, for now. But if she wants to be a cop, I'm good with that. Mostly, I want her to find her passion and run with it."

Perry looked back and forth between Amy and Justice. "So, it's like that is it?"

"Yes," Justice declared just as Amy denied it.

"Whoa boy." He nodded to Justice. "I'll just back away now. I don't fish in another man's pond."

"You what the what now?" Amy sputtered. "I'm no man's anything, let alone his pond."

"You've got that right," Justice laughed. "You're your own woman. All the way. And I like you just fine." He gave her his best 'you've got this' grin. It blossomed to cover his entire face when she smiled back.

"If you guys are all done being kissy face, this is Tweet." She gestured with an elbow toward the slight, timid girl she'd been talking to. "She might have seen Hannah. Tweet, this is Justice, he's Hannah's dad. He's a good guy. I told you, he saved my life. He's my hero."

"Please, join us." He nudged toward Amy who scooted over to make room at the table. Tweet hovered for a moment, sitting only when Casey sat beside Perry.

"She looks familiar. She was here for a couple nights. Her hair's different. She was filthy and spent like an hour in the shower until they booted her out. Late last night, she sneaked away after lights out. Said something about her mom's place. She's going there, even though her mom don't give a rat's ass about her. Too busy with her new boy toy. Don't know why she didn't just go there instead of hanging at this dump."

Her idle thought matched Justice's.

Tweet stared hard at Casey. "Pay up."

"Justice?" Casey said, half question, half demand.

He pulled out his wallet and handed over another forty bucks and his business card without blinking. No price was too high to get his daughter back. "Thank you, Tweet. If you ever need anything, call me. Anytime. Collect." At this rate, he'd have to open a shelter if these girls started showing up at the ranch. He paused in the middle of putting his wallet back. The idea actually had merit. When he got his daughter back, he'd find a way to help teens in need.

The money disappeared in a flash and Tweet scurried away. They watched her go.

"Do you think she's telling the truth or was she just after the money?" Perry asked.

"Does it matter now?" Amy replied and stood. "I say let's go back to Ellen's place and see what we find."

Perry froze in the middle of rising. "Back to Ellen's?"

"Yeah." Casey slung her arm around his waist and pulled him up. "We might have checked it out when we got to town. No biggie. Justice was married to her. They're, like, one big happy family. More or less." She winked at Justice.

"Baxter, you owe me a big one for this." He sighed. "Let's go."

· ❤ · ❤ · ❤ · ❤ · ❤ ·

Chapter Twenty-One

They waited impatiently at the end of Ellen's lengthy driveway. Forty-five minutes after they arrived, one of Perry's coworkers finally showed up with a warrant to search the house for signs of Hannah. They were lucky, Ellen's ranch fell just inside city limits. Before long, it would be surrounded by subdivisions.

"Not one word about being here before," Perry warned them.

At the door, the other officer turned to them. "This place has an alarm. It's going to get loud."

"I know the code. My daughter does, did, live here."

Amy didn't know how Justice had convinced Perry to let them come into the house during the search, but he had. It would have killed her to wait in the car. Justice never would have survived it.

Perry knocked and announced their presence. He tried the door. it opened easily. "Unlocked." He gave Amy a questioning look.

She shook her head. They'd locked the handle when they left.

Perry stepped inside. "The alarm is off. Someone's here, or has been here. I'll take this floor; you guys are with me." Then he gestured to the other officer and his partner. "You've got upstairs."

A cursory search revealed nothing until they hit the kitchen. Dirty dishes were on the counter. Amy popped open the fridge, there were fresh groceries inside. "Someone has definitely been here," she declared.

A door thumped softly down the hall. "The garage," Justice cried and bolted toward the sound, Perry hot on his heels. Amy chased after them and Casey scrambled to keep up, hobbling as fast as her broken ankle allowed.

Perry elbowed Justice aside and drew his firearm as he went into the garage. "Stay back," he warned.

Justice plowed in right behind him. Amy crowded against Justice to see.

Perry stood on the step; his gun pointed at a terrified girl standing in the open door to an old muscle car.

"Don't shoot," she cried, her voice trembling. "This is my house. I l-l-live here."

"Hannah, baby?" Justice reached around Perry and pushed gently down on his hands, forcing the man to lower his gun.

"Daddy?" The quiver in her voice broke Amy's heart. Behind her, Casey gasped and clutched Amy's hand.

"Baby girl? Get over here? Where have you been? I've been so damned worried about you? What were you thinking?" He advanced slowly toward her; his hands outstretched. "Are you okay? Are you hurt?"

"Daddy!" she exclaimed and slammed the car door shut to bolt toward him. She threw herself, sobbing, into his arms. With a little leap, she had her legs wrapped around his waist like a toddler. She wept openly; her sobs clearly audible despite her face being buried in his shoulder.

He pivoted half a step and rested against a car, slowly rocking back and forth, comforting his daughter.

Amy covered her mouth to hide her own emotions. Tears of joy and relief washed down her face, matching those on Justice's. Her heart hurt with the beauty of their reunion. There'd be hell to pay once Justice got over his joy, but for now, this moment was the most perfect thing Amy had ever seen. This man knew how to love.

Pushing the last thought away, she turned to hug Casey. The teen smiled through her tears. How bittersweet to see such a joyful reunion when your own reunion was impossible.

"You've got me now," Amy whispered, hugging Casey tight.

"Okay everyone," Perry spoke, drawing their attention to him. "Let's take this inside where it's comfortable. We've got a lot to discuss." He holstered his weapon and radioed an update to the other officers.

·♥·♥·♥·♥·♥·

Chapter Twenty-Two

"We're going to talk about this," Justice warned Hannah.

"Do we have to?" She groaned. "I'm not a kid anymore." Her frown was nearly his undoing. He was so relieved to see her; he'd have given her anything she wanted. Luckily, he knew better. Now was the time to be kind and strong. He'd have to channel his inner Sue and act like his mother.

He was tempted, damned tempted, to let the whole thing slide, just to keep her from running again. One thing his parents had taught him was the easy way wasn't always the easiest in the end. Sometimes, taking the hard road was simpler and less problematic.

"I can see that. You've grown into a beautiful woman. I can't even begin to understand what you went through during the last two years. But I'd like to." He paused. "Besides, these officers," he nodded toward the police who had accompanied them into the living room, "need to know what happened. At least enough to wrap up your file. And more if someone has done something wrong to you." He let the statement hang, giving it the feel of a question.

"Crap." Hannah groaned and flopped onto her mother's expensive leather sofa. "Can't we just go home to the ranch? Or our house in town. Don't Grandma and Grampa want to see me?"

"They do. I've texted that we found you. They're crazy excited to see you. But it's irrelevant at this moment." It was ridiculously difficult to walk the line between parent and friend at this moment. He'd blown it once; he didn't want to screw this up again. His phone vibrated in his back pocket. He ignored the summons. It was probably just another family member with questions.

"I can't wait to hug Grandma. And race Grampa on the horses," she enthused.

"There won't be any racing anytime soon. At least not against your grandfather. He had a heart attack. He's fine, but he has to take it easy for a while."

"Jesus, Dad. Couldn't you have kept him safe?" Hannah glared at him.

Her rude, concerned response should have annoyed him. Instead, it tickled him. Her apparent comfort was a good sign. Wasn't it? "He's been ill. Hiding it from everyone. But, he's on the mend now. He'll be thrilled to see you. And, stop avoiding the issue."

"Fine," her response was full-on five-year-old petulance.

"I'm going to make notes while we talk," Perry said, flipping open a small notebook. One of the other officers opened a tablet and sat poised to type. "I'll have questions later," Perry added. "For now, just tell your story."

"Whatevs."

"Hannah, mind your manners," Justice chided.

"Oh, for shit's sake, Dad," Hannah cussed.

"Watch your mouth," Casey warned. "Your dad is a hero. He saved my life. Show the dude some respect."

Tears filled Hannah's eyes. Justice's heart crumpled like a dry leaf in a fist.

"I leave for a while and you get a new kid? For the love of f...fudge." She burst into sobs.

God, save him from bawling women. Tears had always been his undoing. Justice moved to sit beside his daughter. She'd changed so much. She was a good two inches taller and so much thinner. She'd matured but still held a child's fragile vulnerability. "Honey, I could never replace you. I searched for you every single day. I was looking for you when I found Casey. That's another story. One for later. Right now, I really need to hear your story. Please."

She sniffed and wiped her nose on her sleeve. Unless he missed his guess, she was wearing her mother's clothing. She was taller now. She'd probably outgrown her own.

"Fine," she snapped. "But I want details later." After a few deep breaths, she started talking.

"I wanted to be a jockey. I really did. I still do. Nothing is as important as horses."

Justice refrained from mentioning they'd had that particular argument dozens of times. "I realize that," he pushed understanding into his voice.

"You said no. Mom said no. She said she was selling all the horses. She fricken lied too. I went to the stables, they're all still there and more. God, she's such a b-witch."

"Your mom always did like to ride. It's how we met. So, she was going to sell the horses..."

"Yeah, to keep me from riding. So, when a guy came to visit and I heard he needed a jockey, I volunteered."

"What guy?" Justice asked.

"Keller Knight of Knight Stables in California. Anyway, he said I was perfect. Mom said no." Her anger at parental refusal rang in Hannah's voice. "Knight gave me money. Said to catch a ride to his place. I waited a couple weeks and headed out. I told her I was staying at my friend's and took the bus to his place."

"Hannah," Justice chided. "You know better."

"Yeah. Yeah. You were right. You're always right."

He suppressed a chuckle at her pique. "And?"

"And it was good at first. Then, it turned to shit. Knight Stables my ass. More like Nightmare stables. He didn't let me ride. Nothing.

Not a single horse. I spent all my time mucking out stalls like a slave. At least with you, if I did my work, I got to ride, even if it wasn't jockeying. He lied. Why do adults all lie? When I said I wanted to go home, he said I owed him room and board and had to work it off. I was working eighteen hours a fricken day, without pay, and I owed him?" Her voice rose in indignation.

Lost for words and battling the urge to find Knight and beat him senseless, Justice said nothing. He massaged Hannah's shoulders encouragingly. He was going to need a therapist after all this. No doubt family counseling was in order. He'd be having words with Ellen as well. Why the hell hadn't she realized her own daughter was missing?

"I got sick of it. Shoveling shit all day, sleeping in a teeny, tiny box of a room. Sharing a bathroom with twelve people. It sucked. I decided to hitch my way home."

"Oh, honey." He embraced her. His heart wrenched. She'd been through so much. "Why didn't you call me?"

"I was afraid, Daddy. You didn't want me to jockey. I needed it so bad. I wanted it with everything I had. If I called you, you'd know what I did."

"I was worried sick, Pumpkin. I needed to know where you were, if you were safe. I would have come to get you in a heartbeat." He suspected there was more to her story than she let on. Secrets she was keeping. He hoped they'd come out in time. He swallowed his anger and misgivings over all she'd done and been through and asked the question most preying on his mind. "Did Knight, or anyone else touch you?"

She jerked back out of his arms. "Gross, Dad." She winced. "No. I'd have cut his balls off." She reached into the back pocket of her jeans and extracted the jackknife he'd given her for her thirteenth birthday.

He couldn't help but chuckle. "That's my girl."

"Uncle Jason taught me some fight moves when I worked at the butcher shop when he was babysitting me. I'm going to get him to teach me more."

Her vehemence startled him. "Are you sure nobody hurt you?" he asked softly.

"I'm sure. But Knight lied. He said I could jockey. I'm so mad I just want to punch him."

"Oh, baby, why didn't you call me? Send a message? Call one of your uncles? Your grandparents? Anyone?"

"'Cause you'd be mad. You'd ground me. I'd never ride a horse again. I had to do the mature thing. Find my own way home. I'm not a kid anymore. I'm an adult. I needed to do it my way."

Half of him understood the emotion behind her statements. Half of him wanted to shake her until she realized how foolish and unsafe her choice had been. Rather than act on either sentiment, he hugged her. His heart rejoiced at the pleasure of being able to embrace her again. Motion on the other side of Hannah caught his eye. Casey squeezed into the small space between Hannah and the end of the couch.

"You did good. It's tough on the streets. I lived there. I was in some tight spots. Not tough like you, at least I wasn't in a foreign country alone. But you should have called. You've got family. A ginormous family. They'd do anything for you. I know. They helped me. Especially your dad and Amy. They rescued me when I thought I'd die in the woods." She slid her arm around Hannah, dislodging Justice's embrace.

"Really? He saved you?"

"Damn rights." She grinned at Amy in obvious apology for cussing. "I was lost, my leg was broken. I had to beat off a coyote with stick."

Whoa. That was the first Justice had heard of that event. He glanced at Amy; she looked as shocked as he felt.

"I hit him and threw pine cones at him until he went away. I was stuck. When I moved too much, I passed out. I ran out of food. I was starving. Nothing but snow, grass and maybe a berry the birds missed. But then this goofy guy crawls through the bush and finds me. I would have died before I went with another man who might abuse me. I swear on my life. But he talked about you, and how you were missing and how he'd find you if it killed him. That's when I knew he was one of the good ones. He even shared his Mars bar with me."

"Seriously? He won't let me eat them. Dad? What's up with that?"

"Desperate times call for desperate measures. How could I not give up my favorite food to save a girl's life?"

"From now on, you're gonna share your Mars bars with me," Hannah demanded.

"If you promise to stay home and talk about what's bugging you, you can eat all of my Mars bars," he agreed readily. "I'll buy you a case of the damned things. But now, we need details of your trip. We know about your stop at the library in Shelby, Montana. Amy and I went there looking for you when we found your email but we missed you."

"Yeah, they were cool. They let me stay all day. But Mom never answered. She never checks her email." Justice could almost hear her eye roll.

"True."

"I should have emailed you, I guess." Her voice was small and uncertain. "I didn't want you to be mad."

In that moment, she reminded him so much of the little girl she'd once been, his heart ached. Now, she sat beside him, a fully grown woman. Mature in ways he'd never understand and having lived nearly two years of unthinkable difficulties. Reforming their once close bond wasn't going to be easy.

"Honestly, Hannah. I am mad. Mad and disappointed you didn't think you could trust me. But above all else, I love you and I'm glad you're safe. Let's get these police reports done and go home."

Chapter Twenty-Three

Justice drove into the deepening evening. Night came early in winter. Hannah sat quietly in the passenger seat; Amy had nodded off in the backseat. Initially, he suspected she'd feigned sleep to allow him time alone with his daughter. Casey sat quietly in the back; her foot propped up on Amy's lap. She'd drifted into sleep a few minutes ago. For the first fifty or sixty miles, nearly half the trip, he had no clue how to talk to his daughter. Some of the tension between them had eased while discussing her trip with the police, but it still felt like a huge wall between them.

Finally, he gathered his courage and spoke. "I'm glad you're back. Your grandparents are ecstatic. It'll be well past supper when we get home, but we're going to the ranch for a late meal. Everyone wants, needs, to see for themselves you're okay. I know you're tired and have been through a lot. We'll need to talk more about it. Eventually. Tonight, we party with the family. Is that okay with you?"

To his surprise and mortification, she burst into sobs. Her entire body shook with emotion. He pulled into a roadside turnout and parked the truck out of harm's way. "Take a minute to calm down, then we'll talk." He dug into the center console and handed her a box of tissue.

At length, the shaking and silent tears ebbed and she looked up at him, blinking solemnly.

"Want to talk about it?"

"No," she sniffed.

She'd never been one to share her feelings on impulse. When his marriage was imploding, he'd learned to wait Hannah out. Eventually, she almost always found a way to articulate her feelings and come to him to talk. Falling back into old habits, he sat and waited. He looked up, Amy caught his glance in the rear-view mirror, smiled and closed her eyes.

Thank heaven she seemed to understand. He leaned toward his daughter. Draping a hand casually over her shoulder, he tugged her close. "Love you, Hannah Bear," he dropped her old nickname, one he hadn't used since she was six and told him she was too old for it.

"Do they hate me?" She mumbled.

"Hate you? Sweetie, no! Never! They love you. Everyone spent their spare time searching the internet for clues to where you were. They love you, just as much as I do." He took a deep breath and broached what he knew was going to be a touchy subject. "I'm not saying they aren't upset. They might even be angry. I was mad, and scared, and disappointed. But more than that, I'm glad you're back safely. My heart, my world, was broken without you. No matter what happens in the future, we need to find a way to talk about what's going on in your head. I'd rather we fight than keep silent and be upset. Maybe if we'd found a way to talk, we wouldn't have lost two years with each other. Okay?"

His breath stalled in his chest. He hadn't meant to start this discussion, at least not yet. He'd planned to give her a day or two to adjust. But she was right to worry about how their family would react. Even after a long vacation, the Flint family swarmed you when you got home. Births and birthdays as well as anniversaries were family events. He couldn't even imagine how they'd react today.

"You'll be mobbed," he warned. "Everyone will want to hug you and talk to you. There'll be tears and maybe some scolding. Just be prepared."

"What if they ask things I can't, or don't want to answer," she said with a blubber of tears. She sniffed inelegantly and blew her nose.

He nudged the tissue box on her lap and she grabbed a clean one.

"You'll eventually have to answer most of their questions. For today, answer what you can. I'm sure, if you ask for time to adjust, they'll back away. But, please, don't push them away unless you can't stand their closeness anymore. You had it rough while you were gone. I can't even imagine what you went through, neither can they. But it was no picnic being here without you. Worrying."

"Daddy, I'm so sorry."

He heard the aching truth in her words and it eased the pressure in his chest. She was still in trouble; he'd probably ground her or find some other way to show her she was still under his authority. Two years she'd been gone, a lot of time to make up. She'd run her own life while she was away. She would have to re-adapt to having rules. Return to being a child, at least for a while.

"It's okay. We'll get through this. Together. We just have to be honest. And patient with the family when we get there. Okay?"

"'kay," she whispered, sounding more like a three-year-old than a teen rapidly approaching adulthood. His breath shuddered out. God, he'd missed her so much. All because he couldn't compromise on her dream to be a jockey. He'd have to learn some flexibility to keep from making the same mistake.

It was high school all over again. When he'd caught Riley sneaking out to go to a party. His intervention had turned into a brawl in the front yard ending only when their ruckus roused their parents. There'd been hell to pay that night. Riley caught hell for sneaking out. Justice caught hell for not minding his own business. Even after the mild punishment was meted out, he didn't regret his actions. He'd do it all over again. That hadn't been the first, or the last time he'd played substitute parent to one of his siblings. It was a role he fell into and couldn't seem to step out of. Now, with his own child, his success ratio wasn't all it might have been.

"We'll get through this," he declared, kissing her on the top of the head. "You and I, we can handle it. I've got your back."

"Thanks, Daddy. Just don't hate me. Please."

The entreaty in her voice, her desperation for approval, wrenched at his heart. She must have some awful stories to tell. He hoped one day she'd trust him enough to come clean.

"Hannah, look at me."

She hesitated a moment but turned toward him. He looked her right in the eye. "Remember this Hannah Ellen Flint; no matter what you do, no matter what you've done or had done to you, I could never hate you. Not now. Not ever. I love you. I've adored you since I first heard you were growing inside your mother. Nothing in my life, in this world, has ever meant as much to me as you. I might get mad; I might scream and shout. Hell, I might want to paddle your backside. None of that matters. The love I feel for you is stronger than any force on earth. Nothing in this universe can stop my love. Nothing."

Tears cascaded down her cheeks and she gave him a weak, watery smile. "I love you, Daddy. So much." She unhooked her seatbelt and leaned awkwardly across the console to embrace him.

It was the most painfully heart-wrenching moment of his life. So much sorrow and pain. Love and joy. The tangle of emotions was like a steel band around his chest pulling tighter with each moment she was in his arms. He could barely breathe.

"Daddy?" She paused. "You're squishing me."

He released his tight hold.

"You're crying!" She wiped his eyes with a tissue. "I promise never to make you cry again."

He chuckled painfully. "Baby girl. You will make me cry again. It's part of parenthood. Kids make you cry, good tears and bad. Happy and sad. It's part of life. I can't even begin to guess at how many times I made your grandparents cry. You don't talk about it; you just know it happens and let it lie."

"I'll try not to make you cry," she vowed.

"That's all I can ask." Another quick kiss and hug and they buckled back up and hit the road. They were an hour and a half from the ranch and night and full dark was almost upon them. He'd have to focus on the road and watch for stray deer and moose. They were travelling up Highway 43 on a section of road dubbed Moose Row in recognition of all the moose and deer lives lost to collisions with vehicles. Fortunately, although he saw a few animals on the edge of the trees, none approached the road.

Predictably, the ranch yard was overflowing with vehicles. The curtains were wide open, light spilling out onto the snow-covered yard, welcoming them home.

"You could have dropped us at home on your way past town," Amy said from the back seat.

"Not a chance." Justice turned to smile at her. "You guys are heroes. Without your friend Perry, and Casey's contacts and people skills, it might have been months until we found Hannah. And I probably would have had to break into Ellen's house again." He chuckled. "Come inside. Accept the kudos and gratitude you've earned."

"I can't believe you broke into Mom's house," Hannah exclaimed for at least the third time since she'd found out. "Grandma is going to kick your butt."

"I'd rather she didn't hear about it, to be honest."

"Yeah, right. Like I'm going to take all the attention. When things get tough, I'm totally gonna squeal on you. Just to shift their focus for a few minutes."

"You go," Casey encouraged and the girls high fived over the seat before climbing out.

"Get in here already," Beth yelled from the front porch. "We're dying to hear all about your adventure." She hurried down the steps, coatless, in her snow boots, to embrace Hannah. "Thank heaven you're safe. I'm so glad you made your way back to us." She stepped back and shook her finger. "Don't ever do that to me again. If your dad is being a jerk, call me and I'll set him straight. Okay?"

Hannah's smile wobbled but she agreed to her aunt's dictates. "Thanks, Auntie Beth."

"You betcha, kiddo. Get inside before your grandfather has another heart attack or your grandmother wears a hole in the floor pacing back and forth." She gave Hannah a small shove forward and stuck her hand out toward Casey. "Hi. You must be Casey. I've heard a lot about you. Thanks for helping find my niece. I'm Beth, the sister who was away at university. Justice's favorite sister. He loves me best."

"Hi." Casey looked back and forth between Beth and Justice.

"Get over yourself." Justice laughed. "You're my brattiest sister and a big pain in the backside to boot." They stuck their tongues out at each other.

"Wow." Casey grinned. "I thought you guys were adults."

"I am, he's not," Beth shot out before Justice could respond. With a laugh, she bolted after Hannah, catching up with her on the porch.

Hannah paused with her hand on the door handle, reminding Justice of all the times as a child, and as an adult, when he'd been in the same spot. Knowing he should be inside, but needing just a bit more time alone to gather his thoughts. Sometimes the pause was to savor being alone before entering the chaos of family. Others it was to brace himself for the inevitable lecture over the most recent stupid or careless thing he'd done. He understood her turbulent emotions all too well. A lot of life's reflection happened on this porch.

After Beth, Casey and Amy went inside, he drew Hannah back into his arms. "Come on, kiddo. We've got this. Nobody can defeat us when we stick together. This place is always chaos, and I'll bet part of you missed the bedlam."

"Actually, I did. I just don't want to be the center of attention."

"Hannah, you've been the center of this family's attention since you left. Too late to change that now. The only time you weren't was when your Uncle Riley found out he had a five-year-old daughter. The spotlight was all on him then." He opened the door and pulled her inside.

"I can't wait to hear about that!"

"Ask him about it, you might be able to turn everyone's attention away from you. Maybe." He chuckled. "Or, maybe not." Somehow, he doubted they'd be assuaged or diverted by a rehashing of his brother's mistakes. Hannah was in the hot seat tonight and she'd probably be there until someone else screwed up.

The house was uncharacteristically quiet. Justice did a double-take and checked to see if everyone was actually there. They were, they stood or sat quietly, waiting for Hannah to enter the living room.

"Come in, darling," Sue urged. "We've missed you."

Hannah flew into her grandmother's arms, tears rolling down both of their faces. "Grandma, I missed you so much."

Pandemonium erupted. Justice, along with Casey and Amy, watched from the doorway. Every tear, every greeting and happy exclamation stripped away a layer of the wall he'd built around himself, around his heart. Slowly, he began to feel whole. For the first time in two years, he didn't feel like he'd shatter if someone looked at him wrong or said the wrong thing.

"Thank you," he whispered to Casey. "Thank you for bringing my daughter home." Smiling at Amy, he included her in his words. Without them, he might never have his daughter back. "I can't repay you, and there aren't enough words for my gratitude."

"Seeing you two together is enough," Amy said with a grin.

"Yeah, it is," Casey echoed sadly.

"Hey," Amy nudged her with an elbow. "You and I might not have families of our own, but we've got each other, and that's a start. One heck of a good start. Plus, you're my foster daughter, and I have a foster sister. Making her your..." she paused, looking for the right connection.

"Foster-foster aunt?" Casey joked.

"Good enough for me. I can't wait for you to meet her. She's going to love you."

Warmth trickled through Justice. How generous and gracious of Amy to give the gift of family to Casey in a moment where she might have been lost in the shuffle of an enormous family reunion. She was a woman who understood family dynamics and the meaning of belonging.

She was amazing. Was it any wonder he was falling for her?

·❤·❤·❤·❤·❤·

Chapter Twenty-Four

"Can't I wait until after Christmas break to go back to school?" Hannah demanded the next Monday. "There are only a couple weeks left. I've already missed two years. Maybe I could take correspondence or something. Maybe get my GED."

"You need to get back to school." He was hoping, probably in vain, it would be the end of the discussion. "And after school, we're going to try, again, to call your mother and let her know you're safe."

"Yeah, fat lot she cares. I can't believe she just went away and got married. Like I'm a piece of shit on her shoe." She crossed her arms over her chest and glared at him as if he were responsible for Ellen's actions.

"I'm loath to admit it, but I agree with you. I would have spent my entire life looking for you. But—she is who she is. Like it or not. You don't have to be pleased with her decisions and you don't have to like them, but you do have to treat her with respect. We'll call her and you'll be civil." He mimicked her stance. "And, you'll go to school. By rights, you should be put back into grade nine. Instead, I've asked them to let you try grade ten. You'll probably end up in some of Casey's classes. With hard work and tutoring, you can catch up."

"Ugh. I should have stayed away."

His disappointment must have shown in his expression. She apologized immediately.

"It's just so hard," she said quietly. "Everyone knows I'm a runaway. They'll talk about me."

"Probably. There's nothing we can do about that. They'd talk about you even if you were home schooled. Just like they gossiped about your Uncle Ken's separation and Uncle Riley's new daughter. Nothing stops the gossip mongers in Coyote Creek. Live with it. It's crappy, but they'll move on. They always do. They even moved on after Aunt Candy was arrested."

"What? Aunt Candy was arrested. Man, I missed so much. Tell me all about it." She wiggled like an excited puppy.

"I'll make you a deal. You go to school; do your best and I'll tell you about it tonight." He stuck out his hand hoping to shake and seal the deal.

She grabbed his hand and pumped it. His daughter had a firm, strong handshake, he thought proudly.

"You better," she warned, just as the doorbell rang. "Guess that's Casey."

"Are you sure you don't want a ride?"

"And be seen with my dad at school. Ew. No." She wrinkled her nose.

"I'll be there anyway. Getting you registered and doing paperwork. I don't mind driving you. I won't require you to talk to me," he teased.

"No way." She gave him a quick hug and raced to the door. "Bye, Dad," she called over her shoulder and left.

A moment later, a knock sounded on the door. What had she forgotten? He called out, "You don't need to knock. You live here."

The door opened and Amy stepped inside. Dressed in knee high leather walking boots, jeans and a cozy sweater, she was a sight for sore eyes. He smiled. "Come in, please."

"Thanks. She's long gone. She was grumbling something about fathers and stupid rules."

He sighed. "Got time for coffee? I need a hit of caffeine before I stop at the school on my way to the ranch.

"I was hoping you'd ask." She unzipped her boots, stepped out of them and followed him into the kitchen.

·♥·♥·♥·♥·♥·

Amy inhaled deeply. Pancakes and sausages. Yummy. It smelled almost as delicious as he looked. Freshly showered and shaved, his hair still damp, he wore a snug T-shirt and jeans that hugged his legs and backside like a lover. She paused. Surely, she wasn't jealous of his pants. Was she? Yeah, she was.

The little things he said and did for his daughter and those around him kept showing her he was a good, honorable man. The kind of man a woman wanted to get close to, maybe even marry. They'd become friends at Halloween, bickered over her jumping to conclusions, and somehow, in the search for Hannah, had grown closer together.

It dawned on her that despite wanting to keep her distance from the residents of Coyote Creek, she had a relationship with this man and by extension, his family. Now, with her taking the role of new mother to a teenager, and him the father of a recently estranged daughter, they had a million things to talk about. Notes to compare and, probably, wine to drink when things went awry. Right now, she'd enjoy the coffee he poured. Justice made the most delicious coffee. She'd have to ask him his secret. But first things first.

"So, you're the one with parenting experience," she blurted. "What rules do I set, what privileges do I give her? What about allowance? Should she get a job? A phone?" Times were so different now than when she'd been a kid. Nobody had a cell phone then. She'd had a part-time job to earn spending money. Stiff curfews, and rigid rules. She'd survived.

"You're asking me? My rules were at least part of what caused Hannah to take off with the horse racing jackass. I'm hoping the US police can do something with him, though I doubt it. He says she hid in his horse trailer; she denies it. It's a he-said she-said nightmare. I trust her version more than his." He shook his head sadly and leaned back against the counter, his oversized mug cradled in his hands.

She settled, sideways, into a kitchen chair, back against the wall, legs resting on the adjacent chair. She rested one elbow on the oak table with her hand gripping the handle of her coffee mug. "The Edmonton police are handling it. Personally, and professionally, I doubt anything will come of it. Cases with gray areas are often lost in more urgent and straightforward cases. It's unfortunate, but a sad reality."

"I'd love to see the jerk pay for luring my daughter away, but now, I'm just glad she's home safe."

"I can understand that." She already worried about Casey; from the moment she left the house alone until she returned. Like today, when she decided to hobble all the way to school on her crutches when Amy would have happily given her a ride. Casey walked short distances without crutches, but the long walk to school required extra support.

Amy sighed. Parenting was a tough gig. There was so much to know, so much to figure out. Her mind whirled with all the decisions she'd have to make regarding Casey's care. When she'd opted to be a foster parent, years ago, she'd been expecting children much younger and only for short term emergency care. It looked like she was going to keep Casey until she graduated high school. She didn't know where the thought came from, but she couldn't shake the feeling. It was so much like when she'd arrived at the Englots. There was tension and unease, but there was also a sensation of belonging and of being wanted.

"Do you think I'm using Casey to fill some void in my own life?"

"That's a crazy idea. You've given her a home, a place to heal and a sense of stability. In the short time she's been with you, she's already blossomed and become more outgoing. Look at her and Hannah.

They barely know each other and they're fast friends. Best buddies." He looked thoughtful and sipped his coffee before continuing.

She liked the way he considered his words, didn't just blurt out the first thing that came to his mind. He always weighed his words carefully.

"I don't know you well, I know your childhood was tough. I know your breakup was a disaster. Maybe you have a hole that needs filled, I can't say, only you would know. What I do know is you're good for Casey. If she fills a need in you and you fill one in her, isn't that a good thing?" He opened the fridge and grabbed a Bailey's flavored coffee creamer and poured some into his mug. He raised it toward her silently asking if she wanted any.

"No, thanks."

He put it back and lifted his mug. After a long drink and deep sigh of pleasure he smiled at her. His green eyes sparkled and that dimple appeared in his cheek. "You're smart and you've got a lot going for you. You've lived the good life and the rough life. Trust your gut. You can handle this. It's like I told Hannah, the road might be bumpy but we'll get through if we work together. I think you can trust Casey. I'll have to learn to trust Hannah again."

He made some good points. Perhaps, she could do this parenting thing. Who would have thought she'd be the mother of a teenager when she was in her early thirties? Life took some strange turns. Like the one that landed her as Justice's neighbor. And friend.

"Thanks. Your belief in me helps." She glanced at him and caught the stove's digital clock with the corner of her eye. "You probably need to get to the school. First bell is in ten minutes." How had twenty minutes passed so quickly? It seemed like they'd just picked up their mugs and here it was, time to go already.

The next morning, and every morning for a week, they repeated the coffee ritual. Bright and early the next Monday, Justice popped over to her place when the girls left for school. It became their habit to share a hot drink and commiserate before they started their days, unless she was already gone to work.

"You're okay to be on call for Casey while I'm on the night shift?" she asked for the third time. "I hate to leave her alone, but at fifteen, she's old enough to stay alone."

"At fifteen, I was babysitting my brood of siblings. She'll be fine. Hannah and I have no plans so she can come over or call if she needs anything. This is part of the trust we talked about the other day."

She groaned. "I know, but—"

"No buts. Zero buts. Neither of them did anything wrong or stepped out of line this week. We have to trust them. In fact, after school, we're going to get Hannah a cell phone."

"I thought you were going to make her wait." She raised one eyebrow and grinned.

"I was." He sat across from her at the table. "She made a valid argument about being able to contact me easily. She's made her bed every day since she's been back and she helps cook and do dishes. She's proved herself responsible, though she does grumble about the rules."

"Can you blame her? She spent the last year and a half, or more, living on her own, doing her own thing. It must have been difficult, but she survived. Now, you're watching her like a hawk and your family is everywhere." She emphasized the last word with a heavy dose of teenage-style angst.

"I suppose." He didn't sound convinced.

"How did the paperwork go with Ellen?" With her work connections, she'd been able to locate his ex and Justice's lawyer had faxed her updated custody paperwork and new support payment agreements.

"She signed the custody update but balked on the removal of child support payments."

"That's nuts." Amy couldn't fathom expecting child support payments when you were rich. Justice wasn't poor, he had enough to live on, and more, or so he said. But his ex wanted child support even after she turned full custody over to Justice. She wouldn't even leave her extended honeymoon to come see Hannah now that she was safely home. Incredibly selfish. "She wants money for nothing? Doesn't she have enough already?"

"You'd think so. It's not like she's poor and neither is her new husband. The guy owns a trillion-dollar, multinational shipping conglomerate. And a distillery in Ireland."

"Maybe it depends on how you were raised. All I ever wanted was a place of my own and a family. I get together with my sister Mindy as often as I can, though not often enough. I still feel bad for ditching her to look for Hannah. Coyote Creek's great real estate market let me buy my first house. I have a steady income, it's all I need. Shouldn't that be enough for Ellen too?" It was a rhetorical question; she knew everyone had different standards. She wanted Justice to know what hers were.

They had similar values but was it enough to bring them together? Could they be a family, all four of them? She wished she wasn't so hung up on him. She was fast losing her desire to leave Coyote Creek. Could she spend the rest of her life here?

Heaven only knew. She certainly didn't.

Chapter Twenty-Five

Justice stood in the barn, leaning on the handle of the pitchfork he'd used to clean stalls. He glanced at his watch. Amy was supposed to bring the girls out for dinner with his parents. He expected them nearly half an hour ago. He was starting to worry.

Tonight wouldn't be a huge family gathering, just his parents, Casey, Amy, Hannah and himself. No doubt his sisters who still lived at home would be there. At least they'd be down his brothers and their kids. Sometimes half a brood was better than a full one. It wasn't that he didn't love his family, he did. It was more that they could be overwhelming. He wanted Amy and Casey to get to know them a few at a time. This was also for Hannah. After her time away, Hannah needed to re-adapt to living in the fishbowl of a large family where nothing you did went unnoticed.

Amy's car pulled into the driveway and he went back to work, pretending he hadn't been watching for them.

"You're not fooling anyone," Sue said coming out of the tack room. "Everyone knows you've fallen for your lovely neighbor and her daughter. You should just admit it."

"I was thinking we could hire someone to help with the work around here until Dad gets better." He was not having a discussion of his love life or more accurately potential love life, with his mother. Not here. Not now. Not ever.

She strode up to him, her salt and pepper hair gleaming in the falling daylight filtering through the dusty barn windows. She patted his cheek.

"Justice Flint, don't you try to change the subject with me. You might have been a man when I joined this family, but I'm still your mother. I watched you grow up. Your mother and I were friends long before you came along. I know you. I know how your mind and your heart work. Amy Baxter is a lovely woman. Smart, kind, caring. You could do a lot worse. Plus, I see the love in your eyes when you look at her. She fills an empty place in you and makes you whole; as you do her. You'd be well off to admit it."

One thing about Sue, she didn't miss much. He hadn't thought about how long she'd been in Coyote Creek. "How long have you lived here?"

"Since I was in grade two. I met your Mom when I moved here. We became friends on my first day of school and stayed friends until she passed."

"I had no idea you knew her that long. You must have gone to school with Dad too."

"I did. He was the only thing your mother and I fought over. She wanted him, as did I." She chuckled. "We actually had a hair pulling fight over him. I backed down. They dated and fell in love. I met Barry Webb, my first husband when he moved here to work at the garage. He was so handsome and strong. Everything worked out perfectly. Your mother and I stayed friends."

"And you ended up with Dad anyway. Odd."

"That's fate. Who knew what might have happened if your father and I had gotten together back then? It might have worked. It might not have. Fate gave us a second chance and we're making it work. Though I'll tan his backside if he doesn't stick to the rules the cardiologist gave him."

"You and me both." So far, Robert was listening to the doctor. He was taking it easy, eating healthier and following the strict exercise regime. It was going to be a long, slow road to recovery for his father, but with Sue's help Robert would get there. "What do you think of the idea of hiring someone?"

"I don't know. Your father won't like it but it's probably advisable." She chuckled. "We just have to find a way to make it his idea. Then he'll get it stuck in his head and make it happen. There was a young fellow out here the other day, a retired soldier. He might do."

"What does a soldier know about ranching?" The suggestion was odd. Hiring someone from another ranch made more sense.

"Well, he'd be responsible and probably trainable." She made the idea seem more like an offhand remark than something she'd given serious consideration.

"It's neither here, nor there, unless Dad comes up with the idea." He put the pitchfork away and double checked to ensure all the stall doors were closed. "Come on, let's go get supper. I'm starving."

"You're always starving. I swear your leg is hollow." She hugged him tightly. "Just think about what I said. Amy's a fine woman and unless I miss my guess, she's stuck on you."

He wasn't even going to dignify that with a response. He clasped her hand in his and they walked back to the house after closing the barn doors.

"Where are the girls?" Justice asked his father when they entered the house and found him alone in the kitchen.

"Upstairs. Candy and Jennifer are giving them makeup lessons," Robert replied. "Amy's sitting in, supervising. Dang foolishness. Women don't need to be painted up to be beautiful."

Justice thought about Amy's natural beauty. His father was right; she was lovely, with or without makeup. Come to think of it, she rarely wore any. "I'm not sure I'm ready for my daughter to start painting her face."

"Relax," Sue advised. "You know your sisters, neither of them wears heavy makeup, just a bit here and there to highlight their best features. You'll hardly know she's wearing it at all."

"Ugh." He sighed. So much had changed while she was gone. She'd been his baby girl when she left and now she was back, practically an adult. This was going to take some getting used to. "I suppose I'd better brace myself for buying makeup."

"And don't skimp, dear," Sue advised. "Take her to the drugstore's beauty counter. They have the same lines as the city's high-end shops. They'll set her up with a proper skin care regime and the right makeup for her skin type and coloring. I did it with all my girls and they never once looked like they'd applied makeup with a spackling trowel."

He knew exactly what she meant. A couple girls in high school had worn a ton of makeup. Some of the guys had liked it. All he could ever think of was how gross it would be to kiss all that paint. He shuddered. "Fine. We'll do it your way. I don't suppose you have clothing advice?"

"Keep the girls covered." She laughed and Robert choked.

"Of course—whoa! Wait! Tell me you did not just refer to my daughter's...chest," Justice whispered the word, "as the girls. Please tell me you didn't."

Sue and Robert chuckled loudly and Amy joined in from the doorway. "Suck it up Justice. You've got a high school girl now and she's developing into a beautiful woman. You're going to have to deal with it. The sooner the better."

"This is easy for you. You're a woman."

"Glad you noticed," she said wryly. "Casey and I are going to the city next weekend. You and Hannah should join us. We're doing some Christmas shopping and getting her some new clothing. We bought the basics here, but as everyone knows, a girl needs a few special things. Outfits other girls in town don't have."

"Everyone knows that? Who knows that? I don't know that."

"Suck it up son. I'm a man and even I knew that," Robert chimed in, a bit breathless from his earlier bout of mirth.

"I'm done for. Doomed. I'm toast." He played up his dismay. He'd been waiting for the next blow. This one, shopping, he could adapt to. Keep it modest and Hannah could choose what she wanted, within reason.

"What do you think?" Hannah asked from the doorway, her voice trembled with uncertainty.

Justice turned. She stood motionless, a hint of makeup smoothing her features. Her hair had been trimmed neatly and layered. It barely brushed her shoulders but looked tidy and healthy. They'd curled the ends a bit. She wore one of Jen's gypsy skirts, a white T-shirt and a lacy white sweater. She took his breath away. His baby was all grown up. She was a woman now, and she was beautiful. He blinked away a tear.

"You look, nice. Very nice." He turned to his sisters. "You guys did great. Thank you."

"You're welcome," they replied in unison.

"Who cut her hair?"

"I did," Jen exclaimed proudly. "I've been practicing on old dolls. I'm getting pretty good, dontcha think?"

"Really good," Justice praised. "She looks fabulous and you saved me the price of a haircut." He teased knowing full well he'd pay her.

Casey stepped up beside Hannah. She was wearing clothing he'd seen her in before, but like Hannah, she wore just a touch of makeup. It softened the gauntness of her cheeks and helped hide the weight she'd lost during her ordeal in the forest. Two lovely girls fast becoming ladies.

· ♥ · ♥ · ♥ · ♥ · ♥ ·

Chapter Twenty-Six

Amy took a deep breath to fortify herself. She'd joined forces with Justin and brought the girls to the city. West Edmonton Mall was a zoo. With only weeks until Christmas, they'd had trouble finding a place to park. Justice circled the parking lots over and over until Amy spotted a parking stall in the far northwest corner. It was a bit of a hike to the doors and they hurried through the cold, jacketless to get inside.

"I'm freezing," Justice grumbled as they stepped inside.

"Beats carrying your jacket all day," Amy quipped. "You'll have enough to carry being our shopping Sherpa."

"Your what?"

"Shopping Sherpa. You know, the guy who carries all the bags while we pick out new clothing and find Christmas gifts," Hannah said with a giggle.

"I don't know what's going to hurt worse at the end of this day. My back or my wallet."

"Probably your head," Amy winced as they stepped through the second set of doors into chaos. Sound echoed and reverberated around them. Music thumped in the background. People chattered, kids cried and laughter rang out. It was bedlam.

"I can go wait in the truck. I'll give you my bank card."

"No way. She's your daughter. You're stuck helping us. I'll guide you but I'm not doing the work for you. Come on, Justice. Let's get this done. Step one, find a coffee. A super jumbo extra large mocha with layers of whipped cream. Once we're fortified, we'll hit the stores." She knew he was joking. She admired his sense of humor and how he tried to make the best of what was sure to be an ordeal for a man. She didn't know a single male who thrived in a mall.

They shopped until even Amy wanted to drop. Justice, burdened down with packages, found a seasonal coat check willing to watch their purchases. Amy grinned when, grateful for their help, Justice gave a very large donation to the animal rescue charity the coat check supported. Bag free, they resumed shopping after a quick bite to eat in one of the mall's food courts.

"You're doing great," Amy whispered. Initially, he'd vetoed several outfits as too revealing when in reality were fairly modest. If he had his way, Hannah would be covered from head to toe in flannel. Baggy flannel. Amy found herself giving him a quiet lecture on choices and decision making for teens and he'd lightened up. It wasn't that she was an expert, more that she'd lived through it herself and remembered her own arguments with her foster parents.

"You guys stay here," Hannah suggested. "Sit over there, on those couches and we'll go Christmas shopping. We've got our new phones. We'll call you if we need you."

"I don't know if I like that idea," Justice objected.

"That'll be fine," Amy countered. "Let them go. They'll be together. We can't be hovering when they buy us gifts."

"Yeah," the girls chorused in unison and shared a fist bump.

Justice reluctantly agreed, and they set a time and place to meet. The girls hurried off to spend the money they'd been given.

"Look at them go," Amy chuckled as the girls raced away. "It was brilliant of your mom to suggest giving them gift money. With all the recent upheaval in their lives, neither had the opportunity to earn money to buy gifts."

"I hope they're responsible and don't get into trouble. Is it even safe to let them go off unsupervised? The mall is a zoo. Hundreds of people, thousands. Any one of them could be a threat to the girls. They could get lost, or injured. what if they get abducted?"

Justice's chest constricted, impeding his breath. Oh man, having Hannah home might be worse than having her gone. She was here, but out of his reach. He couldn't protect her if he couldn't see her. He never should have left her go off alone.

"Relax, Justice. They'll be fine. They're smart girls. They survived on the streets; they'll be fine in the mall. We're only a phone call away." She patted his shoulder.

"What if something happens? We're not there to protect them." His anxiety spiked. He wasn't ready to let Hannah out of his sight.

"What if they're fine?" Amy countered. "This is a mall; the girls are nearly adults. They've become good friends. Friend's who'll watch each other's back. The mall has security on patrol, stores have cashiers to ask for help if they get in a pickle. And, they have phones."

"Text me and see if mine is working," he demanded, knowing he was being ridiculous. He couldn't help himself. Hannah had been gone for so long, now that she was back, he wanted her within his reach. They'd already had a dozen fights because he was holding her too close.

Last night, she'd woken up and found him standing in her doorway, watching her sleep. She'd gone ballistic. If they hadn't been making the mall trip, she probably wouldn't be speaking to him.

How did he balance this? One part of his brain was scared to death something tragic would happen. The other knew she was tough and could handle herself. He'd left her and her friends alone in the mall at thirteen. Now, she was sixteen and he was nearly breathless with panic.

"It'll be okay. She's a good kid and you're a great father for letting her go, despite your fears." Amy leaned in and kissed his cheek. "Come on, let's stroll. Maybe we can take your mind off of the girls for a few minutes." She grabbed his hand and laced their fingers together. Tugging gently, she urged him forward.

The touch of her lips and the soft warmth of her hand short circuited his brain. He stumbled along at her urging, lost in conflicting thoughts. Was the kiss a distraction technique or was she starting to feel something more toward him, more than friendship? He'd be fine with that. No, it would be great. He'd fallen for her weeks ago. He was totally gonzo in love with her. He'd tumbled into love and hadn't even tried to stop himself. He was so wrapped up in finding Hannah that Amy had slipped under his defenses. Now, not only did he have Hannah to worry about, he had Amy and Casey as well.

He paused and jerked Amy to a stop. "Why did you do that?" he asked.

"Do what?" Her brows bunched together as she turned to look at him.

"Kiss me." How could she misunderstand the question? It wasn't complex. Well, the emotions rampaging through him were, but the question was simple.

She shrugged. "I don't know, because it felt right. You needed a distraction, I provided one. It's what friends do. Come on, let's shop a bit more. I'd like to get something for your parents. They've been so great with Casey and I."

He followed her into a housewares shop, barely aware of where they were going. In and out of stores. Up and down aisles until she finally found something to purchase. He paid no attention to what they were doing. He followed along blindly, his thoughts torn between his feelings for her and his total panic something would happen to the girls.

"Well, that's it. My shopping is finished. How about yours?"

"Mine?" He gawked at her. He must look like a total fool. It took a moment for the actual question to sink into his muddled brain. "Oh, yeah. I made a lot of my gifts and I purchased the rest. I've ordered a few things online; they should arrive soon."

"Time's nearly up. Let's head back and meet the girls. We don't want to be late; we'd never hear the end of it. Come on, Dad. Let's get back to our girls."

Her words engulfed his heart, like a warm hug. Dad. She sounded just like Sue when she referred to his father as Dad. Like she had when his grandparents had still been alive. She'd be talking to her husband and say things like, "Come on, Dad, Grampa and Granny are waiting." Amy's echoing of Sue's mannerisms felt so...intimate. So perfectly right.

They sat on the bench, waiting. Ten minutes passed by, then twenty.

"Something's gone wrong. Where are they?" he demanded. Deep down, he knew fear was making him irrational. The girls had a ton of life experience and this was a mall, an enormous one. It was Christmas and the place was packed.

"Give it time. They probably just got caught up in the fun. They'll be here."

"I'm going to call her." Whipping out his phone he punched in the preprogrammed number. It rang and rang. He shot off a quick text. "See, I told you. Something's wrong. Why doesn't she answer? What kid doesn't return a text? You better text Casey."

"I will not. Give them a few more minutes. It's early to panic. Don't you remember being a kid and getting distracted? Weren't you ever late?"

"I was, but I never ran away. I was never gone for two years, leaving my father sick with worry. When she comes back, I'm grounding her for a year."

"Whoa. Slow down. You're not over her running away. I understand. Don't let your fear ruin your relationship before you even rebuild it. Wait until she comes back, then, when you're calm discuss it with her. Don't speak in anger."

"You're giving me parenting advice? You've been a parent for a couple weeks and you think you know it all? That's rich." He was being irrational. Fear was driving him crazy, making him lash out; just as he'd lashed out at his ex and his family when Hannah disappeared. He was losing his mind. He was spiraling back into that hell-hole and couldn't stop himself.

"Justice Flint, get your shit together. You need to be calm. We'll give them a few more minutes and then I'll call Casey. This is killing me too, but I have to trust her. Just like you need to trust Hannah. Chillax."

"Chillax?" He rolled his eyes. For a cop, she didn't know crap all about teens. He was about to blow his stack.

Something inside him shifted. Amy didn't deserve his anger. She was trying to keep him calm. Hannah, on the other hand... "Sorry, I'll try and relax."

When forty-five minutes had gone by, Amy called Casey. She'd barely punched in the numbers when they saw the girls coming down the mall.

"Keep cool," Amy advised, ending the call and sliding her phone back into her pocket. "If you lose it, you'll push her away."

"Stop giving me parenting advice. She's late. Way late. She'll be grounded for sure." His face grew hot, his shoulders tense. His fists bunched and he forced himself to relax. "I'll parent the way I see fit."

"Suit yourself, but you're about to make a big mistake. At least give them a chance to explain."

He heard her words and understood their wisdom. Fear, love, panic and a dozen other emotions battled him, stealing his reasoning power.

"Where the hell were you?" He demanded the second the girls were within earshot.

"Shopping. You know that," Hannah smiled as if she'd done nothing wrong. "The store was crazy but I found this perfect gift and the line was so long. I totally forgot to text you. We were just talking, you know, becoming friends. Casey's so cool."

"You're grounded until I decide otherwise. We're going. Now." His anger flowed out of him unchecked. Hannah's face went from happy and excited to annoyed and morphed into disappointment and anger.

The disappointment was echoed in Amy's stunned expression. Casey just looked shocked, and a bit afraid.

"Can we just—"

He cut his daughter off mid-sentence. "No, we can't. We're going home. Now." He pointed to the exit they'd come in. "Out."

Hannah and Casey looked at each other and glared at him.

"I'd like to collect the packages we left at the coat check," Amy suggested. "If it's okay with you?" Her words rang with sarcasm.

"Fine." He stormed toward the charity coat check, retrieved their purchases and returned to where they stood, looking shell shocked. He stormed out of the mall without looking back. He was overheated with anger and frustration. By the time he reached the truck, the icy winter air had cooled his body and most of his anger.

Humiliation and chagrin slipped in to take its place.

He'd lost it. Totally. Completely. One hundred percent lost it. The ride home was going to be interminable and probably unbearable. He was in trouble, and he couldn't see a way out.

Chapter Twenty-Seven

They gassed up the truck without speaking. Amy never said a word to him. In the back seat, the girls were quiet. They carried on a soundless conversation via text messages and glared at the back of Justice's head. He pretended to ignore them.

Amy stared out the window wondering how to start a conversation. Was there a way to break the ice? To open communications? She was usually good at this. Part of her understood his anger and fear. She'd been worried too; but she trusted her foster daughter to find her way back. There was no denying the girls had screwed up. They'd been late and they'd forgotten to call and let their parents know as they'd been instructed to.

Perhaps punishment was in order, but this icy cold shoulder was going too far. She'd thought Justice knew better than that. She'd seen the good in him. The dedication. The strength of his love for his daughter. Couldn't he understand Hannah and Casey probably felt safe and secure for the first time in months, perhaps since they'd run away? Feeling safe might have made them careless. Both girls had the street smarts to stay safe. They'd learned them the hard way. He should have taken that into account before he'd come unglued.

Not a single word was said during the entire three-hour ride back to Coyote Creek. The radio was off, the truck filled with uncomfortable silence and wordless accusations recriminations. They parked on the street in front of Justice's house and everyone climbed out into the late night cold. It had been a long day. A three-hour drive into the city, four at the mall and three hours home. It felt like the drive home had lasted at least twice as long as the rest of the day.

"Thanks for the ride and the shopping," Amy said as she gathered her packages from beneath the cover on the box of the truck.

"Thank you, Mr. Flint," Casey said quietly.

Amy turned back from her porch to peek at Justice. He stood, arms crossed over his chest as Hannah picked up her packages and stormed up the front steps and waited impatiently for her father to unlock the house. It looked like it would be a frigid night at the Flint house.

·♥·♥·♥·♥·♥·

Work was hectic the next few days. Besides taking some online training, Amy was wrapped up in helping out with a police charity drive collecting gifts and food for Coyote Creek's less fortunate. Gifts were sorted and wrapped. Food was organized. More was purchased and everything was prepped for delivery. She didn't have time to worry much about what went on in the Flint house.

She did anyway.

"Mr. Flint is still being a jerk," Casey informed Amy that evening, while they prepped for supper. Amy had asked her foster daughter, more than once, to stop giving constant updates but the girl refused to keep quiet about their neighbors. Finally, Amy had enough.

"Look, I understand you girls are friends. I'm glad you found someone your age to get close to. But I believe Justice has to work this out for himself. He was wrong to reprimand you girls as harshly as he did. Frankly, he treated us all poorly. I'm not saying you didn't deserve to get in trouble, you did. You're both old enough to be responsible. You should have called. You didn't. That's why there's no television for a week. You're lucky I don't take your phone." She paused.

"Sorry. I got off track there. The point is, Justice owes us all an apology and until I get one, until *we* get one, I don't want to hear about what goes on over there. Unless he's breaking the law, it's none of my business. Okay?"

"Fine. I guess so. It's just...Hannah's my friend. And, you and Justice like each other. Liked each other," she corrected. "You should still be friends. If you guys got together, the Flint's would be my family and Hannah would be my real sister."

"Don't even go there. Justice and I were friends. That's all. Besides, you know my plan. I've been open about it from the start. We stay in Coyote Creek until you graduate high school and then I'll transfer somewhere else while you are in the city continuing your education."

"I know, but—"

"No buts. Is your homework done?"

"Yup. Can I go out tonight? Some of the kids from school are going to Tammy's for coffee." Tammy's, a local restaurant, was a popular evening hangout for teens.

"I shouldn't let you go. You should be grounded." She extracted a frying pan from the cupboard and set it on the stove. She placed a couple porkchops into the non-stick pan and flipped the burner on. "However, because you've been good and done all your chores from the day you moved in, I'll let you go, just this once. We'll need to solidify your rules and curfew as well. Once you've caught up in school, I want you to consider getting a part-time job or find another way to earn your own spending money."

"Okay. Maybe I could babysit, or get a job at the bakery. I have a bit of money left over from the mall. Remember? I told you and you said to keep it. I'll use it tonight, if that's okay?" Casey started setting the table for dinner. It was one of her evening chores, along with helping with the dishes and being sure the garbage was taken out.

"You'll need to be home by ten. It is a school night. Do you need a ride?"

"A ride would be great. Thanks. My leg is getting better, but it's a long walk to Tammy's. I hope they have peanut butter pie. I had it once and it's incredible."

"Who all is going and when do you need to be there?" She seasoned the chops and started cutting veggies for a salad.

"We're meeting at seven. Hannah's going, I think." She rattled off a few other kids, girls and boys.

"Boys too? No shenanigans," Amy warned with a teasing smile.

"Ugh. I'm so not ready to date. You on the other hand..."

Amy whipped a balled-up tea towel in her daughter's direction, making her laugh. "Never mind."

Casey half skipped, half hobbled, out of the kitchen. "Call me when food's ready. I want to read for a few minutes. I'm in the middle of this great mystery."

She adored how much time Casey spent reading. Evenings were often spent in the living room in front of a fire, each of them lost in their own book. Justice was a reader too. She'd seen his impressive stack of books. Fiction and non-fiction both. Casey had informed her Hannah and Justice both read, though usually separately because there was still a lot of tension between them.

She checked the chops and finished the salad, trying not to wonder what Justice was up to tonight. Before the disastrous trip to the mall, they probably would have gotten together for tea or wine while the girls were out socializing.

Not anymore.

She sighed. She missed him, but it would be a frosty Wednesday in Mexico before she admitted that to anyone. She ignored the constriction in her chest and called her daughter to dinner.

·♥·♥·♥·♥·♥·

Chapter Twenty-Eight

"Be good tonight," Justice said. "Please call me if you need a ride home."

"Thanks, Dad."

"Hang on a second." He joined her at the front door. She looked adorable standing there in her heavy winter boots and baby blue winter jacket. She had a small purse in her hand. God, he'd never get enough of looking at her. The haircut she'd gotten from his sister still looked good. Today it was straight; sometimes she curled it into what she called beach waves. There was a hint of makeup on her cheeks and her lips were a light pink. She looked so grown up. He might never get used to her looking like an adult. She was beautiful, like her mother was. Luckily, she had a warmer heart than Ellen. She was great with her cousins and had started helping with the after-school care program at the school.

"What's up? Amy's waiting."

Amy. He almost sighed. Sooner or later, he'd have to find the balls to apologize to her for flying off the handle. That was a battle for another time.

"Okay. Here it is." He hugged her tightly, loath to let go. "I might have been out of line at the mall. I freaked out and panicked. You've only been back a couple weeks. I was scared to death something happened to you. And Casey. You've both been through more than any kid should have to. I'm sorry. I'll try to contain myself in the future." The apology flew out of him in a rush of words. He'd been working up to it for days. "I'll always worry when I can't see you, but I'll try to trust you."

She flung herself into his arms, nearly knocking him off his feet.

"I'm sorry I didn't call, or text. I promise to do better." She kissed his cheek. "Love you, Daddy. I'll be back by ten." She flew out the door, the screen door slammed behind her.

He eased the inside door shut and leaned against it.

Happiness flooded through him, washing away the chill he'd been unable to shake since the mall. He'd missed her smile. He was glad he'd finally found the right words to apologize. Now, if only he had the words to express his regret to another important person.

Suddenly anxious to do so, he showered quickly, and waited. Five minutes after Amy returned home from dropping off the girls, he was knocking on her door, bottle of wine in hand.

He waited one minute, then two. Just when he'd given up and turned to go, she opened the door.

"Flint." She crossed her arms over her chest and glared at him.

"Amy." Dang, she was cute. She looked set to kick his butt off her step, and he didn't doubt that she had the skills to do it. He lifted the wine. "I came to apologize."

"And?" Her gaze didn't soften. In fact, her frown deepened.

"I'm sorry I lost it in the mall. I treated you badly. I crapped all over the girls for a simple mistake. I overreacted. Hannah has forgiven me and I intend to apologize to Casey next time I see her." Her frown eased, but her arms remained crossed. That was progress, wasn't it?

"You had good advice and I didn't listen. Hell, I didn't even hear it. I slammed you for not being a parent. I treated you like crap. I apologize for it all. I'll try not to do it again."

"You'll try?"

Was that the hint of a smile?

"I'd promise not to, but I don't make promises I can't keep. I will, however, try my best not to be a jerk again." He offered his best smile, hoping to break through her icy exterior. Standing there, he was hit with renewed clarity of how important she was to him. She wasn't just his friend, somehow, when he wasn't looking, she'd snuck into his heart. He had to make this work. He fondled the small box in his pocket for strength. It held the ring Amy had admired in his garage the night she'd been sneaking around, spying on him. He was going to give it to her as part of his apology. Now, it felt like the ring represented so much more.

"I'm going to be honest here. I like you, Amy Baxter. I like you a lot. I'm pretty sure I've fallen in love with you. I need you in my life. We can be neighbors. Friends would be better. But frankly, I'd like to be more than that. I think we developed a pretty serious relationship over the weeks since you moved in. I love you Amy Baxter, almost as much as I love my daughter."

"Almost?" Her voice squeaked.

He shrugged and grinned. "She's a tough act to keep up with. I doubt anyone will ever come close, but you're not far behind."

"Come on in." She stepped back and opened the door.

He stepped past her, the light, floral scent of her shampoo tickled his nose. Another step and he was overcome by the aroma of chocolate. He sniffed heavily. If she wore chocolate perfume, he'd have to marry her on the spot. Next to bacon and steak, chocolate was his favorite smell.

"Stop sniffing," she chided him. "I made brownies this afternoon."

"You can eat brownies with red wine, right?" He grinned at her over his shoulder.

"I'm not sure I'm ready to share my brownies with you. Come in anyway." She closed the door and eased past him into the house.

He'd just declared his love and she wouldn't share brownies? Harsh. Very harsh. He'd much prefer some kind of hint she felt something similar for him. For a fraction of a second, he debated pushing for one. He discarded the idea. It was enough, for now, to know how deeply he cared for her. He suspected, and hoped, she returned his feelings, and he could wait for her to feel comfortable enough to share them.

"So, no brownies then?" he asked.

"Maybe one."

"Technically, if you don't cut them and just hand me the pan and a fork, that's only one. Right?" He hung his jacket in the closet and slipped off his boots before following her into the kitchen.

"Typical Flint, always pushing the limits. Too bad they're already cut." She laughed and smiled at him.

Dang. The upward curve of her lips stole his breath. It was all he could do not to step forward and kiss her senseless. Well, kissing her would knock him senseless, but if she wasn't moved by it, she might actually, physically, knock him senseless. He'd heard she had a great right hook. Occasionally, she sparred with the guys from work. She'd given her boss a black eye. Best to save the kissing for later. If the opportunity presented itself.

He sighed in mock grief. "I suppose one brownie will have to do. I hope they're big ones."

She rolled her eyes at him and served them each a moderately sized brownie. He found the corkscrew and some glasses and carried them, and the wine, into the living room.

He sat on one end of the couch; she took the other. She held her wine in one hand, and sat facing him, her arms wrapped around her knees. She looked stiff and wary, but not as unapproachable as when she opened the door. He could have reached out and touched her. He wanted to, but he restrained himself. Barely.

"So, how have you been?" Great, now he even sounded nervous. The uncertainty of his position in her world was making him crazy. Weird how his life had turned around since Hannah came home. Everything was so much better, but still so up in the air. Time would settle things out, he hoped.

"Good. Casey's healing nicely. She saw the doctor after school. Work is good. You?"

"Good. I spent the day at the ranch. I apologized to Hannah. I think we've gotten past my stupidity. We're not comfortable yet, but I think it'll come. How are you and Casey getting along?"

"Great. She's got chores and does them without complaint. She's working hard to catch up in school. I'm proud of her efforts."

Their words were serious, raising kids was no joke. At the same time, they felt like inanities. Could this conversation be any lamer? Probably not, but he couldn't seem to find a way to work past the discomfort his stupidity had caused. The only comfort was knowing he'd managed to work his way into her house and at least they were talking.

"Be right back." She stood and strode down the hallway, taking her wine with her.

He heard a door close and water running and shut off. The toilet flushed; the water ran again. He waited and waited. He wondered if she was ever coming back.

· ♥ · ♥ · ♥ · ♥ · ♥ ·

Chapter Twenty-Nine

Amy stared at herself in the bathroom mirror as she glugged the remainder of her wine. What the devil was wrong with them? They used to be friends and confidants. Maybe more. She couldn't push past the idea that he loved her. How could she cope with his declaration of love?

He wasn't supposed to love her.

She hugged herself, rubbing her shoulders, trying to chase off a chill. She was leaving Coyote Creek as soon as Casey graduated. Granted, grad was a couple years away. Until then, he was supposed to be her friend. Not something else. How was she supposed to deal with a confession like that?

She couldn't tell him that despite his idiocy at the mall, she'd fallen for him too. If she confessed her feelings, she'd be trapped here. She had a career to follow. She had plans for her future which didn't include Coyote Creek and Justice Flint. She'd come here to escape her mistakes, not to find a man and a foster daughter. Crap, he had a daughter too. If she stayed, she risked hurting Hannah too. The girl had been through enough already. Nothing like adding stress to an already difficult situation.

She splashed water on her face and buried her face in a towel. Leaning against the bathroom door she pondered her situation.

Justice wasn't her ex. He was honest, caring, giving. Yeah, sometimes he was bossy and he'd certainly overstepped his bounds at the mall. Then, he'd found his way to apologize. He was stubborn but not too stubborn. He'd saved Casey's life and had virtually given up his own life to find his daughter. He'd stepped up his role at the family ranch in light of his father's health issues. He was always available for his siblings and nieces and nephews. He'd helped her muddle through some parenting issues. Look at how he'd helped Casey during the search and rescue. Amazing.

Damn. He was a great guy.

Just what she wanted in a man.

And good looking too. Handsome, sexy, smart.

There was no avoiding it.

She was in love with him.

She'd known it for a while.

Even as she admitted it, she was tempted to deny it. Again.

She'd been avoiding it for weeks now.

Okay, so she loved him. What did that mean? Her plans didn't include Coyote Creek and he'd never leave here. It didn't bode well for the future at all. What to do? What to do? She needed to work off some stress. She needed a run. Or a kickboxing session. Maybe some sparring with the guys at the station.

Calm hit her like a bolt of lightning. One minute she was pacing and wringing the towel between her hands and the next she was breathing slowly and deeply. Calmer than she'd ever been. She wanted this. She wanted him and this silly little town where people were nosy, friendly and helpful. She liked it here.

She opened the door and strode into the living room.

Justice perched on the edge of the couch, poised for flight.

That wouldn't do. It wouldn't do at all.

She walked up to him and pushed him back onto the couch. He stared up at her looking a little stunned. Good. She felt a bit stunned herself. Could you be stunned and calm? She shrugged it off. It was what it was.

She straddled his legs.

His eyes widened in shock.

"So, I've decided to forgive you."

His grin was like sunshine to her heart. Great, now she was calm, surprised and happy. "Justice Flint, you're an enormous pain in my backside, but I love you anyway." She pressed her lips to his.

He leaned back at stared up at her, a bemused grin on his face.

"Yeah, you heard me. I love you."

He grabbed her by the waist, swung her sideways and threw her onto the couch. Kneeling on the floor beside her, he leaned in and brushed his lips across hers. He tasted like chocolate, wine and minty toothpaste. It was a weird, heady combination. She lifted her head, pressing their lips firmly together. She snaked her arms around his neck and devoured him.

The kiss deepened, became softer, more loving. It shifted again, becoming more frantic. She fumbled for her buttons, trying to answer the need building in her. She'd wanted him from the moment he'd saved her from falling off the stupid ladder. Now, he was hers and she could have him.

"Wait." He leaned back on his heels and stilled the motion of her hands with his.

"You're turning me down?" She blinked, feeling like an owl. What the heck? He didn't want her? He said he loved her. They were in love, so why not?

"I'm not turning you down. Well, I am. But for a good reason. I think." He was obviously fumbling for coherent thought. He was breathing as hard as she was.

He grasped her hand and placed it against his heart. "Feel that. My heart is pounding for you. Only for you. I've been alone since Ellen and I divorced. Before that even. I want you, never doubt that." He moved her hand to his groin. "See?"

She squeezed the bulge in his jeans lightly. He groaned and she giggled. "Explain."

"This is new. To both of us. I don't want to screw it up. We both have responsibilities. Huge responsibilities. I want to wait until we're married."

"You want to wait until what? Is that some kind of backhanded proposal?" Her heart redoubled the pounding his kisses had caused. Could he mean it or was it just a heat of the moment thing? She so wasn't ready for this.

He flopped to his backside and stared up at her, grinning like a maniac. After a moment, he shifted one knee. Proposal style.

"Amy Baxter, I'm a stupid, stubborn man. I'm not perfect but I think you might be. You make me happy. You challenge me to be a better man. I've loved you for ages." He pulled the ring box from his pocket, opened it and held it out to her.

Wow! The ring she'd admired. "I thought that was sold?"

"No, I said it wasn't for sale. It's for you. If you'll have me. I know Coyote Creek isn't your destiny. Being together might mean I have to leave the town I've grown up in. But for you, I'll do it. I'll move. I'll go anywhere you want to go. Amy Baxter, say you'll marry me and take me with you."

"You'd move for me?" His words and awkward proposal stunned her. He'd give up his life and his family for her? What kind of man did that?

"Yes."

"Then, yes, Justice Flint, I will marry you. I might even agree to settle down in this crazy town. They should call it Crazy Creek, but I'll marry you and we'll figure out what comes next later."

"So, we'll marry this weekend?" he asked, sliding the ring onto her finger.

"No," she blurted. "I think the girls will need some adjustment time. They've been through a lot. More than any kid should have to go through. I'm not giving up Casey. She's my daughter now. Can you accept her as part of the package?"

"I wouldn't have it any other way." He kissed her again.

"I was thinking we could marry a year from now," she said, breathless from the kiss.

"Too long. I can't wait that long. Unless we move in together." He grinned at her.

"I'm not going to live in sin with you, what would the gossips think?" Laughing, she pulled him close for a kiss. "But I might agree to move up the date. A bit."

"Look at that, our first compromise. We're going to rock this marriage thing."

"Justice?"

"Yeah?" He looked at her.

The love shining in his beautiful green eyes thrilled her to her soul. There wasn't any place she wanted to be besides here, with him.

"Shut up and kiss me," she whispered. There were so many details to work out, but staring into his eyes, she knew they'd muddle their way through.

"We've got this. We'll make it work. With both of our daughters." He captured her lips with his and for a long time, the world around them disappeared.

"Oh, gross. They're making kissy faces," Casey's voice penetrated the fog of their kiss.

Amy leaned away from him as heat stole into her face. Justice looked flushed as well. From the kiss or chagrin at being caught necking?

"Casey. You're back." She turned to face her daughter. "Hannah. Hi. You guys are home early. Anything wrong?" She righted herself on the sofa, Justice sat beside her, his arm slung over her shoulder.

"Not really," Casey responded. "My ankle aches and it was crazy busy at Tammy's. We decided to catch a ride home."

"Grandma and Grampa were in town," Hannah added. "We got a ride with them. We're invited to dinner on Sunday. All four of us." She gestured toward the adults. "So, what's up with this?" She quirked one eyebrow at them.

"You look just like your grandmother when you make that face," Justice laughed. "This," he pulled Amy closer, "Is us, Amy and I, being engaged. We're getting married. Blending our families. If you two have no objections."

Amy's heart melted all over again. He was so kind, including them in the engagement, asking their permission to marry her and making it clear Casey's opinion was just as valuable as Hannah's. She kissed his cheek.

The teens blinked, looked at each other and grinned. They high fived. "Yes," they declared in unison.

"We're going to be sisters," Casey declared. "I have a huge new family."

"Where are we going to live? Do we have to share a room? Can we get a bigger house? Can we live on the ranch? Yeah, we should build a ginormous house on the ranch." The girls hurled questions at Amy and Justice, making Amy laugh.

"Hold your horses, there are a lot of decisions to make," Justice declared. "And we'll make them together. All four of us. As a family. But for now, go to your room. Amy and I have things to discuss."

"Gross, they're going to kiss again," Hannah declared. Laughing, they hurried down the hallway toward Casey's room.

"Kids."

His chuckle rumbled through them both as he leaned in to kiss her. She raised her lips to meet his. His smile was wide, his eyes sparkled. Her heart swelled as she brushed her lips across his. This was where she wanted to be, right here in his arms, with teenage laughter trickling in from down the hall.

·♥·♥·♥·♥·♥·

Love the novel you just read?
Your opinion matters. Please Review this book on your favorite book site, review site, blog, or your own social media properties, and share your opinion with other readers.
Thanks in advance,
Katie.

I hope you enjoyed Justice and Amy's story.
Check out Book One: A Lesson in Love for Riley and Tricia's story.
Watch for Book Three: A Secret to Shatter, Ira and Honey's story.
Coming soon to a retailer near you.

Books by Katie

A Silver Fox Christmas Box Set
Heart's Haven:
Running Home
Building Trust
Saving Grace
Loving Winter
Heart's Haven Box Set
Three Moon Falls:
Fire Magic
Water Magic
Earth Magic
Midnight Magic
Air Magic
Stand Alone Books:
Carly'sHeart
MatchmakerChristmas
Cupid'sCharm
GingerbreadDreams
Christmasin Silver Creek
Fake Dating at Half Moon Bay
Playing for Keeps in Half Moon Bay
SleighBells Inn
Heartsin the Spotlight
Toa Tea
BulletproofHeart
ProtectingJosie
RekindledFire
Winningher Love
Ticketto Her Heart

KO'dby Love

$\cdot \heartsuit \cdot \heartsuit \cdot \heartsuit \cdot \heartsuit \cdot \heartsuit \cdot$

About Katie O'Connor

Katie O'Connor lives in Calgary, Alberta, Canada. She married her high school sweetheart and is living her happily ever after. She is the mother of two grown daughters and is extremely proud of her five grandchildren.

Katie's career path has been long and twisted, with most of her life devoted to her family. She's been a waitress, chambermaid, cashier, store manager, as well as a lab and x-ray technician. She is an avid quilter and crafter. She finds inspiration and relaxation in the wilds of Alberta.

She's dabbled in writing since high school because something drives her to create stories. She swears it's impossible for her NOT to write. Unsatisfied with one genre, Katie writes contemporary romance, erotic romance, fantasy/paranormal romance and erotica. Recently, she's crafted her first cozy mystery with the intention of publishing a cozy mystery series.

She believes in all things magical; including dragons, fairies, UFOs, ghosts, and house pixies. But most of all she believes in love, romance and hope.

Where to Find Katie

Website: https://katieohwrites.com
Email:katie@katieohwrites.com
NewsletterSignup: http://eepurl.com/Q2nRr
Facebook:http://www.facebook.com/katieohwrites
Bookbub:https://www.bookbub.com/profile/katie-o-connor
Instagram:https://www.instagram.com/katieohwrites/
Goodreads:https://www.goodreads.com/author/show/5362469.Katie_O_Connor

Contact Katie O'Connor

Katie loves to hear from her readers. Feel free to contact her anytime.

Website:

Email: katie@katieohwrites.com

Facebook:

Reviews are an author's life blood.

To thank readers generous enough to leave a review, I hold a monthly draw for a free e-book.

To enter, simply email me the link to your review. (katieoconnorwrites@gmail.com)

Each month's winner will receive the e-book of their choice from Katie's publications.

Thank you in advance, Katie.

www.ingramcontent.com/pod-product-compliance
Lightning Source LLC
Chambersburg PA
CBHW020832260626
47169CB00003B/953